MAGIC BREAKER

MARIE BILODEAU

To every person
who keeps reaching for the light
when the darkness is thickest.

ACKNOWLEDGMENTS

While writing this series, my life took a turn when my mother was diagnosed with dementia. My first published book, which started this entire series, *Princess of Light*, was dedicated to my mother: "For always seeking the light."

Every book since has been partially dedicated to her, for her strength, her love of life, and her kindness. Through her/our new reality, we've met lots of amazing people who have supported, helped, and shared laughter, and tears, with us. Everywhere mom goes, she brings that same kindness, that relentless stubbornness to find *les petites joies de la vie* (the small joys of life), no matter what.

So, as always, a major thank you to my mother, who consistently reminds me that life is about moments and *petites joies.*

Through it all, my partner, Kerri Elizabeth Gerow, has been relentlessly supportive with baked goods, fun, and lots of laughter. My family, as always, is a well of strength:

Jessica Torrance, Jean-François Bilodeau, George Henri Bilodeau, Ada-Marie Bilodeau, Karen and Dave Henderson, and Kathy and Martin Gallant.

Every writing life is made better by those we surround ourselves with. Major thanks to my little community: Brandon Crilly, Jennifer Brozek, Lydia M. Hawke, Ed Greenwood, Julie E. Czerneda, Derek Künsken, Evan May, Kevin Hearne, Kate Heartfield, 'Nathan Burgoine… and so many more.

Thanks to my beta readers: Kerri Elizabeth Gerow, Nicole Lavigne, Lina El-Samrout, and Christina Yother.

If you're thinking AI cover art is "good enough," you're missing out on A-good art, and also B-working with an artist. Simon Carr brought Shirina to life for this cover, and helped me solidify some of the thinking around Circle wear (seriously, working with an artist is amazing, and Simon is among the best)! Also thanks to Deranged Doctor Design, who took Simon's wonderful art and turned it into a cover.

And, as always, a major thanks to fans of the first series, *Heirs of a Broken Land,* for still being here after all these years, cheering the characters, and me, on. I can't even begin to describe how your notes and messages encourage and lift me up.

The road may get darker and at times is hard to see, but the journey is always, will alway be, worthwhile, and in no small part thanks to all of you.

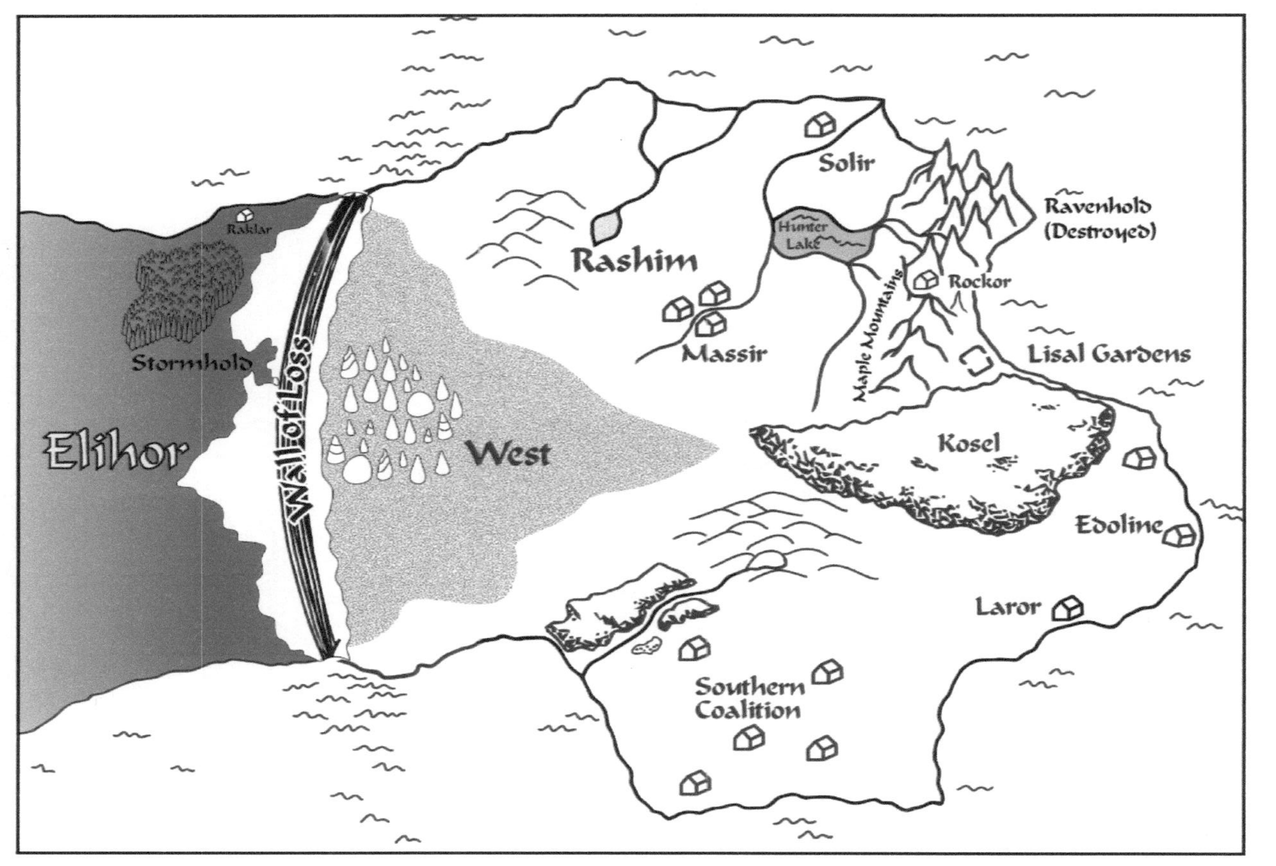

Elihor
Raklar
Stormhold
Wall of Loss
West
Rashim
Solir
Hunter Lake
Ravenhold (Destroyed)
Maple Mountains
Rockor
Lisal Gardens
Massir
Kosel
Edoline
Laror
Southern Coalition

1

The air crackled with Elihor's magic, strands that Shirina could not see but could sense whipping the wind in a frenzy as Rojon's magic unleashed. The blade, intended for Cassara, had pierced the apparently still alive Avarielle through.

She thought she'd been dead. Shirina had grieved her. And now, unless she moved quickly, that grief would amplify with missed moments.

Twenty years of preparing for Siabala's return and Shirina had failed to spot the den of snakes forming right beneath her feet. Her shoulder ached and her heart ached more but, with a groan, she pushed herself up and headed into the torrent of magic.

Elder Tally's body had satisfyingly been tossed aside, but the old woman struggled up, refusing, or unable, to stay down. At least the nasty wound at her neck blocked her voice, and hopefully her casting.

Shirina ignored her. She knew little of the magic of the heirs of Elihor, but she thought she knew enough. Kale had spoken of it and had died by it.

That I could save you, too, old man.

Him, and the Circle. And her witches, running, powerless, away from the green flames of the rebels, which consumed all in their path.

So many had died. She thought she'd lost Avarielle, and now she actually might.

Shala, loyal to the last, running down corridors, trying to save what had taken years to build…

No. Enough. She'd had enough. She would lose no one else. With or without magic, she would find a way to win this day.

Feet firmly planted on the ground, she fought against the magic slamming into her, a vortex of energy swirling her crimson cloak, stealing her breath. She reached Cassara first, the magical bonds still holding her.

Their eyes met, and nothing needed to be said. She grabbed Avarielle's shoulder, felt energy coursing from the warrior into her, keeping her standing despite the blood pooling at her feet. Shirina almost slipped in it, using Avarielle like a lever to pull herself forward. The warrior stood as though frozen in place, Elihor's magic wrapped around her.

Rojon is trying to keep her alive! Freezing her in time. Holding her breath captive, even though her blood still trickled down.

Siabala's magic would not be undone so easily. Even

without the Sight, Shirina could see red strands wrapping around the warrior, one hand holding back her son, the other clutching Graysword's pommel.

"Rojon." The winds whipped the name out of Shirina's mouth. Rojon's face twisted in agony, fighting against Siabala and bleeding out Elihor's magic. He would be pulled apart unless he managed to get his magic under control.

Shirina slipped in the blood and almost went down, grabbing Graysword's pommel, its magic buzzing at her touch, but not hurting her. She pulled herself up using it, hoping she wasn't pushing it deeper into Avarielle, magic rushing against her skin. The rush turned to blistering heat, but she did not let go until she had a firm hold of Rojon, despite the powers of Elihor pushing her away from him. She grabbed his shoulder, held herself steady.

"Rojon," she shouted, closer to him. Eyes filled with tears turned to her slowly, red and dark strands of magic coiling around his body. Siabala would not abandon his prey easily. Right now, Shirina just wasn't certain if that was Rojon, or Avarielle.

They needed to stop the flow of Siabala's magic, while focusing on the magic that might save them.

"Rina." His voice echoed in the winds.

"Rojon, listen to me," she placed her hand on his cheek, willed him to focus on her. "You can save everyone with Elihor's magic. You need to think of Cassara, your mother, and me. And you need to let go of Graysword."

His voice like a howl on the winds: "The magic will kill me."

"I won't let it," Shirina said, trying to peer outside the veil of magic but unable to. "I promise I won't let it."

Shirina couldn't find the strands of Graydon's magic, but she'd created her bracers to filter Elihor's magic. And, right now, Elihor's magic was plenty. All she needed to do was filter it and cast a teleportation spell. She had no idea where they were, which would prove dangerous, if not deadly. But the rebel had managed to teleport them both, so it stood to reason she could bring them back.

To Kosel's Circle. Or perhaps to the Lisal Gardens, where strong magics took root and her witches could help. *If they've not been destroyed.*

No. She flicked the destructive thought away and focused on Rojon.

"Rojon," Shirina repeated, still connected with his cheek, still looking in his eyes—all black, with sparks of red magic.

You cannot have him, Siabala!

"I can get us out using your magic. But I can't teleport safely with Siabala's magic, nor with the magic holding Cassara. You can end both of those."

"I don't want to die," his whispers became the wind. "I don't want anybody to die."

"Your mother will if you don't trust me, Rojon." Avarielle's features were taunt, turning a worrying shade of gray. "Let me save her. Let me save you."

"Mom?" he said, and his magic exploded outward, with

such force that his arms were flung at his sides, releasing Graysword. Avarielle collapsed to her knees, as did Cassara, the bonds releasing her, undone by Elihor's magic. Shirina managed to keep hold of Rojon, standing with him in the circle of magic. But Graysword flickered still within Avarielle's wound, the magic reacting to her touch, which would undo any attempt at crafting a teleportation spell.

"Cassara!"

"I'm here."

"I need you to pull Graysword out of Avarielle." Shirina winced at her own words.

Cassara's eyes widened, mouth opened as if in protest. Then she seemed to understand, and she nodded, features set in grim determination as she grabbed hold of the sword. The queen's touch seemed to diffuse its magic, Graydon's magic silenced, but apparently not destroyed.

There was hope yet, and Shirina clung to it. Moments passed, like an eternity wrapping around them as her muscles strained.

"I have it," Cassara shouted. "Shirina, if we're going to save Avarielle, we have to do it now!"

"Hold Avarielle and grab hold of my ankle." The queen did as instructed, wrapping her arm around Shirina's ankle as she wrapped her legs around Avarielle, Graysword kept at bay but secure in her other hand.

Shirina focused back on Rojon, his eyes brimming wells of the universe.

"Trust me, Rojon," she whispered.

And then she willed her bracers open, to welcome the magic of Elihor. He screamed, the magic fighting back, pounding into her bracers, unwilling to be manipulated. She clung to it, forcing it within the metal shells, turning it into strands of magic she understood, and cast a teleportation spell.

The bracers melted under the angered magic, burning her skin so deep she was certain it fused with her bones. She gritted her teeth against the white-hot pain and stench, and focused on her magic, and saving her friends, on the words that needed to be spoken with the right cadence, on holding back the cries of pain that threatened to escape.

All that mattered was her spell. She prayed to Elihor and Graydon that she would not get them all killed as the shimmer of magic blocked her vision, not risking using the Sight to look at Graydon, too focused on getting all of them to safety. Teleporting two additional people would have strained her. Three felt like running through a field of barbwire, every inch of her body screaming in agony.

The scent of roses exploded around her, and Shirina knew she'd reached Lisal Gardens, against all odds. Voices joined hers. Her adepts. Her Circle.

Even though powerless to use their magic, their words helped ground her as she dropped the teleportation spell. Rojon collapsed to his knees. Before his magic completely evaporated, she grabbed more of it, wrists blistering beneath her melted bracers as she turned to Avarielle and pushed healing magic deep within her. The warrior didn't even shift as Shirina mended arteries and skin, bones and muscles, the wounds deep. Left arm a sea of cracks, blood flowing freely, too quickly.

She couldn't afford the time needed to focus the spell, pumping as much as she could into the warrior before the magic of Elihor left her, ignoring the pain of her wrists, focusing only on the blood around the warrior's midsection...

"Shirina," Cassara said, placing a hand on her shoulder, kneeling on the other side of the warrior. "It's done."

Avarielle breathed gently. Her features were set in pain, but she no longer bled. Cassara squeezed Shirina's upper arm. Nausea crept up her throat, a fever breaking across the back of her neck.

"Let me help you," the queen said softly, in that voice Shirina had heard Cassara use on the gravely injured.

Shirina tried to speak, but found she couldn't, the world spinning around her.

"Crimson Circle Elite!" One of her adepts cried out. *Tinat.* Her youngest adept. She'd come to her as an orphan, willing to work and learn magic. She would make Crimson Circle Elite someday.

Shirina tried to comfort the adept, to tell her she was fine, but lost the thread of thought. Cassara held her tightly as she slipped into darkness, wishing she could pull on magic, but glad she'd made it back here, in the end, to where her Circle had begun.

2

*A*varielle felt every inch of the blade sliding out of her, though it didn't burn. It coated her, left a piece of itself behind. Magic writhed within her, like snakes settling in her core, finding her arteries and veins, traveling up them, razor sharp fangs leaving a trail of scars all the way to her heart.

And exploding in agony. Avarielle gasped, thought she heard Cassara say something, but was dragged back under, plunged into the flames growing within, spreading from her heart into her mind.

She fought to swim up, to find the surface again, but her mind shut down, waters turning to angry flames.

Siabala's Rage.

She was back in the ancient prison, trapped, gasping for air, tortured. Her left arm—which had been broken so often—snapped again, the wounds healed but the scars chiselled on her bones reopening. She fell, again and again, sulfur burning her nostrils, until the floor met her, and always, waiting for her, was Siabala.

She couldn't see him, but she could *feel* him.

Deep inside her, where Graysword had claimed her blood.

No. Her son needed her. She pushed against the flames, her bones charred, skin blistering, heart turning to ash.

Always, Siabala stood, waiting. Watching.

You are just an illusion.

She fought back, reached up, felt a hand take hers.

"Hang on, Avarielle."

Cassara. She was here, with her, keeping her safe. Avarielle found the strength to squeeze the queen's hand, who held her more tightly in turn. She would not let her go. They would not let each other go. Never.

This is the oath I will follow, she spat in her mind. *To protect the descendants of Graydon. To keep Cassara safe.*

The voice hissed in answer.

Oath Breaker.

Monster. Siabala was a monster, and she would break her oath to him as often as possible to keep the one that mattered. To keep Cassara and her family safe. To protect Rojon, like he'd protected her.

Pulling on her remaining strength, every inch of her body screaming in agony, she pushed back the shrinking flames, extinguished them, the scars within her hardening. The wound at her core. The magic trapped within.

As she finally drifted into oblivion, she heard the voice, perhaps riding on a memory. Or a nightmare.

Siabala, who haunted her still.

Impressive.

3

The beds bookended Rojon's chair, where he'd taken vigil since regaining consciousness. Shirina's hands rested over the blanket, wrists bound tightly with bandages. They'd scraped the metal fused to skin off, made sure the pain would not bother her, and that she would sleep. From her relaxed features, Rojon doubted the sorceress felt much of anything.

On the other bed, his mother's tanned face was ashen, eyes drawn tightly shut, breath ragged. He thought he'd lost her. And now, he might. At least this time, he'd be with her.

His leg twitched nervously beneath him, and he forced himself to relax, for his hands to stay on his thighs and not reach for his mother's hand. To reach for her would mean reaching for something darker. Deeper. To reach for her would be to reach for Siabala. To reach for Graysword.

He could feel it, the crackle of magic coming from her.

Could hear the spark of darkness traveling her veins. He loved her. Fiercely. Always had, from his youngest memories to his most recent ones.

Except now he knew that she'd made a deal with Siabala. She'd run his father through with Graysword. Just like Rojon had done to her. After he believed her dead, lost in a deep forest, never to return. He'd grieved for her, the mother he'd always loved.

Now that she was back, he found that he hated her, too.

She'd been his hero, and a hero to so many others. He'd witnessed how respected she was in Graydon, heard tales of her heroism. She'd always shrugged it off, told him that stuff didn't matter. That had made her more heroic. Sword-wielder, bow expert, quick footed and assured, and uncaring of what others thought, too.

But he'd seen beneath the veneer of who she was, to the darkness that lurked beneath the surface. The *monster.* Which she'd made a deal with. The one who'd killed his father. And that she'd failed to destroy, in turn, only killing his body and not his soul.

He didn't want her to die, yet he wished she'd stayed dead. He could feel it, Siabala's magic snaking in him, still, though he knew it was no longer there. He'd almost lost to it, and then his mother… She'd stepped in front of him. Used her own body to protect Cassara.

Would she have done the same to save him?

She protected the queen because of an oath she took, but if she already had a blood oath with Siabala… Why had she not wanted him to take the oath to protect the descendants of Graydon, too? She'd said she'd wanted more for him. But she must have known that Siabala would come for him, eventually.

His heart and mind twisted together, coating him with nausea and exhaustion from the magic. He wanted nothing more than to curl up beside his mother, to be near her familiar presence in this strange world that he no longer understood. But he wanted to run away from her, too, and never speak to her again.

She ran my father through with Graysword!

The door opened and Cassara slipped in. She checked both sleeping women, then winced as she sat on a beat-up wooden chair at the end of Shirina's bed.

"How are you feeling?" She asked in a whisper, studying him.

"You knew about my mother's oath with Siabala?" he asked, voice equally low. He hated knowing the truth. Speaking it, even less so.

"I found out recently, when she finally told us." She didn't need to elaborate for him to guess she'd also told Shirina. "She wanted to make sure we kept Graysword from you. I'm sorry we failed you, Rojon."

"No," he said, voice harsher than he'd intended, a quick motion of the chin toward his mother. "She failed me."

"Rojon," Cassara started, but he stormed off before he could hear what else she had to say. She did not follow him, which was just as well. He didn't feel like talking to anyone. Everything he'd known was a lie, and he couldn't handle the queen's calm and thoughtful presence. Right now, he wanted to rage.

He pounded down the wooden stairs, away from the guest room, where the healers had clumped their patients. He crossed a library, several adepts wisely moving out of his way, multi-colored cloaks a spattering against filled bookshelves.

The scent of stewing meat teased his stomach to life, growling.

But he wasn't done storming. He needed to get rid of this anger, this darkness, which choked his throat and crushed his chest.

He turned left, down another wood-panelled corridor with no decorations on the walls, and found a simple wooden door. He pushed it open, his senses slammed with heady perfume in the warmer day. Lavender. Roses. Other tantalizing scents he'd never before encountered.

He'd only seen Massir's gardens in Graydon, so far, and those were on palace grounds, not in the earth itself.

These... this place made him pause. He stopped dead in his tracks, looked slowly around, each bloom lifting the crushing weight as his breathing returned to normal. Finely woven mesh protected parts of the garden, brick walls crisscrossed to create interest, along with more recent wooden walls holding herb planters and securing tall and ripe purple and red tomatoes. A much earlier crop than in Elihor. Vines covered the brick mansion, making the building appear to be a feature of the gardens, not the other way around.

Pink and purple flowers bloomed along the vines, a variety he wasn't familiar with. Surrounding the stone mansion were what he guessed to be berry bushes, even if currently no fruit graced the thin branches. He skirted the building, taking different paths which led to mini gardens, demarked by bushes or old, half-crumbled stone walls. Some were all herbs, others all flowers, some vegetables, but most seemed to be a mix. Great trees cast shades in some areas, while sun shone through in others.

Stones had been laid down to create paths, the large slabs surrounded by white-flower-bearing moss. He let his feet follow the feast for his eyes, holding back from touching plants as he circled. A few witches walked by, observing him with curiosity. Most seemed worried but kept working diligently at tending the plants. Gathering crops. Splitting plants and putting them in the ground, an activity too late in the season to do in Elihor. Different plants, different ground, different heartiness.

He wanted to know everything about them. His hands practically twitched with the need to wield something different than a cursed sword. To feel the earth between his fingers, to smell plants blooming around him. To create, instead of destroy.

His mother had run his father through with Graysword.

He took a deep, shuddering breath.

"If you're just going to wander aimlessly with long soulful looks," an old woman said, "then at least make yourself useful."

He turned to her, a woman at least eighty, he guessed.

He looked at her with surprise, a simple blue cloak on her, instead of the more advanced orange or crimson cloak.

"What?" Her smile was rueful and unapologetic. "Life isn't a one destination journey, young man. Now, come on. Help an old woman prune these shrubs before they take over Lisal Gardens." Another Blue Circle joined them, apparently her sister.

They didn't ask his name, and he didn't offer. But he did take the offered shears, took a deep breath of earth and life, and put his hands to work.

4

Cassara watched Rojon go as she forced herself not to stop him and remain seated in her chair. She knew him just enough to know he needed space to gather his thoughts. She turned to Shirina.

"I know you're not sleeping."

"And how would you know that?" Shirina answered, voice thick with fatigue. Or pain. Cassara took Rojon's vacated chair at the head of the beds and offered the sorceress some water.

"You could have said something to Rojon. You know him better."

"You're much better at that stuff than I am, Cassara."

"Yes, I definitely did great," she muttered, putting the cup back on the table between the beds. Shirina's lips quirked up at Cassara's words, the amusement vanishing as quickly as it had appeared.

"How do you feel?" Cassara asked.

"Like I did something stupid and paid the price," she answered. Her eyes slid open, barely.

"Your wrists are burned pretty badly, but you'll recover."

"No magic here either, then."

"No," Cassara answered in a whisper, heart beating faster.

"Avarielle?"

"You healed her enough that she'll pull through, but she's still pretty badly off."

"She's too stubborn to die. I'll never think she's dead again, lest she fool me twice." Her voice faltered, cracked. "How are you? Your injuries were not fully healed, and you were too stubborn to stay in bed, from what I recall."

"I'm fine." Her breath hitched up, betraying her lie.

"I'll heal you as soon as I can," the sorceress said, voice drifting.

"I'll let you rest," Cassara stood up and headed for the door, not bothering to point out that Shirina couldn't access her magic.

"Cassara," Shirina croaked out. Cassara turned, door handle in hand. "I'm sorry I couldn't pull out Altessa, too."

"I'm sorry, too," Cassara said, then rallied. "But she's resourceful, and I'm sure she's found a way to find safety."

"Her mother's daughter," the sorceress said with a thin smile, before sliding back into sleep.

Cassara's head spun as she stepped into the hallway,

letting the healers back into the room. They'd already tended to her and done what they could, though it felt like a vice squeezed her midsection. She took the stairs, intent on getting some fresh air, for fear her worry might choke her.

She wasn't sure of anything, at all. Not of her daughter, nor her husband, nor of her kingdom.

The distance between them made her stomach turn and her heart ache. Part of her wished she'd stayed behind, to face whatever they faced. At least Alexavier and Traina were safe in Edoline, with her brother.

But Altessa and Dayshon… She didn't want to outlive any of her loved ones. Not again. She'd face Siabala without her magic time and time again, if it meant not burying anyone else she loved.

She'd already done enough of that for a lifetime.

5

The city held its breath, muted under the attack on its palace, a smothering smoke filtering down from the fires still raging in parts of it, hours after the alarm bells first rang. Great cracks travelled down the length of roads and up buildings, and wells which had been dependent on Circle magic to bring up water, had gone dry. The city cisterns would provide water for at least a few days, as long as they hadn't been damaged.

I have to find out, Altessa thought, breaking from the rebel to go speak to some nearby guards, mobilized throughout the city. The rebel grabbed her hand and kept her near.

"There are spies everywhere, princess. Trust me." Sweat lined the rebel's dark skin, dripping from her chin. She was exhausted, and risked everything to save her. They'd never seen the attack coming. How many spies did Elder Tally have looking for her at this very moment?

"She'll be looking for you," the rebel harshly whispered, as though sensing her fear. Altessa had no reason to doubt her, but no reason to really trust her, either. Except that she'd saved her life. That… that would have to do, for now. Right now, she was the one person she was certain wasn't actively trying to kill her.

Altessa followed the rebel for most of the day, down the streets of her beautiful city, blanketed with fear. They moved cautiously, avoiding large pockets of people, the rebel taking time to rest when the rebel's spell became too much to hold.

The city bristled the further down they went. Some looked toward the palace, others hid. Some ran, others stood in place, unable to break free of the sight of destruction in the heart of Massir. A reversal of how it had been twenty years ago, when its perimeter had been destroyed, but its palace protected.

Sunset began to cast heavy shadows all around her.

Wearing what she considered her relaxed yellow dress made her stand out like a sore thumb. Even her most casual garment outshone those in the area where they currently moved quickly. Thankfully, they were still under the rebel's spell, a green mist hiding their presence. Green magic that should never have existed, that had been somehow implanted in the woman now trying to save her. A few times the rebel faltered, exhausted. But she didn't want to take any more breaks. She just wanted to get to wherever they were going.

Her hand was clammy around Altessa's, still holding

hers, as though the princess' safety was as important as her own. They stumbled in the lower strata of the city, outside the old wall, but inside the newer one. She'd never been this far down in her own city, this area derelict and full of thieves, according to her maids. Not a place for a princess.

Yet here she was, surrounded by dark shadows cast by the walls buttressing them, the scratches on wood unmistakable as the Elom attack which had ravaged this part of the city. While her grandparents closed the gate leading to the palace, abandoning their people. Saving some. But dooming so many.

The rebel opened a wooden door and slipped into a house, pulling Altessa after her. Only after the door was shut did the green mists slip away. The rebel took a deep breath, leaned against the door, and slowly slid down it.

"Water," she croaked. Altessa headed for the counter to the side of the small home, quickly found a pitcher filled with stale water. She grabbed a clay bowl from the exposed wooden shelf, the only thing she could see that resembled a cup, and brought it to the rebel.

She took it without question, water dribbling down her chin as she gulped it down. Altessa refilled it, and she downed that one, too.

"Even poor people have cups, your highness," she said, handing back the bowl.

Altessa flushed. "I chose expediency over propriety," she bristled, then added in a whisper, "Thank you for saving my life."

The rebel shook her head and crossed her legs, still leaning against the door.

"It was a stupid thing to do and is probably going to get us both killed." Her voice was gruff, without care, and Altessa liked the sound of it.

"It was a brave thing to do," Altessa whispered, slowly sitting on the ground near the small wooden table, so she'd be level with her. "But I must admit that I'm not quite clear on why you saved me. I mean, you're with them, aren't you?"

The rebel looked up at her, eyes dark brown, skin only slightly lighter, dark hair in braids. And those eyes pierced her, now, studying her. Deciding if she could trust her. Then a lazy smile spread across her face, though her eyes lost none of their intensity.

"You're really slumming it, aren't you? Sitting on the ground in a Scratch home?"

"Scratch?"

"That's the name of this area, well, what the locals call it. Others call it Bait. Some call it the Sacrifice. I prefer Scratch, myself. Makes it sound more badass."

"Oh," was all Altessa could say.

"Want to know why all those names apply?" The grin was still there, frozen on her face. Altessa forced herself to look her in the eye.

"Because my grandparents closed the gates, to save what they could of the city, when the Eloms attacked."

Anger flashed in the rebel's eyes.

"When your grandparents *murdered* so many," she

hissed. Altessa bit her tongue, forcing herself not to say anything. It wouldn't help, and she was in no position to pick a fight with the woman who'd just saved her.

"I'm sorry," she finally said. "I wasn't even born then." She added, as if that somehow absolved her from her ancestors' actions. Would she have done any differently, in their shoes? It hadn't saved them, either.

"But you still live in their shadow, no, in their light, with the riches and powers of the throne."

Altessa wanted to argue that one. It wasn't all perfect roses and plump strawberries, but in the presence of the woman's anger and obvious lack, she didn't feel she had much of a leg to stand on. She simply stared at the woman.

"And your mother abandoned the armies to their death, on the eve of the final battle."

That, Altessa could not let sit, anger bubbling out of her before she could think better of it.

"My mother went to fight Siabala. A lot more people would have died if she hadn't done that!"

"So you say." The rebel shrugged. "There's no proof your mother ever even had magic. Maybe her friends just tried to shore her up so she could get on Rashim's throne."

"Why would she do that?" Altessa scoffed.

"Her own kingdom was almost completely destroyed by Eloms. She could gain more power and pull our armies away." Victory flashed in the rebel's eyes at her logic.

"It doesn't matter what you think," Altessa said softly, but didn't dare meet those eyes, looking down at her hands, instead, feeling the weight of fatigue crush her again. How many other people believed that of her mother? How many now cheered that she was gone? She wished she was back home, mad at her mother for being too careful, getting to know Rojon, laughing with her father.

Where were they now? Rojon was gone. Her mom had been taken, along with Shirina. Her father… She hoped the guards had snuck him out, but if there were traitors among their ranks… The tears came before she could stop them, from exhaustion and fear, or grieving her family. From feeling so lost and alone.

She wanted to wipe the tears away, to maintain composure before the rebel. For all she knew, her parents were dead and the throne was hers. But did any of it matter?

Altessa forced herself to look up at the rebel, expecting victory in her eyes still, as though her tears marked her guilt. But the rebel's eyes had softened. With a deep breath, Altessa tried to reach her once again, though she knew too many layers of pain and lies drew trenches between them.

"I'm sorry my family has caused you so much pain," she said, voice trembling, meaning every word. "But I will not pay the price for actions I did not commit. I can learn. I can become better and do more. But I will not bear the burden of generations. And I will not give up on them, either. Now—" she focused on the rebel, the woman observing her, fists clenched, "—do you have a plan to turn me in to them? Because if you do, just get it done with. If not, can we please adopt some semblance of civility?"

Both eyebrows shot up. Then a slight laugh escaped her lips. Altessa looked to the small home, the flowers in the window, the handwritten notes on the walls. This place was clean, and felt cozy. Safe. Like her home had, not long ago.

"I'm Altessa," she said.

"I know," the rebel looked at her with incredulity.

"Well, may I know your name, please?"

The woman let a moment pass. And then seemed to decide her worthy. "Ramelia," she answered.

"Thank you for saving me, Ramelia," Altessa said, her mind cleared by the release of tears. "Will you be missed? Will they come looking for you here?"

The rebel's eyes widened and she pushed herself up, though she was unsteady on her feet.

Altessa didn't want to assume she wanted help, and so just stood up with her, ready to step in while maintaining her distance.

"May I borrow some clothing to change into? I'm rather conspicuous at the moment."

Ramelia nodded, pointed at a room to the right. As simple as the rest of the home with a small bed and dresser, it nonetheless held everything the princess needed. Including, on a shirt, a familiar insignia, no doubt belonging to the rebel's parents. She tucked the information away, in case it should be needed later on.

Altessa threw on pants, tightening them with a belt, then picked a cotton shirt, and a heavy coat. She wrapped her hair in a scarf, wiped some of her makeup off. Avarielle had taught her how to vanish quickly. *Your hair is too noticeable. Hide it, cut it off, dye it. Don't be pretty, get dirty. People don't pay as much attention to dirty if you're out in the streets. It's clean and proper that stands out when you're on the run, and you don't want to stand out.*

She swallowed hard. *Thank you, Avarielle.*

Then she stepped out, where Ramelia had grabbed a few things. She looked with surprise at the princess, and Altessa fought the urge to stand up proud. Her posture was as part of the disguise as the dirt.

"We'll need to get out of the city," Ramelia said.

"My father is in the palace."

"Your father is dead."

Altessa's trembling hands turned to fists at her sides.

"What would you have me do? Run from my own family? My own kingdom? My people?"

Ramelia scoffed at her, crossed her arms, some of her energy returning in anger. "It's what your family does, isn't it? Abandon its people?"

"Get out of my way," Altessa commanded through gritted teeth. "I'll do this myself if I must."

"What will you do?" Ramelia asked. "You have no magic. You don't know who you can trust. What will you do, walk up and demand they obey you? You think that'll work?"

Altessa reached out for Graydon's magic in pure anger

but found the wells as empty as before. Had the Wall of Loss fallen, now that the magic had vanished? If Shirina and her mother were dead, was she the only one who knew her mother's magic had held the Wall in place? If they'd managed to survive, wouldn't they be back here already? The flames of her anger turned to ice as cold dread settled in. But it also brought calm. Her hands loosened at her sides, her mind stopped buzzing.

Rashim would be destroyed if the magic was unleashed. She needed to shore up her people's defenses, and make sure they knew what was more than likely about to happen.

"What did they intend to do to my mother," she asked softly, words leaden.

"Kill her." Ramelia's words were harsh, but her voice soft.

"Are you sure?" She looked to the rebel, to see if she could spot other possibilities in those dark eyes.

"There was only one plan for her."

Altessa's stomach turned once with grief, and she pushed her fears down, ignoring them for now. She'd break down later. Now, she had few options, even fewer allies, and almost no other potential outcome.

Siabala was free or would be shortly. The moment her mother had so feared was coming to pass, and the enemy seemed to have dismantled all their defenses and robbed them of their protective magic.

"I need your help," Altessa said, voice surprisingly calm. The rebel scoffed.

"To walk back into the palace? I just spent all day getting you out. If you want to go die there, that's on you. My conscience is clear."

"No." Altessa crushed down thoughts of her father, possibly trapped in there. Of her mother, already dead, or soon-to-be. She pushed back the faces of the maids and cooks and guards that formed her world. Of the home she'd grown up in, and both loved and loathed. She pushed deeper still her growing terror of doing everything wrong, despite striving for right. She pushed all of it down and focused on the rebel.

"I need to warn the people of an incoming attack," she said. For once, Ramelia didn't scoff at her or have a quick retort. "With Graydon's magic down, with my mother dead—" her voice faltered, "—or soon to be dead, that means the Wall of Loss will fall, if it hasn't already."

She said the words so simply, so calmly, that it took an instant for the full impact to hit Ramelia.

"You're kidding," she said. "Why would it come down? It just...it's safe, right? It held for a thousand years before."

She looked her straight in the eye, knowing she needed her trust. She needed an ally, and this was the only one she was sure wasn't out to kill her. Plus, part of her wanted vindication for her mother. To show them she'd been wrong, and her mother had been the hero Altessa had always believed her to be.

"Because after she defeated what she could of him, my mother's magic reformed the Wall of Loss," she said. "She gave it all up, almost died, to ensure he remained trapped."

Ramelia's mouth hung open, trying to form words that wouldn't come out. "And now that your people have killed her—" another hitch stopped her voice, but she pushed forward, "—and the magic of Graydon is muted, I can only imagine that Siabala is free. We must prepare for invasion."

Ramelia stood still for a few moments, studying her. The moments dragged on as their eyes remained locked. The rebel seemed to make up her mind and she nodded, lips thin.

"If I find out you're lying…"

"Our chances of survival will be much higher, and then feel free to give me a piece of your mind."

Their whispers and fears still thick in the house, they slipped out into the night, hoping the darkness would offer them cover, while Altessa wondered how, exactly, she would help her kingdom.

She had no magic. No Circle. No army. No allies.

All she had was the knowledge of what needed to be done, and the fear of failing her family, their blood casting a shadow over all of Rashim.

6

If Shirina paid close attention, she could see the warrior's chest rise and fall, lines of pain smothering her features, scars pale on her tanned skin. A thin sheen of sweat covered her face, a slight tremor on her left hand.

Her mind still pieced together the magic she'd filtered to get them here. She remembered the flow of power in her bracers. The pain, terrible and acute. Pumping it into Avarielle, even as Rojon lost his connection to it.

Avarielle's arm. Shirina remembered feeling dozens of fractures, if not more, on every bone of her left arm. She pushed herself off her bed, slipped into the chair, legs weak beneath her. The bandages around her wrists stung and itched, meaning the healing poultice was doing its job.

Graysword leaned casually against the wall near Avarielle's bed, and Shirina studied it, though she dared not touch it for fear some of Siabala's magic lingered there still. She'd never really had the chance to look at it so closely, even though it had been the reason she'd met the warrior in the first place. Sent to hunt down the Grayloft and her magical sword, Avarielle had not made it easy. They'd formed a tentative truce when it became clear they needed each other to save Graydon. And when Cassara had made it clear they needed to work together for each to accomplish their goal.

She'd never once asked to look at the blade since, knowing the warrior's distrust of her would easily, and understandably, be reignited. The red stone set in Graysword's pommel seemed to glow, though no light emitted from it.

Avarielle's left arm. Something bothered her, but she focused on the sword, instead, letting her mind slowly drop the threads of sleep and pain. The crafting on it was beautiful, there was no denying that. A solid blade constructed to kill, and to impress. Once it had been the sword of the leaders of the West. Had things been different, Avarielle might still be in the West.

Shirina frowned, turned away from the sword and looked to Avarielle's left arm, lying uselessly at her side, where the slight tremor courted her hand. Her right hand lay still.

Fractures. Memories gelled and she remembered healing Avarielle once, long ago, when she'd had little magic left except what she could draw from her staff. The damage had all been done by Siabala, a result of his torturing the warrior in his Rage.

Why had the fractures returned? It had been twenty years, and they'd healed long ago. Not to mention that one of Avarielle's useful but annoying traits was her ability to self-heal.

No. That wasn't *her* ability. It was Siabala's magic, holding her together. She'd once believed it to be Graysword's magic, but now, after seeing the magic infiltrate the warrior, she feared she'd been greatly mistaken about the origins of the warrior's abilities.

She'd healed Avarielle, and the warrior should be awake by now. She'd seen her more injured than this and still standing. Too stubborn to die. Too ridiculous to quit.

Shirina gently pulled back the thin cotton blanket covering Avarielle. They'd removed her armor, a clean cotton shirt covering her bandaged abdomen. The sorceress carefully undid the expert bandage, ignoring the pain of her wrists in favor of putting her fears to rest.

She breathed a sigh of relief as no fresh blood covered Avarielle. The muscles of her stomach held a nasty scar where Graysword had pierced her through, but it seemed closed and the stitches holding. Poultices had been applied to ward off infection, and no signs of inflammation could be seen. She placed two fingers on the skin near the wound, to sense if it held heat.

Avarielle hissed.

"Your hands are freezing," she slurred. "Take them off or I will."

Shirina couldn't feel heat, and so gently covered the warrior again.

"Why are your cold hands on me, anyway?" Avarielle seemed to rally, opening her eyes slightly. "You're not a healer, and if you were, you wouldn't be a good one anyway."

"I'm glad getting stabbed through didn't lessen your charms, Avarielle," Shirina said with no bark.

Avarielle shifted, then started pushing herself up, forcing her eyes open.

"Rojon."

Shirina held her down, to be rewarded by a scowl.

"He's fine," Shirina reassured her. "He used his magic and helped us escape."

That seemed to calm the warrior, and she stopped trying to push herself up.

"I knew he'd tap into his magic," Avarielle whispered, looking up at the ceiling. "But I was afraid, terrified, it might kill him."

"He's fine," Shirina repeated.

"How did he manage to get us out. Where are we, anyway?"

"The Lisal Gardens," Shirina said. The warrior had never been here, a long time Circle outpost even before Ravenhold's fall. It was here that Shirina had chosen to establish her new Circle, based in earth and plants, in life and hope.

"How would Rojon know where…oh." She turned and looked at Shirina, forced her eyes to focus, and reached for the sorceress' hand. With a gentle touch Shirina had never known from the warrior, Avarielle lifted it up to examine the thick bandage on her wrists.

"Your bracers," Avarielle said. "You used them to channel the magic of Elihor. Rojon's magic."

"It was enough to get us all out, and to heal you, but I've spent it all." A wry smile. "As you can see, I destroyed my bracers in the process, so should you get stabbed by your son again, healing you won't be an option."

"I'll keep that in mind," Avarielle whispered, lowering Shirina's hand but not letting go of it just yet. The warrior's breathing began to steady and slow, her tired body needing more sleep to recover from her injuries. Just when Shirina thought she'd fallen asleep, the warrior spoke.

"You saved him," she said, so low Shirina strained to hear.

"I'm sorry he got Graysword, Avarielle," Shirina said. "It shouldn't have happened. You trusted me to keep him safe, and I failed you at the first test."

Her only answer was a slight squeeze of her hand, and then the warrior's breaths grew longer as she slipped away. Shirina waited, counting those breaths, looking at the lighter red of Avarielle's hair, now sprinkled with gray, though not as much as her own. Age and battles had stamped time on the warrior's face, but her strength seemed as unfailing as ever. A sign of a well-lived life, or of magic coursing through her? Magic from Siabala, she now understood. Trapped in her sword, and so not in the

Wall of Loss. A strange blessing as monsters attacked Graydon and Elihor once more. Had Tally created the monsters? How had she communicated with Siabala after all this time?

Shirina let her mind decipher and catalogue possibilities, remaining seated near the warrior. Her mind was no longer tired, though weariness steeped her bones. Whatever had happened had already come to pass, and Shirina's lack of magic meant that no amount of hurrying on her part would change things.

And so Shirina waited until Avarielle was well asleep, and then she waited a few moments more before gently disentangling her hand and pulling up the warrior's blanket to make sure she wouldn't catch a chill, and slipped out of the room.

She needed answers, and she doubted she would find them here.

7

$\mathcal{E}$lder Tally had died before. She couldn't say she'd particularly enjoyed the experience, but she was familiar with it. One had to embrace death to embrace Siabala fully.

That's what the Grayloft fails to understand.

With a heave, she pushed herself off the bed, her head feeling more attached now that the skin had healed around it. No more blood flowed to her brain, since her artery had been rudely severed, but the magic maintained her well enough. Still, the change was undeniable, like a thick blanket had been laid over her senses.

She was lucky to still be alive, and she knew it.

"Thank you, My Lord," she whispered, thankful for the oath she'd sworn. An oath she never intended to betray. Not that she could, even had she wanted to.

With tentative steps she managed to reach her kitchen. Everything was as it had been yesterday, and yet completely different. Dust had settled over everything, from the crushing stones. A section of Massir had collapsed into her underground realm, killing so many. Not just those who dwelt above, but her rebels, too. And the outcasts, living under her wing.

It proved an annoying complication, but one she could deal with by settling elsewhere, of course. Her magic came easily, and she warmed up a cup of tea, cradling the earthen cup in her palm as she walked toward the exit of her home and planned her next steps. Of course, that proved difficult to do as details were sketchy in her mind.

But she knew many had been lost. With a deep breath, she smelled the death and fear surrounding her. It should taste like victory, but somehow, they'd been thwarted. Had the bloody Crimson Circle Elite figured out their plan in time to stop them? Or the queen drawn on her powers?

Perhaps. She couldn't quite recall, memories shadowed by the Grayloft's treachery.

"Elder Tally," Elder Morik stepped up to her, his fully dark eyes a perfect match to his black robes and cloak, showing he was an Elder of Larkhold. He sought her out with those eyes. "You have recovered…surprisingly well."

"All things are possible in the shadow of Siabala," she replied, nodding her head slightly, as much as the still repaired stone skin allowed.

"So it would seem," he uttered, showing his lack of belief. Tally was hardly surprised by it. Morik had survived Elihor's destruction by hiding beneath Larkhold with other Elders. They'd only showed their faces once the danger had passed. A coward's move, or a wise man's move, depending on your goal.

Dust from the collapsed cave clung to the bottom of her red robes. Barbwire ran through her veins, Siabala's magic snaking deep within every vessel, shredding her from within even as it kept her whole.

Were she younger, she would spare a thought or two worrying about what it might entail. Why she'd been spared, when others had been killed. So many hadn't survived the fall, but she had. Were she younger, she would have wondered what else her god was capable of, and how much his powers now infused her.

But she was old, now, and had lived a good long life, filled with choices that had led her to this moment. To this life, and this calling.

To do Siabala's bidding.

Their little village stood buzzing with fear. Some of her people had run, rebels welcomed from the edges of Massir and the lands of light and darkness. The outcasts that didn't quite fit in this new world. Those who had lost everything and couldn't climb the new echelons of this world.

And there were always echelons, no matter how well meaning the rulers might be. Which so few were. There were always those who had, and those who didn't. She'd reached for those who didn't, welcomed them into her fold. Offered them a home, for those who were homeless still. Offered them hope, for those who were too broken. And offered a purpose for those who were still angry.

To give the spark to their flames that would lead to the explosion that would consume Graydon.

Just like Siabala robbed Graydon of hope, and sparked anger within it.

Anger against the descendant of Graydon. Against the Circle. Against those whom some misguided souls worshipped as heroes.

It was a new day, and it was time for them to step into the light and show the world what they were capable of. She smiled as her robes turned white, the dust clinging at its hem in stark contract. She'd started in Graydon's Circle, after all, and their robes still belonged to her. As an Elder of Ravenhold, she would cleanse the Circle and finally set it free.

That was her gift from Siabala. And she would always owe him for his kindness, and guidance. And for the chance to leave the world a better, more powerful place for the witches who would follow in her footsteps, a clear trail marked crimson with the blood of the adepts who failed to swear their allegiance to Siabala.

8

This place reminded Cassara of her childhood kingdom Edoline, with its beautiful sprawling gardens surrounding the ancient mansion, accented though hardly contained by meandering low stone walls. Trees cast deep shades over rocky gardens, paths led to fountains and tree trunks. If she closed her eyes and listened to only the wind dancing in the leaves, she could almost convince herself she was home. Almost. But the air was wrong, not carrying the usual scent of the sea. The Lisal Gardens were near the water, but not close enough to hear the crashing surf like in Edoline.

She missed her childhood home, and wished deeply she could find herself there. To make sure her children were safe, and her brother. To walk the gardens and play her flute peacefully among them.

A pursuit for a different life.

A life she'd left behind twenty years ago, after

monsters ravaged her small kingdom, killing her father and taking her brother captive. She'd vowed to get him back, and she had. Well, Avarielle had, anyway, but they'd all played their part, like the weaves of destiny intertwined them together.

Avarielle, with her quick wits and feet, neither of which had slowed down. Shirina, with her magic and deep knowledge of Graydon. Except now she no longer possessed her magic. But she still had her knowledge. And her determination.

Cassara let her feet guide her, not paying attention to where she was headed, lost in thought. She crossed thin bushes, a path leading her amidst rows of lush roses. The Lisal Gardens always had something in bloom, Shirina likening the patient tending of gardens to the patient caring for magic, both necessary for life and growth.

Except there was no more magic. At least, it didn't seem there was. Cassara had no idea what had happened, but Shirina's magic had stopped working. Her daughter's no longer worked, either. Her heart skipped a beat at the thought of a defenseless Altessa hunted down by rebels. Her steps faltered, anxiety churning like angry groundhogs in her stomach. She hated this. Being so powerless to help her family, or her people. All because some had decided they wanted the power for themselves.

Dayshon. He would have been in the palace in meetings during the attack. Would Captain Tralin and his royal guards have managed to save their king? Had they all died trying? Would she ever feel her husband's gentle hands on her again?

Her hands flew to her midsection, pain lancing her from yesterday's—had it really only been yesterday?—attack. When Altessa had saved her by tapping into Graydon's magic.

Ages ago. When magic danced in the air around us.

With a deep breath, she forced her feet to keep moving forward, as rows of marigolds greeted her, row upon row of red, orange, and yellow hues dancing in the slight breeze.

Where am I? She glanced back and couldn't spot the mansion for the tall trees but imagined it to be somewhere to her right. Her feet moved of a will almost their own, bringing her to the cut trunk of a once large oak. Its rings were worn by time, but didn't feel dry, like sap still brought life to it from somewhere deep within. In its center grew a sapling, a single leaf clinging to it.

Cassara walked up to the trunk. It was large—the tree it once fed must have been magnificent, and visible from as far off as the Maple Mountains. She stepped on it, its strength supporting her, and headed to its centre, focused on that single leaf on the sapling.

The breeze caressed it and it shifted gently, pure green, new growth in a beautiful garden. Once, long ago, when all the trees of Graydon had seemed to be dying, a new leaf would have been a miraculous sight. Now, less so, but something about this leaf, in this moment, called to her. Its fragility, its refusal to die, its desire to cling to the possibility that life might exist... Cassara fell to her knees slowly before it, wanting to touch it, but fearing her fingers would prove too clumsy and damage it.

Her heart ached for her flute, left back in Massir, the instrument that helped ground her since she was a child. To hear her notes break free, to let her heart dance in the wind with them, uncontained and unstoppable... She'd never found a better way to express her emotions, nor to release them.

Her knees grew warm against the trunk, like it emanated heat. It grounded her, kept her in the moment—here, in this place she'd never before been, her two friends injured, her family lost, her kingdom too far away for her to intervene.

The breeze lifted her hair, the pale yellow dancing almost too slowly. The leaves sang around her, the fresh scent of marigolds teased her senses to life, the warmth spread from her knee upward, and still, she focused on that new life, on its gentle curve, on the dew drop trapped in its curled center.

All she had was this moment. Here. Now.

Her mouth opened and, lacking her flute, she instead softly began to sing, the words non-sensical and inconsequential as she focused on the leaf, and on the leaf alone, like it was the most important thing in the world.

Like it was the *only* thing in the world.

9

The adepts—*her* adepts—all cast her worried glances, as though trying to decipher through her what had happened to their magic. She'd informed the current Crimson Circles to gather everyone in the main hall in an hour and she would speak with them, mostly to comfort them. She had precious few answers to give but could offer words of comfort. First, she had to try to figure out what had happened to the magic of Graydon. All she knew was that it no longer danced in the air as it always had. As Elihor's dark strands danced in this land, the two weaves separated by the Wall of Loss.

She paused, looked over to the West. From here, the Bloody Mountains were a distant shadow. Did the Wall still glow above it? Or had it also fallen in the wake of Graydon's magic, releasing what remained of Siabala and infesting her land with magic that couldn't be channeled?

Shirina had pondered time and time again what his

escape would look like. Without a body, he wouldn't jump off his mountain and start destroying all in his path. But he'd have his magic, and he'd burned Elihor before. Would he unleash his magic? Or would he bide his time, like a poison silently destroying its carrier, detected only when too late? And did Elihor's magic still work? She had no idea, and the lack of knowledge made her bristle.

"Rina," Rojon's soft voice made her pause. She turned to see him stand up from where he'd been crouched, apparently tending to a patch of flowers which had seen better days. She'd been so focused on her thoughts that she hadn't even noticed him.

"Rojon." She examined him. The youth had been temperamental with Cassara, but always seemed to be when in proximity to Graysword. Wielding it had certainly not helped. He seemed calmer, his features back to their usual passive selves, a mix of worry and embarrassment lining them. This was the boy she'd watched grow up.

"Are you all right?" They both asked at the same time. He gave a short laugh, and she waited him out patiently with a smile.

"I'm fine," he said. "I mean, I've had better days. But I feel okay."

"Good." She glanced into his dark eyes, the tired rings beneath them. "Have you rested at all?"

"A bit, but only because I passed out," he said, looking embarrassed again. "I was worried about you." He paused. "And Mom."

She noted the hesitation, decided not to pursue for now.

"You used your magic," she said gently. "That will exhaust you, Rojon, on top of everything else that's happened in the last few days."

"I'm not exhausted, though," he shrugged.

"Define that for me," Shirina said. He looked physically exhausted. "Is your mind racing so you can't sleep? Are you too infused with energy to sleep?"

"I don't think it matters, does it?"

"It does to me," Shirina whispered. "Rojon, I'm worried about you, and I'm not sure how using the magic might have impacted you. I need to make sure you're all right."

He softened at that and gave a hefty sigh of his own. "Honestly? I *am* exhausted. But my mind is racing. No, that's not even it." He looked down at her, embarrassment creeping back on his features. "I'm numb, Rina. And I don't know how to shed it."

Shirina softened her voice. "I understand how you feel, Rojon. I've felt that way before, when overusing my magic. And—" she took his hands in hers, touched the dirt on them, "—I think you know exactly how to ground yourself again, Rojon. Don't underestimate your instincts."

A grin popped up on his face, then slowly vanished away to wonder. "Do you think that's how we ended up here? This place is like a garden haven."

"Perhaps it helped boost my spell," she conceded.

"You saved me," he said, as though remembering. "I

remember now, you reaching for me. Thank you."

"Always."

"I used my magic," he said in a whisper. "And I lived."

"You did, and now we're very much in uncharted territory. I do believe you're the first descendant of Elihor to survive her magic."

He nodded slowly, her words weighing on him. Then he cocked his head, looked to the west.

"What's that song?"

Shirina strained to hear, barely able to make out the music. Rojon walked toward it and, curious, she followed, heading into the heart of the Lisal Gardens. Not the mansion, but the location of the oldest, and most important, tree on this land.

When they approached, she recognized Cassara's voice. And then she recognized the music, if not the words: The Traveller's Song, which had once allowed her to wield the most powerful magic in Graydon and seal Siabala back in his wall.

Where hopefully he remained trapped.

Cassara's untrained voice was far from perfect, but it seemed to lure Rojon as effectively as the promise of rain during a dry summer. Concentric circles of red, yellow, and orange marigolds surrounded the large cut tree circle she knelt on, singing to a sprig growing from the long dead tree. Or perhaps not so dead, a green leaf unfurling, making way for another. And another.

Shirina had not seen a twig from this—the ancient oak planted by Graydon himself—since twenty years ago, when the last one had been cut and turned into a staff so she could safely use her magic. Grasky, the keeper of Lisal Gardens, had tended this tree himself, and refined it. He'd died in the final battle, saving Circle younglings, taking his secrets with him.

Yet here Cassara sang, and the sprout grew and thickened, more leaves appearing, as though responding to the Traveller's Song—that was what Cassara called it, anyway. A song gifted by Siabala's brother—the being who, by all accounts, had gifted Graydon with its powers—had called it his Song of Awakening. *Could it be?* She cocked her head and focused on the music.

Rojon stepped up beside her, and she examined him. He stared, lips parted as though a part of him wanted to join, but didn't quite know how. Shirina focused back on the song. She did not understand the words the queen uttered, a seeming assortment of random sounds and syllables.

Shirina took a deep shuddering breath and summoned the Sight. The magic refused to court her, and she could not see the threads of magic that made the tree grow. Nor could she see any magic in the air. But the sapling kept growing, slowly, and she'd learned long ago not to underestimate Cassara's magic.

In another time, she'd used a staff to wield the magic of Graydon safely when it had merged with that of Elihor, killing all those who wielded the combined threads. That staff had come from here. From this trunk. Much like this sapling.

"Wait here," she told Rojon, and she stepped on the large oak ring, her robes billowing slightly, as though power emanated from below.

This has to work, she thought as she reached Cassara before shifting to the other side of the sapling, the queen seeming unaware of her. With a trembling hand, she touched the sapling gently. It felt warm and welcoming.

Like the magic of Graydon. With more assured fingers, she wrapped her fingers around it gently, careful not to impede its stunning growth or damage its young branches. Power thrummed in her hand, like she could sense the lifeblood of the tree pounding beneath her palm.

Shirina took a deep breath, closed her eyes and relaxed them, let go of expectations, and reopened them slowly while focusing on the sproutling. It glowed softly with magic. At the sight, Shirina's knees felt weak, relief flooding through her.

The magic wasn't gone. It hadn't abandoned them. It hadn't abandoned *her*.

She looked to Cassara, and the queen did not glow with power, as she once had. She frowned, looked back to the sapling.

With the tip of her finger, the queen touched the uncurling leaves, and the magic danced up her hand. But it withdrew back to the sproutling as soon as she removed her hand. The magic might not be gone, but it had changed. Could it be hiding? Why? And how? Was Shirina simply attributing human-like behavior to it because she lacked answers?

Cassara removed her hand from the sapling, and the Sight immediately failed. Quickly, as though her life depended on it, the queen took hold of the sapling again, to be rewarded with magic, and relief.

Rojon walked forward, drawn by Cassara's song. The queen's eyes turned a deeper blue, affected by magic in a way that Shirina didn't quite fully understand. She was a descendant of Graydon, and her powers were quite different than the sorceress's.

Shirina took a deep breath, turned toward the West. She could barely see the distant tips of the Bloody Mountains between the dancing leaves. She stood still and gazed as the leaves shifted, spotting it between the world's breaths. She turned to the sapling, seeing the magic. Back to the mountains.

Her elation at using the Sight crumbled as it failed to spot the Wall of Loss, always a shimmering magical presence between worlds. The wind grew more intense, lifting the leaves, as though desperate to show Shirina something else. And then she saw it. And her stomach plummeted.

From the Bloody Mountains, washing over the West and even Massir, dark streams of magic unfurled, like a great wave washing over Graydon.

"Cassara," Shirina whispered.

The queen seemed to snap out of her magical stupor at the mention of her name.

"Shirina?" Cassara's voice trembled from exhaustion or fear as she slowly stood. The sapling stopped shifting beneath her palm, no longer growing without Cassara's urging.

"Elihor's magic…it's filtering into our world. I see it. No magic of Graydon in the air. Just the dark strands."

Cassara now stood beside her, her hand on Shirina's upper arm, squeezing. Shirina could feel Cassara's heartbeat through her palm, her anticipation so high, her fear so great. Or perhaps it was Shirina's heart that beat so wildly, as she couldn't bring herself to utter the words.

Shirina released the Sight as the strands approached, and dropped her hand from the sapling, for fear she might hurt it. What little magic she'd found was already lost to her, at least not without some safe means of filtering it, lest it devour her from within. She'd destroyed her bracers securing their escape. This sapling might help them, but they lacked the expertise to harvest it safely.

Which only compounded their problems. There was only one way the magic of Elihor would spread over them, now, as it had once before, to disastrous consequence.

The Wall of Loss had fallen. The day they'd dreaded for the past twenty years was finally here.

Siabala was free. It was only a matter of time before he made himself known.

With an unintended flourish of her cloak, she turned around, Cassara and Rojon following closely as she called to her Circle witches to come to her.

The time for battle had come. And they had no magic with which to fight him.

10

ltessa had often decided not to join her parents during their community days, a decision she now deeply regretted. It had always seemed unnecessary, or at least not *currently* necessary. What had occupied her time so if not to get to know her people and prepare to take over the throne? She couldn't understand the person she'd been just yesterday, like a chasm separated her from who she'd been mere hours ago.

The fireplace lit the face of Builder Hilar, who led the quiet night shift ready to aid if needed, though it was rarely needed. Their duties were too important not to always be prepared, however, from breaking the spread of house fires, to closing the gates against invaders, in case of another attack, like the one that had cost so many lives during the Days of Blood.

The Builder did not know her personally, and it had taken some doing to convince him of who she was. Even then, he seemed more confused and annoyed than attentive.

"Princess Altessa," he said, "I'm sorry that you've been through such a trial. The palace will need massive repairs, as will parts of the city that collapsed. That's my domain, and the Builders are hard at work day and night ensuring the people's safety and comfort."

"I understand that, Builder Hilar," Altessa said. She found it difficult demanding attention and respect when covered in dirt and baggy clothes, and with none of the trappings of the court like guards and gilded walls. Here, in the Builder's Hall, at night no less, her royal power became much more ephemeral. "Yours is a respected and important position." The man nodded in agreement, dark shadows on dark features. Her mother mostly worked with Builder Gramire, but she'd spoken of Builder Hilar and how she liked this man and respected him. Altessa disagreed with her mother's assessment. As far as she could tell, this Builder was only haughty and obnoxious.

Maybe it was her appearance that led him to look down at her. Or her age. She fought hard against her annoyance, to keep the edge out of her voice. The only other person in the room, Ramelia, stayed silent as she leaned against the stone wall, looking like she was witnessing, and enjoying, a bar fight.

"With the Wall of Loss fallen," she said, "there will be an attack from the West. It's important to shore up our defences beforehand, just in case." The Builders would be the ones to keep the walls standing, while the army, under General Akhalon, would fight off any incoming attack.

Hilar shook his head, as though still having a hard time wrapping his head around the Wall of Loss having fallen, even though it was the third time she'd mentioned it.

"How do you know that the Wall has fallen, princess? I was at the front lines the last time the Wall fell. It was concussive. Your mother's magic, long live the queen, saved us all."

"I share that magic," she said. He looked surprised but did not argue. "And I saw that it was gone." It was a slight lie. She assumed it was gone or would soon fall. Because her mother was gone, taken by them. And once she was dead…

"But where is the queen?" He asked, looking down. "She would not let this happen."

Altessa wanted to scream. *They took her, and I couldn't stop them.* A deep shuddering breath rattled her core, as the Builder stood straighter, sensing her tension.

"She has been taken by Siabala," Altessa whispered, as though she couldn't say the words too loudly.

The man muttered a curse and whispered something about revenge.

My mother is dead. Or will soon be. It doesn't matter anymore.

"And now we must honor her memory," she swallowed hard, "and make sure her people live. The people she sacrificed so much for."

A slight snort from Ramelia, which both Hilar and Altessa ignored.

"She had us build multiple walls and reinforce the homes at the base of the city," he said.

"Keep the poorest as fodder," Ramelia said.

"Another wall is coming up, as the city extends out," Hilar said, brows knitting together. "It does enlighten a few things. Like why she wanted walls before repairing parts of the city. If she knew an attack would come…wait, how would she know? How did she know when the Wall of Loss would fall? It had stood a thousand years the last time. Yet she moved as though she believed it would fall within her lifetime."

Altessa held herself a bit straighter. "She reformed the Wall using her magic only. As long as she lived, the Wall stood."

Had it been weakened because Altessa had used some of its powers? Had that alerted the enemy on how to take down the Wall? She pushed her guilt far below, forming a pool beneath her that threatened to swallow her whole.

"A queen as bright as the sun," Hilar's hand trembled toward the sky. "We will never know another like her."

Altessa both flushed with pride and embarrassment. She would be their next queen, after all. And she had a lot to prove.

"Will you help ensure the people are safe?"

Hilar didn't answer immediately, looking up confused at his hand, still above him. Altessa looked up with him, and Ramelia slowly pushed herself off the wall. A string of blood formed across the middle of the Builder's forearm. Blood started to dribble down the perfect line.

"What—" Altessa's words faltered when the top half of his arm fell to the ground, blood gushing upward from the fresh cut. The Builder's eyes grew wide, his mouth opened wide with a trapped scream. His eyes rolled back in his head as it slipped off his neck, body crumpling to the ground, theatrically slow.

Altessa stared at the mutilated man who'd spoken just moments before, trying to wrap her head around what exactly had happened, blood pooling slowly toward her feet.

Ramelia jerked her back as a silver thread snapped at Altessa, cutting her cheek. Altessa cried out as it burned. She fumbled to her feet and started running, but a wire caught her leg, and she tumbled down, Ramelia losing her hold on her.

Altessa tried to scramble up, but something tugged at her legs and dragged her toward the pool of blood. Several strands of silver formed a web over Hilar's body, reflecting the low light as they coalesced, forming the body of a woman cast in silver.

Her wide smile wasn't complete, and Altessa could see threads wiggling in its hollow, revealing the wall behind her, like she'd somehow lost half of herself and didn't have enough threads to form a full figure.

"Hello, princess." She tugged playfully at the wires holding Altessa's feet. "You can come willingly, or I can cut your feet and carry you." She waved her hand gently at her side, and the strings on Altessa's legs drew blood. Altessa bit down a scream. "What do you say? Do you take after your father and choose the most painful path?"

Father! Altessa's blood turned ice, and her voice found no purchase in her dry throat. The woman laughed, the sound like a shuffling of tinsels, silver wires moving out of synch, her body growing even more disjointed as wires separated and vibrated with the strange laughter.

Green fires slammed into the silver attacker, flinging her back as she shattered into a thousand silver wires. The threads holding Altessa's legs snapped away, cutting deep, but not so deep that she couldn't scramble up.

"Come on!" Ramelia pulled her up, and the two didn't look back, running into the darkness to escape the creature, leaving behind a trail of fresh blood.

11

*R*amelia's mind tumbled with possibilities, none of them good. She wished her parents had been home. She could use their counsel, but they were members of the guards, and had run off to do their duty.

Always running off to someone else's bidding. The familiar anger coiled in her belly, snaked in her blood. They were honorable, kind, fierce. Yet they'd bound themselves to the queen who'd abandoned them in the final battle. The blood-stained battlefield that still held parts of them captive, even twenty years later.

The princess followed her, Ramelia no longer certain where to go. If they found out she'd deserted, they'd go after her home. Her parents.

Would they? Maybe not. Maybe they'd think her dead.

That was too much of a risk to take. She'd just seen someone cut to pieces by a monster who worked for Tally. The Elder had other monsters, too. Ramelia had seen them lurking on the walls of the caverns down below, from the corner of her eyes. Shadows shifting unnaturally. Fear skulking in her gut.

Ramelia sensed she walked alone and stopped, turned to see the princess a few steps back, looking to the south. Her pant leg was crisscrossed with blood, fabric shredded. Dry blood covered her cheek. Her eyes, however, shone with fierce determination. A determination that fascinated and terrified Ramelia at once.

Why did I save her? Her life would be so much simpler if she'd have just walked away. Instead, she'd seen her, lost and afraid, and she'd needed to save her. Not because she was her princess, but because she'd looked so scared. So alone.

Because I'm an idiot, that's why.

"We have to keep moving, princess," Ramelia hissed. "That thing will come after us!"

"The guards," Altessa pointed south. "They'll head to the collapsed portion of the city. General Akhalon will be near to assess the damage and help citizens. I know he will."

"That's also where Tally's troops hid?"

Altessa shook her head. "But it's also our next best shot of getting help. If my father...if he's been hurt..." She stopped, voice shaking.

The silver thread lady hadn't exactly been kind about that.

"They're after you," Ramelia said, wanting to kick

herself even as she spoke, "so you hide, and I'll go get this general for you."

"You were a prisoner in the dungeons and escaped." Altessa's perfectly manicured eyebrow rose slowly. "How would you convince him to trust you?"

"I don't know!" Ramelia forced her voice to grow calmer. "Don't you have like, some kind of code word?"

"We don't," Altessa said softly, regret in her voice. "That would be handy just about now."

"How do I convince him to follow me, then?"

"I go with you," Altessa said, then held up her hand in an annoyingly royal gesture.

Ramelia didn't let her get a single word in. "Don't do that gesture again. It's really annoying."

Altessa sighed and lowered her hand. "Sorry," she offered, though didn't seem to be overly sorry. "Look, we need help. And the general is the next logical step."

"Okay, what will you do when that creature that hunts us cuts up the general before you, as well?"

"Hunts *me*," Altessa said. "Look, if she's with Tally, which it's safe to assume she is, then she'll know you're helping me." Cold dread washed over her. Ramelia had been so focused on getting the princess out, on not bringing the creature to her home, that she hadn't thought that part through. The Elder would guess that Ramelia had helped the princess. And Tally knew about her parents, because she'd told her in a moment of weakness. *This is why you never trust anyone.* The princess's voice softened, apparently aware of the turmoil she'd just ignited in the rebel.

"And she'll come after your parents, and you. You need to get them and get out of Massir as quickly as you can. And your parents are part of the guard, are they not?"

Ramelia blinked, looked surprised.

Altessa shrugged. "I saw the insignia in your home. And they were both gone, with no signs of boots or coats, after a piece of the city, and the palace, collapsed."

Ramelia had been so certain the princess would be too rattled to notice anything that she hadn't really thought about what she might gauge from their visit in her home. She'd have to be more careful—the princess was more astute than she'd anticipated.

"Why would the general not be at the palace, by that logic?" Ramelia asked as they both started walking again, toward the south, toward the broken part of Massir. Because that's where her parents most likely were. And where the princess believed help awaited.

"The priority is always the walls," Altessa said. "First, the walls. Then, the castle. The royal guards will take care of the royal family and system of governance. The military will take care of its people. That's the order of things, as laid out by my parents."

The words surprised Ramelia, but she filed them away for later, much later, while she focused on next steps. Tally would know about her. Unless the silver creature came for them right away, before reporting back, which it might.

Either way, battle was afoot, and the one thing she and the princess seemed to agree on was that they needed help. And it seemed the safest place to try to find it was in the snake's den itself, where the sun now shone, scattering some shadows while creating even deeper ones.

A tingling sensation settled in her middle, where her own blade had cut her. Warm and comforting, it coated the pain that still gripped her, dulled it, then muted it. The warmth moved outward, spreading to her legs, her arms, and her head.

Avarielle took a deep breath, only to find that she couldn't, like something smothered her.

Oath breaker.

She jerked up, throwing her covers aside, gulping fresh air. A sheen of sweat covered her, and she couldn't remember what exactly had woken her, but she felt better than she had for some time. Even the old injuries, the ones that haunted her despite her healing abilities, seemed lessened.

Slowly and carefully, she stood, stretched her arms and legs, then her back, testing her body. Everything moved as it should, and she didn't feel injured. Nor did she feel hungry or thirsty. She took some water regardless, her stomach twisting at the offering.

Another few breaths and it settled down. She had no idea where she was, nor how she'd gotten here. Her hand went to the bandages around her stomach, under a cotton shirt. Carefully, she pulled it away, dry blood making them stiff and brown. She cleaned her stomach, revealing a new nasty scar.

Graysword.

Slowly, it came back to her. Rojon held the sword. Cassara bound. Avarielle had stepped before her, taking the blow.

Had his magic been activated? She seemed to recall Shirina uttering something, but she couldn't pull the words from her memory. Where in Graydon, or Elihor, were they? Shirina… she'd been here. She'd told her Rojon was safe. The twist in her stomach began to loosen at the memory. Her son was safe.

Avarielle secured Graysword to her waist. She couldn't locate her armor but at least had pants and a soft cotton shirt—good enough for now—and she turned to the door to find out where she'd ended up. And how injured everyone was.

The door swung open and Rojon stood there, looking surprised to see her standing.

"Mom—" that was all he got out before she gathered him in a tight hug. After a few breaths, she pulled away from him, still holding his upper arms, and examined him.

"Are you all right? Did that Elder hurt you? I'd behead

her again if I could," she growled, then remembered that the Elder had stood back up again, even after she'd slashed her throat. "I guess I might get a chance at that," she muttered, then looked into Rojon's eyes. There she saw relief, but also something else.

Something darker.

"Rojon?" she asked, her own relief at seeing he was fine evaporating at the sight of that strange darkness, both familiar and new. Familiar because she'd seen it in her older brother's eyes, and in her own. Unfamiliar because it lurked in her son's. Her gentle, kind son. Her stomach tightened again, and she forced her breath to relax.

"I'm okay," he said, his eyes no longer going toward Graysword. That darkness she'd spotted evaporated, and he hugged her back. "I'm glad you're okay."

She held him.

"What did I miss?" she asked when they broke their embrace. "Where are we?"

"Lisal Gardens," he said, worry tinting his words, putting Avarielle on high alert. She found herself missing the snugness of her armor.

"Come on," he said, turning to lead the way. "Shirina wants to see you. And Cassara."

Relieved that her friends were safe, Avarielle followed Rojon and studied him as they walked. He seemed more like himself, and less. His shoulders were squared, as though awaiting a blow, and he glanced around, wary. That was not like her usually relaxed son. The sight of dirt on his hands heartened her, but still, that gnawing feeling at her core persisted.

She looked at those hands.

He'd wielded Graysword. What if running her through had been enough to satisfy the blood oath? Avarielle didn't know what happened to an existing blood oath if a new one was forged while they still lived. She'd never heard stories of such a thing happening. Maybe it wasn't even possible.

She gripped Graysword's pommel, felt the magic respond to her need, eager to be wielded. Rojon didn't slow, nor turn around. He had not felt the magic of her blade, and she had to believe that meant he hadn't taken the blood oath.

She wanted to ask him about it, but Shirina's voice captured her attention. The mansion opened into a large open-air courtyard. Adepts streamed by as they left, some murmuring while looking distraught, some sobbing. Others looked determined, hands turned to fists.

"We will gather again at nightfall," Shirina called to them. "Remember my words. Be careful. Be safe. Be wise."

High hopes for a witch, Avarielle followed Rojon toward Shirina.

"Avarielle," Cassara appeared beside her, grabbing her in a hug.

"You're all right," Avarielle said, relieved as she embraced her back. Maybe this day wasn't turning into a complete nightmare.

"I am." Cassara looked her over. "And you?"

"I feel fine." She shrugged. She remembered Cassara speaking to her, holding her hand, keeping her safe. Avarielle took her hand and squeezed it.

"It's *my* job to keep you safe, remember?"

"You did," she whispered. "You always do."

"It would be stupid of me to die by my own blade, Cassara," Avarielle said with a quick grin.

"No one expects you to die intelligently," Shirina said as she joined them, her jest sounding strained. Rojon stood beside her, looking like he'd swallowed something bitter.

"What were you going on about?" Avarielle asked. "Asking witches to be wise? Is that possible?"

"Not here," Shirina said, leading them down large stone halls toward a study in a private wing. Upholstered wooden chairs and tall bookshelves lined the room, with a large window overlooking the gardens.

"I can't be certain my wards still hold," Shirina said, looking apologetic. "But few have access to this wing, so we can count on some relative privacy."

"What do you mean you can't tell if your wards are holding?" Avarielle looked to Shirina, eyes wide. Cassara looked down, while Rojon stood by the window, examining the gardens.

She wasn't going to like any of this, was she?

"Just tell me what happened," Avarielle focused on Shirina, the only one still meeting her eyes.

"The magic of Graydon is gone," she said, voice impressively steady.

"Wha—"

"That's not the worse of it," Shirina whispered. Avarielle gripped Graysword's pommel. "The Wall of Loss has fallen."

Avarielle turned to Cassara slowly, to meet the blue eyes who now looked at her.

"My magic didn't return," she whispered.

"Not as such, no," Shirina said. "But don't dismiss it yet. If something is affecting the magic of Graydon, it will affect yours, as well."

"How do you know that the Wall has fallen, then?" Avarielle asked, hopeful.

"I used the Sight for a few seconds and saw the magic of Elihor like a wave coming toward us."

"Oh." The only other time Avarielle had known this to happen was when the Wall had been down. "Well, then, where's Siabala?"

"That, we don't know," Shirina said, folding her hands on her desk, as though uncertain what to do with them now that they couldn't conjure magic.

"So, let me get this straight," Avarielle stood up, no longer able to sit. "The Wall is down. Neither of you have your magic, and we have no clue where Siabala is?"

Shirina answered by simply looking at her.

"I thought it would be more dramatic, I'll admit," Avarielle mumbled. "It was the last time."

"How did it fall the last time?" Rojon asked, turning from the window.

"Like a thunderclap," Cassara answered. "Like the

world held its breath for a second. And then Siabala attacked."

"You stopped his fires." Avarielle looked to Cassara. "This time, there are no fires, which is just as well, because you don't have any magic."

The queen winced a though visibly stricken, and Avarielle wished she could take back the words.

"Sorry, Cass," she whispered. "Just a bit on edge. We can't fight an enemy we can't see."

"I have a feeling that he'll make himself known soon enough," Shirina said. Loud voices drew their attention to the corridor, and Shirina stood in one swift motion and headed to the door, Avarielle right behind her.

Standing in the doorway were two black-robed witches with crimson cloaks. The warrior cursed.

"We've been sent by Elder Quilsam to ensure the heir of Elihor is safe." No introductions, no request to enter. Avarielle folded her arms, forcing herself not to hit them.

Shirina, much more gracefully, stepped aside to allow them entry into her study. The two witches looked at Avarielle with some concern. She sized them up, then stepped aside to let them pass.

"As you can see, I'm fine," Rojon said, sounding annoyed. Avarielle raised an eyebrow at him. He'd never admit it, but he usually enjoyed the attention being heir of Elihor won him. Like being royalty without any actual commitments.

"What happened in Stormhold?" Shirina asked.

The two witches ignored her, until Rojon asked the same question. Avarielle took an automatic step toward them. She really didn't like them. The fact that they looked only to Rojon as they answered made her want to hit them more.

"The magic of Graydon just vanished, taking the Wall with it." The first one answered. The second continued.

"We should have never trusted just the magic of Graydon with the Wall. Of course it would fail."

Cassara slowly stood, eyes narrowing, voice shaking slightly as she spoke. Avarielle fought back a grin. She loved it when Cassara lost her temper.

"How dare you," she whispered. Her voice gained strength as she squared her shoulders and stood before them, every inch the queen she'd learn to become. "How dare you come in here and hurl insults." They looked surprised at Cassara's outrage, apparently not having noticed that the Queen of Rashim, who happened to be a descendant of Graydon, sat in the room. "Are you here to help, or will you simply toss insults and continue to display your foolishness?"

They didn't immediately answer, and Cassara made herself taller. Avarielle stood back, enjoying the show.

"I said," the queen asked again, "are you here to help? Because if you are, we welcome you. If not, we ask that you please leave."

"We're here to help," the shorter of the two witches said, turning to Rojon as though asking for help. Her son kept quiet, deepening the grin on Avarielle's face.

"Good," Shirina stepped beside Cassara. "Then begin by telling us how you found Rojon so easily."

Avarielle and Rojon's eyes met, fear lighting his. She gave him what she hoped was a reassuring smile. They'd figure it out together.

"Elihor's magic was used strongly in Graydon recently. In two spots—one underground, and one here. But the latest magic trail was obviously here."

"Shirina…" Avarielle growled. Shirina nodded, and the warrior could see the sorceress's mind already spinning with possibilities.

"Do you know where Siabala is?" Shirina asked, not missing a beat.

"Nowhere," the adept said, shifting slightly. Avarielle didn't think she was afraid. Maybe smug? Again? *She must really not want to make out of here in one piece.*

"We must find out where he is first," Shirina said, heading to her desk.

"No, Crimson Circle Elite." Avarielle did not like how the woman said Shirina's title. "We mean he's nowhere. He was not in the Wall."

Shirina, Cassara, and Avarielle shared a slow look. The sorceress stopped hunting for whatever she sought on her desk and focused back on the witches.

"Siabala was well trapped in there," Shirina said, her voice laced with worry, or a threat. Hard to tell, but Avarielle was willing to bet it was both.

"He did not come to Stormhold, nor did we see his magic."

"It seems," the taller witch answered again, this time with unmistakable smugness in her voice, "that you were mistaken, and Siabala did in fact perish without his body."

"I assure you we were not mistaken," Shirina said softly, narrowing her eyes. "And the very fact that you're willing to believe this implies that you're doing nothing to stop him, for when he does emerge."

"Yes, but—"

Shirina cut her off. "I assume you teleported here?"

They nodded. Now that Elihor's magic permeated both lands, they would still have their powers, unlike Graydon's Circle. A painful irony if they refused to acknowledge Siabala's reemerging.

Or a convenient one.

"Then send a message to Elder Quilsam, telling him that we must speak." The two adepts did not move. "Now," Shirina growled, practically throwing the two adepts out of her study and shutting the door.

Silence smothered the study as they each stood rooted in place. Without magic, they were limited in what they could do. But without allies, they were left without options, while the greatest evil ever faced by both lands roamed free. Somewhere.

"What do we do now?" Rojon asked softly.

"We wait," Shirina simply stated. "And we get ready, as best we can."

Avarielle hated waiting, and hated even more that Shirina was right.

13

Things were moving too fast, and Shirina hated feeling like she couldn't grab hold of events, everything streaming through her fingers, which refused to close and grab them: her magic, her Circle, and her very ability to make Larkhold see her point.

She hated the slippery slope she found herself on. It was more than slippery—it was treacherous. And she'd known treacherous before, just like she'd known humiliation. And having to just take it, because her irritation would solve nothing. The anger of the people of Graydon at the Circle's treachery had been hers to bear, and all the accompanying humiliation as she tried to find footing and recruits for her new Circle. Her white robes covered in the spoiled food and mud thrown at her. A sure sign, she'd comforted herself, that the people no longer feared the Circle.

Eventually, she'd found some foothold with the people

of Graydon, at least. Supporting those who felt abandoned by kings and councils, who needed healing salves and clean water. But still, her humiliation continued. Kings and queens refusing to meet with her, not even bothering to tell her before she arrived to meet at appointed times, turned away without a word of explanation.

Yes, she'd known humiliation and, for the most part, bore it with the grace and dignity she demanded of her witches. They had been the bad guys in the last war, and only hard work and diligence would buy them forgiveness. If at all.

But never before had she felt as hollowed out as she did now, because at least her sister coven of Larkhold had understood what she strove for. Perhaps not supported her always, but they had understood her desire and need to rebuild, even if they hadn't always agreed on her tactics.

The two Crimson Circle Elites from Elihor stood before her, the tall one not even bothering to hide her smirk. Not a single witch or warlock in her Circle could safely use their magic. And Larkhold's magic penetrated every nook and cranny of Graydon, making them the only coven that truly mattered. The only one that could make a difference.

They knew it and reveled in it. Shirina hated them for it, and for the humiliation of having to speak to the Elder through them.

At least he bothered granting my request, she thought bitterly.

But still, that was not what angered her most. The

greatest humiliation of all was not having her Elder cloak yet, so she could stand toe-to-toe with the elders of Larkhold. Her coven would never be seen on the same footing without Black Cloaks amongst them, a fact that made this humiliation all the more painful.

"The Elder says that they have of course looked, and there is no sign of Siabala," the tall Crimson Circle Elite, Patrile, informed her, as though speaking to a child.

"Please inform the Elder—" Shirina wanted to melt into the floor, or ring the neck of the adept, and she wasn't sure which desire would win out, "—that I saw Siabala's soul become ensnared in the Wall of Loss twenty years ago. That I am certain he lives."

She relayed the information, Shirina wishing she could just use her magic. All in all, she much preferred her humiliation to go unwitnessed.

A thin smile crept on the Crimson Circle's face and she narrowed her eyes, looking gleeful. She really hated her. Maybe having Avarielle here would have helped. Surely a glowering warrior would keep them somewhat in check.

"The Elder sees no point in continuing this conversation."

Or Cassara. She'd looked ready to tear a new one into them, and the queen could be scary when pushed.

"He says, and I quote: Crimson Circle Elite Shirina, enough of these games. Graydon has already made us lose enough time protecting a wall that had no purpose, in an obvious ploy not to lose your magic."

"A ploy?" Shirina's eyebrows shot up.

The woman continued. "Larkhold's covenant will undertake the work of both Circles as Graydon's Circle is obviously unable to continue its duties."

Shirina's hands shook at her sides, and she was fairly certain her face was as red as her cloak. And she didn't care.

Patrile folded her hands before her and actually bowed slightly. "The Elder thanks you for your service to the Circle, Crimson Circle Elite, and assures you and your coven that Larkhold will take care of Graydon as well as it takes care of Elihor." The other Circle witch, Kleriss, couldn't even meet Shirina's eyes, focused on the floor past Shirina.

"He thanks me for my service?" Shirina repeated, partly in an effort not to hit the adept, hands shaking as she clasped them before her.

"It has been a long day, Shirina," Patrile said, voice sickly sweet. "We will leave you to rest. You may of course remain in these Lisal Gardens, should you wish. The Circle will have no need of such a...*quaint* place."

Shirina narrowed her eyes and watched them leave, Patrile laughing in the corridor. Is that what the world relied upon? A Circle ready to step onto the still-breathing body of its fallen brethren? Unwilling to listen to them, no, to *her*?

Her own slow steps on creaking hardwood floors brought her back to the now as she looked out the window, onto the gardens that had saved her. This place wasn't quaint. It was a lifeline. Where she'd come after

Siabala had been beaten, with all her new scars and fears, her deeper understanding of the fragility of life and the importance of legacy. And of the Circle.

Without a Keep, Ravenhold deep beneath the sea, she'd chosen this place to begin her new Circle. Built of earth, instead of stone. Of life, instead of dust. Learning from plants born of Graydon, and not just books written by its students. She'd welcomed her witches here and had made a home for them all. Before any other outpost existed in Graydon, this place existed, and gave them a home. They created healing salves, here, that nations still relied upon for survival. So many lived because of their work... work which continued despite it all, reliant on skill and patience, not on magic, because a Circle should be about more than magic—their strongest trait, and their greatest weakness. She had turned no one away from her Circle, no matter if some couldn't connect to the magical strands of Graydon. Anyone who would stand up for Graydon belonged here, as long as they were willing to help cultivate a vibrant future.

The old fatigue crept into her bones and, much worse, the feelings of helplessness. She'd felt that way before, when her magic had been impossible to safely channel. Sick and wounded, and almost powerless, she'd headed to face Siabala regardless. Because it needed to be done.

And it needed to be done again.

My Circle is powerless to stop it. Her fears, kept at bay over years of action and preparation, crushed her. Siabala would win, this time not because he'd found greedy Elders to corrupt in Larkhold, but because they'd become complacent. Because they simply didn't care and wouldn't listen to someone without a black cloak.

No. She needed to think her way through this, and not just succumb to her fears. That would be to Siabala's advantage, and she refused to give him anymore of those.

Where are you? Why hadn't the dark god made himself known? He had every advantage in this fight. Massir had already been struck a massive blow. His Circle seemed to be thriving. The Wall of Loss had collapsed. Why had he not made himself known? The last time he'd been set free, he'd attacked almost immediately.

He would have won, if not for Cassara's magic.

Why did Cassara not have her magic back? Or did she?

Shirina took a deep breath, focused on the gardens below, toward the oak hidden by greenery, and imagined the much larger sprout growing from it. And Cassara, who moved as though her wounds were healed.

For twenty years, she'd envisioned what this day, this moment, would look like. Without meaning to, in a bid to get ready, she'd created mountains of expectations and guesses. And now those clouded her judgment, forcing her to look for expected patterns as opposed to actual ones.

That would not do. It had taken her over a decade to perfect her bracers, and more were being completed, but not yet finished. Without them, her witches could not fight.

She closed her eyes, listened to the sound of the wind

in the trees, the leaves, the flowers below. Felt the earth solid and strong beneath her feet. The Wall had fallen, Siabala and Cassara's magic were both missing. Or, at least, simply not where she'd expected them to appear.

Why had the magic vanished? The question proved more and more vital with each passing second. And there was one person who might be able to give her some answers.

If he could remember.

Shirina squared her shoulders and headed out to find Rojon. She was not defeated yet, and she would be damned if she let some ignorant Larkhold Elder make her feel like she'd accomplished less than she had.

She had not come this far to be stopped by a lack of faith in her abilities. Not from others, and certainly not from herself.

14

ojon busied himself with examining some wriggly plant closely. Avarielle crossed her arms as she scowled at a nearby shrub, anger pouring from her. Cassara stood by a tree, not willing to look at either of them or try to engage them in conversation.

The Wall had fallen. Her magic… her magic should have returned. Fully. Completely. Filled the hollow that persisted within her, to this day, even after having felt it for a few brief moments…

She closed her eyes, took a deep breath, focused on the feel of the air around her. Of the earth beneath her feet. Her heart beating in her chest in anticipation. The breeze singing in the leaves.

She reached out, tentative. That Shirina could not use her magic did not mean that she couldn't. Graydon's magic had never abandoned her before. Not like this. She pulled back, stopped reaching for it, breath trapped in her throat.

I'm afraid, she realized. Then tried to rally. *I don't have time for this.*

She bristled, frowned, planted her feet more firmly.

And reached out again, plunging deep into the wells she'd not dared look within for decades, which had once been filled by her magic. She hadn't looked but had always felt their emptiness coiling around her heart, pouring lead in her bones, slowing her down and making her so tired. An emptiness that seemed to grow with each of her children. With each of her royal duties. That never refilled no matter how *hard* she tried. And she'd tried.

She reached further, willing to drown in those wells if even a minute portion of her power awaited her. Willing to drink it all in, even if it meant death after going so long without it, to simply give it all up for the sake of feeling whole again.

Of feeling full. Like herself. A self she'd left behind two decades ago atop the Bloody Mountains.

I'm afraid, she thought again, the fear gripping her chest as she tried to reach for her magic, as hard as she could, fist firmly against her chest where once it would have clasped her amulet.

Not afraid of failing. No, she wasn't afraid of that.

She opened her eyes, hands trembling, feeling nauseated.

She was afraid that she had found the magic again for a few brief moments, and it had seen her for who she had become: unhappy, lost, trapped in a despair she simply didn't know how to shed. That it could not find the young woman she'd once been, who had been filled with hope and stubbornness. Oh, she'd always been stubborn, sure. Hopeful, even. Because her life mattered—she maintained the Wall of Loss, and someday her magic would return. Except it hadn't. It hadn't, and she was the same, but now without a throne, or her family.

And so she feared deep down that the magic was still there, but it saw her for who she truly was, and found her unworthy. Just like it had grazed her again to help a sproutling grow but deserted her after helping her heal. After dancing within her for a few glorious moments. After visiting the landscape of her mind and heart, twenty years worn.

"Do you think Shirina's slapped one of those smug adepts, yet?" Avarielle asked, making Cassara jump. The warrior stood nearer, leaning against a tree, apparently having grown bored with scowling at the bush.

"Probably not," Cassara said. "That's more your style." She glanced up at the blue sky. The day was perfect. Idyllic, even. She'd never imagined the end of the world would prove so beautiful.

"No, I'd have punched them." The warrior's voice was tense, despite her light words. "Maybe Shirina is a puncher, too, but I peg her for a slapper."

"Avarielle," Cassara turned to her, fear and fury colliding within her. "What are we going to do? Siabala is out. The Wall has fallen. We don't have any magic, I can't *touch* the magic, and I don't know what's happened to my family!"

She could hear the pitch of her voice rising, and found herself incapable of modulating it. Or really of breathing.

I'm not worthy. Whatever the magic once saw in me, it's gone.

Nausea bubbled up, and Avarielle was at her side in an instant. Cassara folded in two and, to her horror, threw up bile.

"We'll figure it out," Avarielle said gently, holding back stray strands of hair and rubbing her back. "We always do."

Hot tears welled down Cassara's face as the warrior stayed near her. She'd been scared for her family before, when a rogue Circle and rebels had attacked. But part of her had known she could always call on her magic, if in truly dire circumstance. Pushed to choose between all of Graydon and her loved ones, she would have called on her magic, she now understood. Because no longer having the option to even draw on it made her feel so helpless that she actually threw up.

"I was supposed to get my magic back," she choked out. She took a deep, shuddering breath, and looked at Avarielle. "Why did it come back for just a few moments, only to desert me again?"

"I don't know," Avarielle said, helping her sit down under the shade of a tree. "But we'll figure that out, too. Shirina will get us help from Larkhold's Circle—"

"I'm afraid I won't," Shirina said as she approached

them. Cassara closed her eyes, leaned back against the trunk of the tree.

"Larkhold confirms the Wall has fallen." The sorceress paused, and Cassara waited, keeping her eyes closed, focusing on the feel of the breeze licking away the cold sweat of her face, the strange tang in the air, the fatigue creeping up her spine. "But they believe Siabala did not escape, because they do not believe he was still trapped in there."

Even Avarielle needed a few seconds to wrap her head around the sorceress's words before exploding into a string of expletives.

"They think we just made it up?" She finally managed to spit out a full statement. "For fun? Just because we were bored and wanted to keep Graydon captive with fear?"

"I don't know what they think." Cassara heard the same fatigue plaguing her creeping into Shirina's voice. "But we have to—"

"No." Cassara opened her eyes, looked to Shirina, the sorceress surprised at having been cut off. "We don't have to do anything. We won't change their minds without Siabala appearing, and by the time he does, it'll be too late." Both Avarielle and Shirina looked at her, Rojon observing from afar, as though afraid to get too close. A breeze lifted her hair, the cooling wind refreshing her neck. She pushed herself back up.

"I'm going home," she continued. "To help my family, and my people. Come what may, it's where I choose to be when he finally does strike."

"Cassara—"

"You don't need to worry about me anymore," she cut Avarielle off. She was done. She'd fought so hard twenty years ago, and all the moments following that battle. She'd given up Edoline, her magic, her future. For what? Shirina could convince the Larkhold Circle to stand and fight, if at all possible. But Cassara was needed in Rashim. She'd fought this battle once and refused to do so again. Her heart belonged elsewhere.

"My magic is no longer linked to the Wall." She turned from Shirina to Avarielle. "If I die, it won't set Siabala free. So there's no need to worry about me anymore."

"Oh, Eli's Tits to you, Cassara! Do you really think that's all I care about?" Avarielle growled. "Keeping you safe because the bloody Wall needs your magic? Or because of some oath to protect your bloodline? I keep you safe because you're my friend! A bloody annoyingly self-sacrificing friend, but a friend, nonetheless."

"I agree with Avarielle," Shirina immediately said, "with less spitting and swearing. We took down Siabala together. We're stronger together."

"It doesn't matter," Cassara spat out before she could stop herself. "We did everything we could the first time. And we killed his body, but not his soul. Now, rebels have risen out of hatred for me. The Circle of Larkhold doesn't respect you," Shirina raised an eyebrow. Cassara turned to Avarielle. "And yours is the only magic we have left, and it's not enough."

"We'll find a way—" Avarielle started, but Cassara cut her off.

"No, we did last time, and it only led us here, in worse straits than before. They think Siabala isn't back! While a rogue Circle slithers beneath my kingdom!"

"Cassara, they—" Shirina didn't manage to get much further either, Cassara's anxiety for her family feeding her words.

"Even if we convince them, what will they do? Will they send their witches to fight the rogue Circle? Did it even occur of them to ask?"

"They don't—"

"They *won't.*"

Cassara fumed as she looked at Shirina, the sorceress holding her peace. When Cassara didn't continue, Shirina spoke.

"May I speak, or would you care to continue interrupting me, your majesty?"

"I can't abandon my people," she answered, feeling better for the outrage, but still numb. This time, Avarielle's voice was gentle.

"You won't. You once found an army to save my people, Cassara. We need magic to save yours, so that's what we'll do. We'll find magic again to save your people."

"It won't help," Cassara shook her head. "It's gone. It should have just returned, but—"

"Rina," Rojon called out from the nearby oak tree, past large wine-colored bushes.

"Can anyone finish a sentence today?" Avarielle

mumbled as the three headed to see what he'd found, the wonder in his voice undeniable. Even Cassara felt energized by it, if only slightly.

Too many hits, too long, too often.

"Look," Rojon said, pointing in awe at the sapling growing out of the oak. Cassara stared. This morning, it had been just a stick with a single leaf. It had grown with Cassara's song, before she lost her connection again. Now it stood taller than Rojon, with several limbs and leaves. A tree in its own right.

"You see, Cassara," Shirina said, voice soft as though afraid of breaking the spell. "Your magic is not as lost as you fear. We just need to figure out where, exactly, the magic of Graydon is, and I think we'll have the key we need to finally defeat Siabala. You teased some of it out this morning. You'll figure it out again."

Cassara didn't answer, breath caught in her throat as she focused on that one leaf, on the tear running down her face, on the greenness of life, and on the strange hollow within her, where her magic had once lived, which still felt empty. On the growing knowledge that yes, Graydon's magic still lurked somewhere and fed this sapling, and on the fear hardening in her heart that it had judged her, and had found her unworthy.

15

The teleportation circle's shimmer vanished from around Elder Quilsam, the stonework of the city of Massir growing solid around him. For a moment, it took his breath away. Elihor had never based its architecture so much on stone as life. Trees with roots you could trust to protect you. Branches that would shelter you. Even if they used stone, which they did for its longevity, it was beautified and surrounded by trees that held the memories of those they loved. Something that the Heir of Elihor had only fortified with his studies, and something that Quilsam knew Rojon Kolder should retake as soon as possible. In Elihor, and not in this land forsaken by even the Great Betrayer's magic.

He gazed down at the city from the top of the palace, where he'd followed Graydon's Circle teleportation trail. The city sprawled beneath him. Smoke drifted up on its edge, where parts of it had collapsed. The sunset in

Graydon was not as beautiful as in Elihor, shadows of the Bloody Mountains stretching around him.

Elder Quilsam wanted to spend hours just observing the architecture below, in this so-called Land of Light. Graydon's magic was not light, despite its pale appearance. No more than Elihor and her magic had been linked to darkness.

He forced his attention toward the castle surrounding him, the stench of fire trickling his senses to life. He knew that smell. When Siabala's fires had raged across Elihor, it had claimed so many. He'd watched them spread out from the safety of Larkhold, helpless to stop them. When it became clear they would not be stopped, they'd poured all of their magic into Larkhold. So many adepts had perished holding back the onslaught of Siabala's magic. Even in Larkhold, the furthest point from the Wall of Loss and the Bloody Mountains where Siabala still dwelt, his power had been too great to stop without heartbreaking sacrifice.

In the end, only a few Elders and adepts had remained. Less than a hundred all-together. An insurmountable loss, he'd thought. Of course, that was before he'd learned of Ravenhold's loss. Not only had Graydon lost its keep—it had also lost all of its Elders. Without at least one black cloak, it would be impossible for a new Elder to step forward. Not even Shirina, their last remaining Crimson Circle Elite, could rise to take the title.

He focused back on the scent of fire, at the burn marks

in the courtyard around him. This was the scent he hated the most. Burnt gardens. Plants. Memories.

If Siabala had meant to rob Elihor of its memories, of the thing that kept them grounded, of their connection to their past and themselves, he'd succeeded. They hadn't lost as many Elders as Graydon, but they'd lost so much. Entire forests filled with the memories of those who'd come before, for generations, annihilated.

His family's trees had all been destroyed. His mother, who used to sing him to sleep. His father, who encouraged his love of learning. His daughter, who died too young, memories only sweet and afraid, a whisper of love. His wife, who'd followed her shortly after. Her memories he'd never dared taste, for fear of only tasting grief and pain. Disappointment at his inability to save her. To save their daughter.

And now, he would never taste them. She was gone, completely, robbing him of his chance to ever find peace. To know how she felt. Because none of the trees could be saved, not even sproutlings surviving.

But these gardens would survive, if well tended. The apple trees were tasteless in Graydon, so it didn't matter. The magic of the land didn't feed the apples here like they did in Elihor. Memories were simply lost in death.

The palace had been gravely injured or attacked. A few of his Crimson Circle Elite witches and warlocks teleported around him. They looked exhausted, even if they'd taken a lengthy break halfway to recharge their strength. They didn't merge their magic like in Graydon to boost their teleportation spells, but perhaps that was one good idea from Shirina. According to his adepts, the Crimson Circle Elite had survived this attack, real or imagined, and had taken refuge in the Lisal Gardens.

And so, she *should* hide. He hated that he'd blindly trusted her. That she'd so easily lied to him and gotten away with it. He'd never been able to confirm Siabala had survived, but why would he even consider that Ravenhold's highest-ranking witch would lie to him?

That explained why only Graydon's powers had reformed the Wall of Loss. Elihor's powers would not be needed for the ruse. But why would Shirina concoct such a lie? That part still bothered him, despite Elder Kush and Elder Marik's belief in her guilt.

He could only think that she was buying herself time while she tried to reform Ravenhold so that his Circle wouldn't just take over. But to what end? Her learning was limited without an Elder or the Keep. She could only get so far. Shirina was many things, but stupid was not amongst them.

Perhaps she'd been trying to keep the strands of magic apart. So many had perished in Graydon when the magic had mixed. That would have been a worthy pursuit, but again, why not just say so? Why lie about Siabala? Did she fear that Larkhold would simply ignore her and doom them?

With the Sight, he glanced around at the magic of Larkhold dancing in the air around him. Graydon's magic was gone. No trace of the bright strands remained, as though the magic had given up on them. Perhaps it, too, felt betrayed at being trapped in the Wall of Loss when it could have simply roamed free. In that betrayal it had chosen to abandon Graydon.

"Where do we go from here, Elder?" Orem, one of his Crimson Circles on the cusp of becoming Elite, asked. Quilsam turned to the youth, dark eyes wide as he gazed at the architecture surrounding him, seeming uncomfortable standing so high up on stone, so far away from the earth and roots.

"We find the descendant of Graydon, Queen Cassara, and introduce ourselves. See if we may be of service as Graydon's Circle has fallen."

The Crimson Circle looked proud at his words. As did the other six adepts who'd made the jump with him, all Crimson Circle, the level required for such dangerous and intricate magic. So many had joined Larkhold's Circle during the rebuild that they neared a thousand, spread across Elihor, though few had the passion and commitment to make Crimson Circle Elite, much less Elder. But, with time, Orem would make the grade, of that he was certain.

Perseverance had seen Elihor survive, and even thrive. They had thirty-three Elders. A sad number compared to before the attack, but they continued to rebuild.

"Elder Quilsam." A Crimson Circle Elite wearing the white robes of Graydon, walked up to him. He bowed respectfully at the waist, hands clasped before him as he faced the Elder. "We welcome you to Massir, Elder, and Crimson Circles of Larkhold."

"I did not think there were other Crimson Circle Elites aside from Shirina," Quilsam said, suspicious, reaching for the magic of Elihor around him, its strength undeniable. He had access to magic. The warlock of Graydon did not. He found that thought comforting.

"That's what the traitor would have you believe." The warlock practically growled.

"Traitor?" Quilsam felt his pressure rising, his anger, rare but powerful, licking the edges of his mind. Larkhold had been betrayed before, by some of their Elders. To be betrayed again, by a Crimson Circle Elite of Graydon's Circle no less… he would not stand for it.

"Perhaps an Elder would be better suited to answer your questions," the Crimson Circle Elite said, visibly trying to reign in his anger.

"You have an Elder?" Quilsam's anger turned to cold dread. He examined where that dread came from, suspecting he liked the thought of Larkhold taking over Ravenhold's duties as well. An uncharitable thought, and perhaps he'd have to readjust his thinking. To have an Elder survive in Graydon would be a boon to them all. They'd lost so much already.

But where had this Elder been hiding all this time?

"Please follow me," the Crimson Circle Elite said with a bow. "My name is Crimson Circle Elite Pol."

Elder Quilsam followed him through collapsed architecture and broken archways.

"You were attacked?"

"By the traitor." This time, the warlock hissed.

"Shirina attacked Massir?" Quilsam hated all these basic questions. The very act of voicing them made him feel simple, something he despised.

"She did."

Quilsam decided he would hold his questions until he spoke with the Elder. His mind spun with possibilities, ignoring the burn marks on the walls and the dark stains on the stones beneath his feet.

Crimson Circle Elite Shirina had crossed through Stormhold just days ago. His heart dropped. She'd been traveling with Elihor's last descendant.

By the time they reached a small study with no windows, a few chairs for comfort and scrolls lining the walls, Quilsam fought against his anger as worry bubbled into rage.

A white-robed Elder stood in the study, her back to him. Her hair still had some brown, though it was mostly white. She looked like she'd fallen on hard times, a distinct lean to her body as she favored her right leg. Her neck seemed bent, perhaps due to injury or simply studying the scrolls before her.

He indicated for the rest of his adepts to wait for him outside the small room. Ravenhold's Crimson Circle Elite, a warlock whose name he'd already forgotten, bowed and exited, closing the door behind him and leaving the two Elders alone. The Ravenhold Elder turned, and Quilsam studied her.

She stood passively before him, waiting for him to draw his own conclusions. Not because she cared what he thought, but because she understood he had to make sure she was of the station she claimed by her black cloak. Quilsam recognized the fire in her eyes, despite the scars and deep wrinkles of her face. An Elder, without a doubt, and so it seemed that indeed not all of Ravenhold's Elders had perished in Siabala's attack.

As Shirina would have had them believe.

He offered the Elder a nod, out of respect.

"Elder Tally." She offered.

"Elder Quilsam," he said.

"Well met, Elder Quilsam." Her throat sounded raw, as though someone had scraped her tongue and throat with a knife, removing a layer of it.

"I must admit to some shock," he said, though was careful not to be too demonstrative in his relief. "I believed all of Ravenhold's Elders to be dead."

He was surprised when Elder Tally offered him a smile. Ravenhold's Circle did not share or lean into their emotions as much as Larkhold's Circle.

"As you can see, I am as alive as you are." She gestured for him to sit in one of the wingback chairs, as she took another. He joined her, unable to shake the strange feeling of dread that seemed intent on holding him captive.

"I can see that," he said, "but I have to admit I'm really not sure how. Where have you been for the past twenty years?"

She looked at him with sharp, piercing eyes. Then,

slowly, she turned her head toward the West. Looked as though she could see through the walls of the castle, through stone and wood, and Quilsam's stomach dropped at the obvious answer.

"Siabala's Rage?" He asked, not believing the words had slipped from his mouth. He'd looked, and there had been nothing. Nothing that he could see… that anyone could see. Parts were open and infrequently used to travel from one land to the other. Others were locked, where Siabala had tortured people and turned them into monsters. But no one had been there. He'd mourned for his fallen colleagues.

"The Wall of Loss kept us trapped," Elder Tally whispered, as though sensing his confusion. "With it falling, we are now free. For twenty years, I have been trapped in time and space itself, with the other adepts."

Other adepts. Like the Crimson Circle Elite. Perhaps Ravenhold's Circle hadn't fallen quite as much as they'd feared. Or as much as Shirina had led them to believe.

Elder Tally shifted and her neck caught his eye, where stone seemed to form over it, lending a stiffness to her movements. She followed his gaze, unsurprised since she hadn't tried to hide her affliction.

"An injury suffered while trapped," she said. "It healed oddly in the land between lands."

He nodded slowly, fighting the urge to reach for her neck and touch the strange skin. Part of him wanted to make sure she was real by touching it, but another part of him was repulsed by the unnatural sheen of the skin. Granite on pasty white.

"Elder Quilsam," she said, her voice regaining the authority he'd expect in an Elder. "Time is pressing. Shirina plans to bring back Siabala by killing the descendants of Elihor and Graydon. She has Rojon Kolder and Cassara Edoline in her grasp. She will bring him back, just as she brought down the Wall of Loss. Time is of the essence."

Elder Quilsam had not known Cassara Edoline was also in the Lisal Gardens, an important fact that Patrile, his chosen Crimson Circle Elite, had failed to disclose. Unless she proved herself worthy, he would see to it she never make Elder. He fought to school his features against his growing anger.

"I doubt Avarielle Grayloft will allow her to harm them." He did not like the warrior, but he knew that she would be too stubborn to let anything happen to her beloved son.

"Have you not heard?" The grief was thick in the Elder's voice. "The warrior was slain some time before the Wall fail. Ask anyone here, and they will confirm this."

"The Grayloft is dead?" The reality of the situation made the Elder's hands numb and turned his voice into a whisper. "They needed her gone to finish Rojon, didn't they? Knowing she would never allow her son to be taken?"

Events from the past few weeks crowded his mind, demanding attention as realization stacked on top of realization. The attacks on the village had been created to divert the warrior and force her to call on the witch's aid. Shirina whispered worries and seeded fears for Rojon's safety in the warrior's heart. She'd whisked them away to Massir, where she ensured the warrior would die, and her son and the queen would be hers for the taking.

And he hadn't stopped her. She'd passed through Stormhold, where he'd been studying, and he'd once again failed to see her treachery. As he stood beneath the very prison that held the Circle of Ravenhold prisoner.

"Did anyone survive from Stormhold?" he asked suddenly, hoping beyond hope that the third Circle survived, as well. That they still held the knowledge of all the magic of Graydon and Elihor.

Tally shook her head, eyes grim.

"Only Ravenhold's Circle was trapped there."

Fear twisted in his gut. Shirina had done something to stop the magic of Graydon from roaming in the lands, or completely destroyed it. He looked wide-eyed at Elder Tally.

"Do you have your magic?" He asked.

"We have some," she acquiesced. "When the Wall failed, we were ready to trap some of it in an attempt to keep it away from Shirina."

"Clever." He began to pace, assimilating all that the Elder had told her. "So, you are with power?"

"Some," she said. "And it's different. Green and red flames. A temporary affliction, I'm certain."

"Indeed." He brushed aside the mentioned colors, not caring for how the magic looked, only that it worked.

He had a choice to make. To believe and trust in this Elder, or to ignore her and hope for the best. Larkhold's covenant had once hoped for the best, and Elihor had paid a hefty, bloody price. Never again. He stopped pacing and stood before the Elder, who looked at him expectantly. He had no reason to distrust her, whereas he had every reason to distrust Shirina. The imprisoned were not the ones who had been pulling the strings of Graydon for the past twenty years.

"I know where they are," he said, breathless. "Two of my adepts are with them now."

"Excellent," Elder Tally said, placing a hand on his arm, her touch cold. "We must retrieve the heirs of Graydon and Elihor as quickly as possible. For their own sake. Do we know who is with them?"

"I did not ask them," he admitted. He hadn't cared about anything except Rojon's well being. "I know Rojon is there. I spoke to Shirina as well. Well, through my witches, as she seems unable to use her magic."

"That's good to know," Tally said. "Two adepts should be able to teleport the descendants of Graydon and Elihor out. How far are they?" Tally asked.

"The Lisal Gardens."

"Of course," Tally scoffed. "That she tried to replace the Keep of Ravenhold with a mere patch of dirt and a ramshackle house is an insult to the entire Circle."

"You know of the Lisal Gardens?" Quilsam asked, the

fact bothering him. If she was imprisoned, how would she know?

"It used to be a Circle outpost," she said, a coy smile on her lips. "And I am well familiar with it. I was an Elder, after all."

"Of course." He backed off. "I will instruct my adepts to get Rojon and the queen and teleport them out of there. Without their magic, Shirina's adepts will be powerless to stop them."

"How far can your adepts teleport them away from the Lisal Garden?" Elder Tally took a trembling step forward, as though hungry for revenge.

Quilsam pondered the powers of his adepts, their strength, and how much magic they'd recently used. It wouldn't be very far, but far enough to be difficult to find.

"They can travel about the distance from here to the borders of the West, with someone in tow."

"That will get them within the Maple Mountains," Elder Tally pondered.

"They will not know the destination, and it would be dangerous for them to do such a jump unaided."

"There is a Circle outpost in the north of Kosel," Tally said. "I've already sent some of my adepts there. The teleportation circle will glow for them, my adepts will ensure it."

"Your adepts will help their spell, as Shirina's adepts combine their powers?"

Tally looked blankly at him. "I have no idea what you mean or why one would even go about doing that. No, the circle will naturally emit magic that they can follow. My adepts will feed magic into it."

Quilsam's stomach fluttered a bit, an uncomfortable sensation. "They're already there?"

Tally nodded. "When the Wall fell, we were ready. We used its falling magic to strengthen our teleportation spells to as many Circle outposts as possible in Graydon. Many more than when last we were here, might I add," she shrugged, "but some proved quite useful. Like the one in Massir."

He studied her, and she continued, looking annoyed at his questions. He imagined he would be annoyed too, if an Elder of his sister Circle questioned him so.

"It was like riding a magical wave," Tally said, "a feat we will not be able to repeat. But one we'd spent twenty years preparing for. Unfortunately, we did not think the Lisal Gardens would be of enough importance to teleport to."

"How did you know Shirina would lower the Wall of Loss?" he asked slowly.

She gave him a wry smile. "She is not immortal, Quilsam, unless that, too, has changed. And Shirina is no fool. She knew she had limited time with which to enact her plan, and so we simply waited her out." It was her turn to study him sharply. "I find it difficult that an Elder of your caliber would not suspect her at all of treachery."

She let the words lie, waiting for his reaction. His pressure rose, his face growing red.

"I suspected her of greed and uselessness," he said, "but not of treason, no." She looked at him piercingly and easily saw through him, even if he could read her with as much ease as he could see through the Bloody Mountains themselves.

"You hoped to integrate Graydon's Circle into your own."

He sighed. There was no point in denying his intentions. "I figured that since she could not ascend to be an Elder, Graydon's Circle would simply be absorbed into Larkhold's, and create a stronger, united Circle."

She smiled gently, a repulsive pull on the skin attached to the stone on her neck. "Of course. And the Circle will be stronger, with more Elders and more knowledge to share. We have much to discuss. But first, we must ensure the safety of the heirs of magic."

Quilsam nodded but kept his eyes open as he cast his spell and reached out to his adepts in the Lisal Gardens.

He would be glad once this entire business was settled, and he could return to his own Keep, away from Graydon drama and politics.

16

The magic of Graydon existed yet, but Shirina was unclear how to access it, or where exactly it hid. She focused on what she did know. It had answered Cassara's song and granted them a gift in the sapling. She observed it from a step back, willing it to grow. The new tree had failed to answer any of Cassara's attempts since then, no matter how vague or specific.

The sorceress filled her lungs with the fresh air of the Lisal Gardens, forced her mind to stop racing and her heart to stop hammering.

She took stock of herself, too—worried, angry, and feeling cast aside and useless. That was how Larkhold's Circle wanted her to feel, and having all her contributions dismissed and her voice muted cut to the quick. Her inabilities to grow, to achieve a greater rank in her Circle and become an Elder, had come back to haunt her.

But, considering her only means of becoming one was

now through the last remaining Elder of Ravenhold, who happened to bow to Siabala… She straightened, forced herself to stop traveling the same familiar path, and looked to Rojon instead.

He needs me to figure this out. Rojon worked on the plants near the oak, a keen eye to thinning out shrubberies where needed. He worked carefully, making sure to follow the rhythms of the plant. His mother and Cassara had gone to ensure the perimeter was secure, in what Shirina had no doubt was a bid by the warrior to keep an eye on the queen and make sure she didn't do anything rash, while also soothing her own paranoia.

But Rojon had stayed and busied himself on the plants. A few other of her adepts worked the grounds, too, with gentle hands, trusting the land and plants to do what they needed it to.

Shirina approached the stump, where the sapling's unfurled leaves basked in the sun. This old, cut oak was said to be a tree planted by Graydon himself, a thousand years ago. The previous guardian of Rashim had once forged a staff for her from this tree, which allowed her to draw on Graydon's magic when it had been corrupted by Siabala.

The sapling fed from Graydon's magic, and so it led that the magic still existed. She couldn't see it, or reach it, yet part of her could sense it.

I don't know how to fix this. She knew that the keepers of the Lisal Gardens had hoarded for generations the secret on how to safely harvest these saplings so they preserved their magic. The last keeper had taken those secrets to his grave, and her staff had broken in the final battle with Siabala. It now hung in her study, a reminder of things lost and won.

Nothing is ever truly won. No victory was ever complete. No battle ever ended.

She stood before the sapling and tried to pull on any knowledge she had of the magic of Graydon. On its plants and earth. On the Lisal Gardens. And came up empty with how to claim the sapling as a staff, in the hopes it would allow her to draw on her magic. The moment she cut it, it would become as useless as her missing knowledge.

Her fear of failure, ignited by so many recent losses, stayed her hand.

Even if I reach the magic, what does it matter? Elihor's magic has drenched Graydon. Shirina tried to dispel the thought, but it intruded in every fiber of her being. She hated feeling this way. So directionless. She'd felt this way before, when the Circle had imploded, and she was given the choice to follow Siabala or try to destroy him, by herself if necessary.

Another deep breath.

She hadn't been by herself because she'd found allies, even if tentative at first, in Avarielle and Cassara. She'd found other adepts, and she'd managed, with them, to stop Siabala, despite all odds stacked against her. Against all of them.

The choice she'd made in her twenties mirrored the one she had to make in her forties. To bow down and give up, or to stand and fight Siabala. Again, everything was stacked against her. She hated this mirroring of life, like nothing ever truly ended, and everything had to be done anew.

Even if a villain was destroyed, or a piece of him, he would rise again. Or another would.

Except this time, she wasn't in her twenties. The situation mirrored her past, but *she* did not. She had grown. Experienced defeat. And she was still standing. She'd worked hard, forged alliances, drawn hundreds to the Circle. She'd rebuilt with magic and earth, hope and knowledge. She'd kept learning, bettering herself, growing.

She was not the Shirina of twenty years ago. She was more, and all that knowledge and experience would support her, if she only trusted herself when everyone insisted that she couldn't be trusted.

Well, not everyone. Her witches were still here. No one had left, and everyone looked for solutions. They tended to the earth not because they had nothing to do, but because Shirina had encouraged them to use gardening as a meditative act, to allow them to connect with Graydon and the magic around them. To let their thoughts wander, while their hands kept busy.

Cassara hadn't run off to her kingdom because she trusted that they'd come up with something together. The queen loved her family above all else and yet stayed, meaning that she trusted Shirina to be her best chance of success. And even Avarielle stayed with her son, sarcasm as ready to deploy as her blade. She believed in what Shirina had been building for the past twenty years. Shala, the first adept to join her new Circle, was in Massir still, probably fighting for her life, if not dead. Her trusted second, who would not claim the same title as Shirina until Shirina had been granted the title of Elder.

Shala trusted in her. She always had.

They all did.

And it would do them a disservice if she gave up now. Not after all this time. She had not bowed to Siabala twenty years ago, and she would not do so now.

Another deep breath, the scent of fresh earth centering her to the problem at hand.

Elder Tally had been good at predicting her moves last time. All their moves. But the Elder wasn't smart enough to have done so by herself. Siabala might have been studying them somehow for the past twenty years, fed information by his vast network of informants.

It was safe to assume they had control of Rashim from its capital of Massir. They had the green magic and Siabala's magic, plus adepts from Larkhold, so their powers far outweighed her Circle's.

She needed her magic. Above all else, she couldn't defend anything or anyone without her powers. She was certain that it was no accident that Graydon's magic had vanished. Tally would have wanted to gain the upper hand, and no easier way than to stop the flow of magic.

But how had she done it? Shirina had been there and witnessed it all. She'd been so busy saving Avarielle and coming to grips with her missing magic, plus Larkhold's disrespect… She forced herself to relax again, to stop her hands from turning into fists.

She focused on the sapling. The one sign they'd received that somewhere, Graydon's magic still existed.

Tally had needed Avarielle's magic for something. Graysword had lit with power. Cassara's amulet had melted in the earth, according to Rojon. *What do we know of the amulet?* It was Elihor's, gifted to her by Graydon. For some reason, the descendants of Graydon still had it, and it worked as an anchor for their magic, as a means to stay grounded, and connect with the magic. But could it be more?

Cassara had used it to draw Graydon's powers into it. And once it had melted into the earth, Graydon's magic had vanished… *no.* Graydon's magic no longer danced in the air around them, where they usually grabbed the strands to cast their spells with.

The sapling had grown after that moment. Fed by magic. Encouraged by the Traveler's Song, an ancient incantation left in his bloodline by Graydon himself.

The magic in the earth.

Shirina's head slowly turned to Rojon's hands, covered in dirt. And to her adepts, silently meditating on what their life would be like if the Circle could not recover from this blow.

All paths lead to Ravenhold. Her mentor used to tell her this, making the loss of Ravenhold even worse, because now no paths led to it. But what if she'd meant only what the keep represented: not a physical place, but the heart of the Circle?

Shirina had started her new Circle here, amongst plants, believing in a gentler approach to magic and that they needed to reconnect with the land, and its people, to truly be effective.

She realized she was breathing normally, for the first time in what felt like days.

If all paths led to Ravenhold, then her path, the path she'd chosen twenty years ago, had led her here. To the ground, the earth, and Graydon.

To the very place where the magic might be hiding.

A plan forming in her mind, Shirina walked back toward her study, feeling energized by the glimmer of hope presented to her, as fragile as morning dew, and intended to grab hold of it before the day swept it away.

17

Cassara's feet felt heavy as she walked beside Avarielle, letting the warrior do checks while she lost herself in her thoughts and fears. It had been years since she'd been in a battle situation. Years since she'd faced Siabala.

Decades.

Despite all the joyful moments since then: every tender touch with Dayshon, her children's laughter, her brother's marriage, the beautiful gardens of Massir blooming, Dayshon leaning on her and trusting her to treat his people—*their* people—with grace and kindness...

Smaller moments. A child handing her a flower on the streets as she walked. A perfect cup of tea. Avarielle's laughter filling her small kitchen. A child sleeping on her lap. Dayshon kissing her sweat-covered forehead after the birth of their children, before taking hold of them, teary eyed... So many small, perfect moments, all of which formed a line from now to her battle with Siabala twenty years ago.

And no matter how many perfect moments she experienced, no matter how much time had passed since that battle, a part of her would always live there. Especially in the moments between awake and sleeping, when she thought she smelled the sulfur from deep in his Rage. When the light turned to autumn glow, and cooler air filled her lungs, dread clutched her stomach. Bonfires made her cry, remembering those they lit to burn the bodies of the fallen. She'd stayed to watch them, to pay her respects. And she still did, no matter the occasion, part of her still standing before those fires. On that battlefield, when summer was cut short by Siabala.

The first snow felt like her magic escaping, like her breath vanishing. Every year, she would find herself on her balcony, as high as she could go in the palace, and stand under that fresh snow. Watch her breath curl before her and look toward the Wall of Loss that she could no longer see, and remember how it had felt to give up her magic.

She'd been willing to give up much more. She was grateful she hadn't. That she'd lived, because of Shirina's and Avarielle's stubbornness. But the shadows of that battlefield still echoed in her heart and mind.

And now, faced with it again, and powerless to stop it, every beautiful moment was cast in that shadow. When she looked back at her life, it became discoloured and ugly under the spell Siabala still held over her. Every moment holding her breath, waiting for him to return.

They'd prepared. Made plans. Shored up Massir's defences, and the Circle's magic. Readied the West for Siabala's onslaught.

And never once had they imagined he was already there, rotting away at their foundation. That her magic wouldn't return, and Shirina's would vanish.

So much power we can't see. Her family had been murdered by a nest of Eloms living beneath Edoline. They'd festered under her beautiful kingdom, and she'd been powerless to stop them. Even the crashing sound of waves made her think of their deaths, now, even though she still loved it.

A nest had been under her new kingdom, too, and had once again whisked away her family.

Here, she couldn't hear the sea, though she had to go but a bit to the East to find it. She could only hear the movement of the wind in the leaves and the plants lining the Lisal Gardens. She glanced sideways at her silent companion. Avarielle had healed faster than she'd have thought possible, even for her. But she walked with the same ease she'd always had, not making noise, looking around them at the place and looking displeased.

Cassara knew that look.

"We're not defended here, if an attack should come," Cassara said, following the warrior's logic.

"Not that we're apparently worried about that," Avarielle said, frown deepening.

"We know better than that," Cassara whispered. "My magic kept him trapped, Avarielle. I know it did."

"I know," Avarielle instantly said. "And don't take my annoyance as a sign that I question, because I really don't. I was there. It's just…this whole thing is grating on my last nerve. And Altessa and Dayshon are still in Massir."

"I have to go to them," Cassara stopped, grabbed her friend's arm in a bid to get her to hear. "Avarielle, I can't—"

"I know," Avarielle gently said. "We just need to figure out our exit strategy."

Cassara suddenly understood. "You don't want Rojon coming with us."

"Of course I don't," she said. "I have to make sure he's safe. Are we certain Siabala won't attack?"

"I'm not certain of anything anymore," she said. "But I don't know that he'll attack here. I mean, he's already found a way to make the Circle powerless. Would he waste resources attacking something that can't stop him? While still recovering? Besides, he'd have been here already, if that was the case."

"If not on the Circle, what will he focus on?"

Cassara pondered the question, grateful for something else to focus on. "I think he'd want to make sure the Southern Coalition was helpless. Their armies helped turn the tide last time. And Solir? And then…I guess Elihor, though they don't have armies like Graydon."

"But they still have their magic."

"True," Cassara said. "So, he'll target Larkhold before Ravenhold."

Avarielle nodded. "That's my thinking, too. Take over Larkhold once the one person who could warn them, Shirina, has been discredited."

"I guess his attack on Ravenhold was already successful," Cassara whispered.

"Seems like," Avarielle grudgingly agreed. "Which is bad but could also work to our advantage."

"Because you can leave Rojon here?"

"Exactly," Avarielle agreed. "But I don't want him staying here. He'll need to move somewhere safer, because eventually Siabala *will* come."

"For Rojon," Cassara looked at her friend, features determined. "Do you think Siabala still wants Rojon to take the blood oath with him?"

"I can't risk thinking otherwise." Avarielle's voice was tense. "But he can't take it without Graysword. So I need to get away from him. Figured I'd help your family along the way."

"We should tell Shirina we're leaving," Cassara said softly.

"You can tell her, because I won't be going with either of you."

Blood drained from Cassara's face. Avarielle intended to head to Massir alone.

"Altessa is a descendant of Graydon," Avarielle shrugged. "I intend to see her safe."

"I can help rally the people," Cassara said. "And I can fight."

"I know you can," Avarielle agreed. "I trained you, remember? But I also know that Siabala wanted you for something, and it's best he not get his hands on you. Rojon will keep you safe, especially when you and he head to Kosel to meet up with Kaden for safety."

Cassara drew herself up automatically, becoming the queen she'd learned to draw on when the occasion demanded it. Which, right now, it certainly did. "I am not going to hide in Kosel while my people suffer."

"No." Avarielle ran her hand through her hair, a sure sign of growing frustration. "You'll stay safe until we're sure Siabala isn't after you. You're of no use to anyone dead, Cassara."

"And if I hide, I'm of no use to anyone alive." She met her friend's surprised eyes. "I'd much prefer dying trying to be helpful, Avarielle, than hiding in the shadows. Would you stay behind if Rojon was the one who needed you?"

Avarielle stopped walking, crossed her arms, not bothering to hide the annoyance on her face. "You'll slow me down," Avarielle said. "And distract me. I'll be worried about you."

"I know that," Cassara said, having already thought through the warrior's objections. "I'll follow behind, and I'll busy myself getting people ready for battle." She'd go into the city and find Builder Gramire. Or General Akhalon.

"Too dangerous, still," Avarielle immediately

countered. "They'll be on the lookout for you, and you're not subtle." Apparently, the warrior had also been preparing her counterarguments. Knowing someone so well that they could predict your responses proved both a blessing and a cutting annoyance. "If you're going to insist on doing something stupid, which I know you will, it would make more sense for you to head to the Southern Coalition."

"But Altessa and Dayshon are in Massir." She spoke the words so softly the breeze caressed them away. Avarielle understood nevertheless and eased her stance.

"I know, which is why I'll go help them." She placed a hand on Cassara's shoulder. No matter how many years had passed, Cassara still found strength in the warrior's presence, even if she refused to go along with her plan.

"Massir is closer than the Southern Coalition," Cassara doubled down, lifting her chin. It proved even more annoying that Avarielle was a foot taller than her. It made it hard to look down on her.

"But you'll go through Kosel—"

"I already told you. I'm not hiding there."

"You'll see Kaden—" she ignored her words, "—and meet his daughter. She's nice. And she can get you there faster, if you ask nicely."

"Pakana. Carsyn and Kaden spoke of her in their letters." She paused when she saw something flicker in the warrior's eyes. Just a moment, but Cassara felt the world shift under her.

"You said I'd see Kaden. Carsyn?" She let the question

hang in the air. She didn't need Avarielle to say anything, the hand squeezing her shoulder answer enough.

She closed her eyes, remembering his laughter. Carsyn, who'd been loyal to her since she was just a child, and to Edoline. Who'd protected her, even against the monsters that had killed her father, the king. Carsyn, grump with a heart of gold. Who she counted on so dearly, even if she hadn't seen him in years.

There hadn't been time. Those words felt so hollow now, no matter how true they were. Such a weak excuse. Not one moment spared to visit the man who'd helped raise her. Who'd watched over her, even as she took ridiculous risks when she was sixteen, going to visit her kingdom's small village at night.

The man who'd tried to keep her safe from monsters, until he'd understood that he couldn't protect his princess from the creatures that stalked her. And he'd handed her safety to Avarielle, a woman from a people he'd always been brought up to distrust.

"He trusted you to keep me safe," Cassara said, voice gaining strength.

"He did," Avarielle said, "and others will step up to protect your family, Cassara. They're not alone. No more than you were when Eloms attacked."

"Most of my family perished in that attack."

"I know," Avarielle's hand dropped. "But I kept you safe then. Let me keep you safe now."

"I hate this," Cassara simply stated, and Avarielle nodded.

"Me, too." She cocked her head, as though pondering possibilities. "We're safe for now, though it's hard to be sure. If they decide to attack here, we might not see it coming."

"What will Shirina do?" Cassara whispered, looking back toward the mansion.

A grin tugged at Avarielle's lips. "Shirina will do what she always does, Cassara. Bang her head on the problem until an answer slips out of her cracked skull. She's too stubborn to do anything different."

Even as Cassara nodded, she found herself looking West. Toward her home. Toward the Bloody Mountains. Toward her lost magic, and the bodies that littered the ground on the path toward it.

18

"We don't know what we're supposed to do," Yorisse, an Orange Circle warlock, spoke from the other side of her desk as Shirina pulled the two pieces of her staff from the wall. Two Crimson Circles stood by him, but he'd apparently won, or lost, the honor of approaching her with questions. She could sense their tension and worry. Their fear at being powerless.

She didn't need her magic to sense how they felt. Their worry overflowed in every corner of her study. Slowly, she turned to face them, clutching the two pieces of her old staff, wood dry and bearing scars of battles and flames.

"Do you know what this is?" Shirina asked, ignoring his statement. He looked slightly put off, but had grown used to her love of riddles and forcing her adepts to seek their own conclusions.

"A staff?" He ventured, though he didn't seem particularly interested in confirmation.

"It is," she said, placing the two pieces on her desk. "This staff was created here, in the gardens, from the trunk of the old oak tree. It was the only safe way to draw magic when the two strands roamed freely in Graydon."

A few more adepts wandered in, eager to find familiarity and guidance. She knew them all. Their names, where they'd come from, why they'd joined. She had a good idea of the ones who would stay, and those who would wander away, drawn by a different life.

She knew them all, having worked with each of them to ensure they understood magic, and its importance. How to wield it well, and respect those it was meant to protect. They'd taken their blows, too, representing a coven which had lost the trust of its people.

Yorisse had joined because he'd wanted to understand the fabric that held the world together. The son of carpenters, he never would have been able to join the old Circle, showing very little potential with magic. But he worked hard, and had a keen, sharp mind that helped him pierce riddles and see beyond the immediate, easiest answers.

Shirina glanced to those assembled, more coming in, as though they'd all been waiting to speak with her. Not the older witches, who spent time tending the gardens, understanding that answers were not always promised and sometimes doing something, anything, proved enough to still the mind.

She spotted the Green Circle Tinat, a young adept who had joined recently. She'd lost her family to disease and had nowhere else to go. She'd showed up at an outpost, and started helping the witches with cooking and cleaning, for a bed and food. Shirina had approached her and asked her if she'd like to learn of their ways. The shy young woman had flourished, already a strong magic wielder. She would go far, given the chance.

Beside her was Yellow Circle Gnarta. She'd been in Larkhold's Circle but had wanted to come to the Land of Light, after going as far as Elders would allow of her in her studies at Larkhold, being weak with magic. She couldn't wield the strands here, but she'd learn of agriculture, and brought much learning with her.

So many had come, under her guidance, believing they could find a home, or make a difference. She'd not told them that Siabala would return within most of their lifetimes. To do so would have put Cassara at risk. Even if, it seems, others had been amply aware of it.

"Crimson Circle Shala spoke to me of this staff," Yorisse said. "I guess I never realized that it was right there." He flushed as he spoke, tipped up his chin proudly as though daring anyone to consider him daft. In the old Circle, the one Shirina had learned magic in, he would have been ridiculed. No, he wouldn't have even made it this far with his lack of magical abilities. He would have been shunned and cast out.

That was not the Circle Shirina was building. She offered learning to those who craved it. Shelter to those who needed it. Peace to those who sought it. And magic to those who could wield it.

She expected them to be respectful, knowledgeable, and to take their duties and studies seriously.

"You didn't notice it because it was always there," Shirina said, feeling pride at all the faces gathered around her. At how they listened and were willing to learn. And to trust.

A trust she dearly hoped she'd not taken advantage of.

"Like the Wall of Loss," Yorisse immediately said, quick to follow her train of thought.

She nodded.

"Why did our magic vanish when it did?" he asked, the same question he'd asked earlier when she'd gathered them all. She hadn't told them everything, then.

She'd trained them for this, even if they hadn't realized it. She'd taught them to work together. She'd made sure their teleportation would get them further, faster, by combining their magic. She'd prepared them to be ready to move quickly. But never once had she imagined that they wouldn't be able to use their magic at all.

"Twenty years ago, our magic intertwined with that of Elihor, making it impossible to safely wield, unless it was drawn through this staff." She placed her hand over the break. Siabala had tried to stop her from using her magic by snapping it in two.

"Or by a witch from Larkhold and one from Ravenhold combining their powers to draw on the strands individually," Gnarta said. Shirina nodded. They'd learned their lesson well.

"In the new Circle, I wanted you to learn to use your magic together, because there's power in combining strength. Never once did I imagine that they would somehow rob us of magic."

She should have. She had been in charge of readying the Circle. But how could she prepare their magical defences if she couldn't draw on magic?

"Who robbed us?" Yorisse asked, voice trembling. At the loss, and the fear.

She met his eyes, then the others'.

"Elder Tally, an old Elder from Ravenhold. She has survived and allied herself with Siabala." The steadiness of her own voice surprised her. A breeze meandered into her study, traveling across each of them, the shifting cloaks and robes the only movement in the room.

"The old Circle is…it's gone, isn't it?" Tinat asked.

"What it was is gone," Shirina confirmed. "Tally is a traitor and has built another Circle underneath Massir. She was part of the attack."

Shala. Please be safe.

"But…there's an Elder…" Yorisse struggled to wrap his mind around what this meant.

"And she will undoubtedly test you, as she probably has tested our sisters and brothers in Massir," her voice grew soft. "If all that you seek is power, she can offer you that. As long as you bow to Siabala."

"We would never do that." Yorisse's mind was made up

as quickly as it had been undone. "You defeated him once and will do so again."

"I helped contain him," Shirina said, keeping her eyes forward. She owed them the truth. Too many secrets, like the old Circle, drowning her. Drowning them all. "We killed his body, but not his soul. And trapped him again in the Wall of Loss." That part they all knew. She pushed on.

"But that Wall was never meant to last long, could never last as long as the old one created by Graydon and Elihor themselves. This time, we used Graydon's magic only. And, even then, only the magic of his heir, Cassara Edoline."

A few gasps, and some widening of eyes. A few eyed her, studied the truth of her words. They were the ones that would have most been likely to be part of her old Circle. Still, some adepts didn't seem to fully grasp the implications, though they would, given more time. Except there was no more time.

"We protected Cassara because if she fell, the Wall would fall. But she's still alive, and the Wall is gone regardless."

"And so is our magic," Tinat said. "Does the queen have any magic?"

"She does not, but she does seem connected to *something* still."

"You lied to us," Yorisse said, not hissing the words as she might have done. But in surprise. That made it all the more hurtful. "You said the Wall of Loss would hold Siabala."

"And it should have. I did not tell you of Cassara's link to that magic, to ensure her safety," she said. "We feared that Siabala still had followers. We vastly underestimated their power and number."

She forced herself to meet their eyes, having dreaded this moment. "I am sorry. I wanted this Circle to be different than the old Ravenhold. Not to have secrets. But some secrets I found to be necessary, while we grew strong enough to face Siabala. We should have had more time."

If they had their magic, they could give him a challenge. Move faster, be more powerful, all thanks to their combined powers. What they lacked in battle experience, they made up for in magical aptitude and the ability to combine strength. Her bracers would have been perfected, allowing both covens to safely wield the magic, even as the strands combined, as they would have undoubtedly done once more when the Wall fell.

"Why would Siabala stop Graydon's powers and not Elihor's?" Gnarta asked, jumping on the obvious question she'd been struggling with herself. Although from Elihor, she was not proficient in magic, and couldn't even see the strands of her magic dancing around them, now. The Sight was for Crimson Circles and above only.

"I'm not sure," Shirina said. "Perhaps it was simply a matter of mechanics. His prison was fully composed of Graydon's magic, after all. Perhaps the only means to break free affected all Graydon's magic."

"And you're certain he's coming?"

"I cannot say that I'm certain as to what his plans are," Shirina admitted. "I did not foresee him robbing us of magic. I did not intend for us to be so powerless."

"What could we have done against him?" Tinat asked, mouth gaping.

"A lot," Shirina said, needing them to understand their strength. "You can combine your magic in a way no one else can, not even Larkhold's Circle. With our network of outposts, we can teleport further than others, with more ease. That principle applies to the rest of our spells, too. Threads amplified by each other. Our numbers, our ability to work together, is our greatest strength."

"But now we have no magic."

"No. But it does not mean we are powerless," she said. "We have learning here and in the old city beneath the West. We can send out riders to go work with them to see if they can find an answer. We can help people reach safety, and make sure trade routes remain open. You may not have magic, but you still have knowledge and the trust we've worked hard to build. All things you can use."

"The staff was up there all along, a reminder that Siabala would return?" Yorisse asked.

"No. It was a reminder that there are so many secrets and truths we have yet to comprehend, including how Graydon's magic truly works. To inspire ideas, like the bracers. And a reminder that by working together, we are stronger. I wanted to forever remember that Siabala could break a staff, but not the Circle. Not our spirit."

"The Larkhold witches say that Siabala was not contained in the Wall," Yorisse said.

Shirina kept silent. When he did not continue, she asked, "What do you think?"

He looked at the staff, then at the books around her, then back to her. He met her eyes, unflinching.

"I don't see what advantage you would have for lying about his survival."

"They say it's because I knew our magic would fail if the Wall of Loss collapsed, so tried to give everyone a reason to maintain it." She fed him their lines, waited.

"Why would you not just work to save our magic, then? Find ways, like the staff, to ensure it continued?"

"Because I'm not an Elder, Yorisse." The words stung, but she delivered them with little intonation. Just stating the facts.

"Could you become one?" he asked, shuffling slightly.

"If I took up Tally's offer to become her pupil, should she still be interested in extending it to me after Avarielle Grayloft cut her neck, then yes, I could become one."

"But you never would. You've dedicated everything to stopping Siabala. You just needed more time."

"I'm not sure it would have made a difference, Yorisse. His roots and treachery are deeper than I could have imagined." She gave him a wry grin. "My lack of imagination seems to have doomed us all."

"No," he said with such conviction that it surprised her. A few other adepts had wandered in, overhearing the conversation. They gathered as if seeking comfort in one another's company. "You don't lack imagination, Shirina, or knowledge. You built a new Circle in Lisal Gardens, once it was clear Ravenhold was out of reach."

Tinat piped up. "You taught us to link our magic so we could do more with it, including further teleportation."

"You led the work to gather knowledge from the cities beneath the West." Gnarta piped up.

"And you did it all without support from an Elder, or much from Larkhold, either." Tinat whispered, her light brown hair streaked with blue dye. Like Altessa's, lost somewhere in Massir.

Shirina found her words could not clear the lump forming in her throat.

"So yes, I believe you that Siabala was there," Yorisse continued, to nods around the room. "I think you'd hoped you'd have more time to prepare us all. And I think that it doesn't matter what any of us wanted, because he's been freed. We just need to figure out where he is, and where Graydon's magic went. So, where do we begin, Crimson Circle Elite?"

Shirina looked from adept to adept—from the young, to the old, the green to the crimson cloaked, the wide-eyed to the steady gazed, the resolute to the uncertain. They all held one thing in common—they looked to her for guidance.

No, this wasn't the attack she'd feared and prepared for. But this was exactly how she'd hoped her Circle would react.

---

19

*A*varielle's entire body felt wrong. Like she'd spent a night in a sandstorm, covered enough to survive, but not covered enough to survive unscathed. Her insides had been blasted by her own blade piercing her, leaving her raw. Her body no longer hurt, but her heart… The more she remembered of that moment with Rojon, the more she understood his sullenness. His anger and the looks her threw her way. It went beyond just Graysword's presence, now.

She hated all of it, and hated how it hurt her, still. With a deep breath she approached him where he tended to some flowers. He sensed her approach despite her quiet steps, stood, and turned to face her. She was certain he'd been thinking about the same moment she had been.

Why wouldn't he? What else could he possibly be thinking about? Cassara and Shirina spoke in quiet tones nearby, planning their next steps, and Avarielle didn't care about them overhearing. She needed to chat with her son before she left, so this wound wouldn't fester in her absence. Its infection could hurt them both so badly. It already had.

Siabala had dealt a harsh blow. Before she could figure out a way to put everything into words, her son spoke up.

"I saw it, mom. I saw you run dad through with Graysword." He looked at the sword, and there she saw it again. The desire to hold it. To wield it.

Cassara and Shirina stopped speaking but kept their distance. They hadn't known the details of Kryde's death—they'd never even known him, only knew of her love for him—and had been kind enough never to ask. This wasn't a secret she'd ever intended to share. Too painful. Too personal.

That Siabala would show her son…

The words sliced through her, deeper than Graysword. Avarielle had faced monsters without hesitating. She'd moved quickly, understanding survival depended on speed and accuracy. But under the hateful gaze of her son, under the crushing weight of memories, she found that she couldn't form the words that might soothe him.

About how much she'd loved Kryde, Rojon's father. That their few months together shone like a bright star in her memories and her heart. How, if she'd have just been better, faster, stronger, she might have stopped him from being taken. Or killed. How much light and passion he'd held, and how, in the end, he'd been left hollow. A shell of the man he'd once been, his soul ripped out by Siabala, his body a puppet he offered *her*. He'd destroyed Kryde to *gift* him to *her*.

And how much it still hurt, every time the light caught her son's features a certain way, or when his grin reached his eyes, like his father's used to.

How Kryde had never even known he would be a father. He'd been caught protecting her, the magic of Elihor only saving her and not him. But he'd also protected their son, without knowing it. Or maybe he had known, on some level.

She looked at Rojon now, saw the anger on his features that she knew so well. The anger of not knowing. Of being kept in the dark.

How could she tell him how it felt to run her sword through the man she loved? How dark those nights were without him, how she'd been willing to let go of everything to claim revenge. How the Wall of Loss had fallen so she could avenge his father, already knowing that it was too late to save him. That what she'd done was out of love, yes, but also hatred.

She had no idea how to put all her feelings, hopes, and dreams into one neatly contained explanation of that final moment. But she knew she had to try, even if it broke her to step back into that moment, to speak of her part in his last breath.

"Siabala had destroyed his soul already." Avarielle's voice shook, and she didn't care. "I simply set his body free."

"He could have been brought back, how do you know…"

"I loved him. I knew," she simply said, unsure how to get him to stop. He looked at her accusingly, and she fought back her temper. She'd done everything to keep Kryde safe. In the end, Siabala had been too strong, and she'd been helpless to stop him.

Just like she felt now, with him hiding somewhere, unwilling to show his face.

"I never got to know him," Rojon's voice quaked, too. She wanted to cross to him and grab him in her arms. But his stance made it very clear he didn't want to be coddled. She turned, instinctively hiding Graysword's pommel from her son, not wanting to see his eyes focus on the red stone. To be drawn in by it. By Siabala, wherever he was.

"And you have Siabala to blame for that," Shirina softly said, the sorceress inserting herself into the conversation, followed closely by Cassara.

"He will try to turn us against one another," Cassara said, "as Tally turned my people against me. He finds cracks that exist, for good reasons—" she looked apologetically at Avarielle, "—and he wedges them wider. That's how he wins, and why he showed you that moment in time, Rojon."

Rojon looked to Cassara, looking bewildered. "You did nothing to deserve that."

Avarielle bit her tongue at the suggestion that *she* deserved his anger.

"I did," Cassara said. "I made choices, Rojon. I did the

best I could, but sometimes there is no good choice. Only the *best* choice. And those choices have consequences. And —" she turned to Avarielle, softened her voice, "—we have to accept them and move on. Otherwise, we'll forever be paralyzed by our own fear of failure."

"We have work to do," Shirina said, stepping between them like she'd decided she'd had enough of this heart-to-heart. The sorceress focused on Rojon, and Avarielle was grateful for her distracting her son.

Part of her heart twisted in the way he softened when he looked at the sorceress. A softness he did not hold for his own mother. At least, not right now.

"Stay with me to help me out, Rojon," Shirina said, then turned to Avarielle and Cassara. "Avarielle, my adepts will head out to connect with other adepts, but specifically they'll look to reach the libraries under the West. There are a few tomes that looked promising but were still being translated. I hope they'll be able to find out more about Graydon's and Elihor's magic. But they'll have to ride through the West, and I would prefer they not receive a deadly welcome from your people."

"I can instruct them on customs," Avarielle nodded, knowing full well Shirina could do so just as easily, but also knew when Shirina was focused on magical, and not mundane, things. At least she would keep her son out of trouble.

"Cassara—" the sorceress turned to her, "—I'll need your help ensuring that we're tapping into the magic of Graydon."

"You are much more skilled in it than I am, Shirina," Cassara answered, probably itching to get going. From the way Shirina spoke, it was pretty clear that Cassara had not yet shared their plan.

"I am," Shirina said, making Cassara bristle a bit. "But you are naturally attuned to it. I am not."

"I'm going to the Southern Coalition," Cassara said. "To get help for Massir."

"Oh?"

"My people need help, Shirina. And I can't find it here, I'm sorry."

"I'll head to Massir to try to find Dayshon and Altessa," Avarielle spoke up. Rojon looked surprised. "Help the royal family out of this mess." She tried to make light of the situation but knew her son wasn't buying it.

"Mom—" Shirina cut him off before he could finish.

"That's reactive and walking straight into their hands," the sorceress said, clutching the two pieces of her old staff more tightly.

"My family needs our help," Cassara said, hands folded before her, visibly holding herself in check, though Avarielle could see that her hands trembled slightly.

"They do," Shirina said, "and I want to help them. But how much help do you think we'll be without magic?"

"I'll find a way," she protested.

"I know you will," Shirina said. "But no one else except us believes Siabala is returning. Larkhold's Circle will help your family, for they're seen as—" annoyance flickered across the sorceress's features, "—innocents."

"Unlike us," Avarielle scoffed.

"Exactly."

Cassara looked to Shirina as though she hadn't considered anyone else but her, or Avarielle, saving her family. "You asked Elihor's Circle to protect my family?"

"Of course," Shirina said, an eyebrow rising slightly. "They have the power to help them now. They can protect them against the rogue circle. And Dayshon can start extinguishing the fans of rebellion. While we worry about the thing we are best suited to deal with—stopping Siabala."

"I still…I need to help them, Shirina."

"I know," Shirina said. "And you are."

"By standing around here?"

"By helping me. By helping my Circle connect with its magic again. Without it, all we have is Avarielle's magic, which can't exactly kill a soul."

"Give me a chance and we'll see," Avarielle growled.

"I'm sure you'll get that chance," Shirina said, "but, last time, with all of my magic, all of yours, and all of Cassara's —" she turned to Rojon, "—plus Elihor's magic through the cries of Rojon, we still could only contain him. We'll need both Circles to stop him this time. And for that, my adepts need access to their magic."

"How did I access my magic when I was born?" Rojon asked, focusing on Shirina still. Avarielle was glad that he was focusing away from Graysword, but she was also heartbroken that he wasn't sharing that look of understanding with her instead of Shirina. It would have been better had it been with Cassara, even.

"I'm not entirely sure of that," Shirina said, "but I believe it was because both strands of magic were freed. So you didn't access it so much as influence it."

"You were so small and so terrified, Rojon," Cassara said. "I did not comfort you, but let you cry out your fears, instead." She gave him a sad smile. "You don't remember, but I've always wanted to apologize to you about that."

"I wanted to meet you so badly because I felt connected to you, not just by the stories my mother told me," Rojon answered. "And not in a negative way. So whatever you had to do, it didn't scar me."

It didn't scar me. Those words cut Avarielle. She'd scarred her son. By keeping some things from him. By leaving him so often. By trying to keep him away from Graysword. By the curse running in her blood. In *his* blood.

"A long time ago, this staff was forged by the Keeper of Lisal, before he fell in battle," Shirina told Rojon. "I'm guessing the sapling growing here is due to similar circumstances, but he took to his grave the secrets of how to forge the staff. I thought that if you examined the broken staff and looked at the sapling, perhaps you'd be able to use your knowledge of trees and plants to forge a staff I could wield?"

Rojon took the two pieces of staff and looked up at Shirina. "Can't you figure it out? Or one of your witches? I'm no adept."

"You are not. But you work with plants and magic. You specialize in encouraging plants to be more than just that —to create buildings, or aqueducts. I thought you might better understand how to change a plant from its original form into something still functional, but completely different." She paused. "Without killing it, preferably, or cutting off its magic."

Avarielle fought against her instincts to step up and tear one into the sorceress for putting such pressure on her sensitive son. If he failed, he'd essentially be destroying their one chance of Shirina connecting back to her magic. That was unfair pressure for her son, and she forced herself to stand her ground as Rojon studied the staff. He was nineteen. He was old enough to know what he could and could not do. And Shirina wasn't fool enough to ask just anyone for help in this crucial duty. If she asked her son, that meant she needed him.

Rojon grew absorbed in the issue, and Shirina seemed pleased with his reaction.

She stepped away from him and the three of them formed a circle. Shirina focused on Cassara. "I don't mean to minimize your worries, Cassara, nor yours, Avarielle," Shirina said, voice level and annoyingly logical. "But unless we get ready for the next attack, we won't survive it, and neither will Graydon. We cannot allow that to happen."

"I have no magic," Cassara said, "I'm of no use to you in this fight."

"But you will get it again," Shirina said. "With the Wall

of Loss down, there is no reason for you not to draw upon your powers."

"Why didn't he also take away Elihor's powers?" Cassara suddenly asked.

"I imagine because he had more access to Graydon's powers, since your magic is what trapped him," Shirina shrugged. "Or Tally helped him get the power he needed. I'm not sure, but it's best to assume he'll eventually rob Larkhold's Circle of their power, too."

"Is that something Tally would know how to do?" Avarielle asked, forcing her eyes away from Rojon, who had stepped into greater light to examine the ends of the staff. Not where it had broken, but where it had originally been forged.

"I don't know," Shirina said, meeting her eyes. "I'm not an Elder and not privy to their secrets."

Avarielle crossed her arms. "When you become Elder, you'll be heads above her, anyway."

A slight smile played on the sorceress's lips, and then she grew serious again. "Help me make sure the Circle is in the best position to defend Graydon—" she implored Cassara and Avarielle, "—before Siabala makes himself known."

Avarielle waited on Cassara. She wanted to run to save Altessa, too, having seen the girl grow up since she was a baby. She loved her, and her oath to protect Graydon's descendants extended to her. But she also had no doubt that their greatest chance of success lay in Shirina and her Circle.

What a tedious annoyance. Were she twenty years younger, she would have gone to face Siabala by herself, if needed. She *had.* And had failed and brought down the Wall of Loss. So, she knew what her best chances of success were, and it wasn't on her own, thinking she could cut through everything with her magical sword. She knew better than that, now, even if she hated it.

She glanced again at Rojon, wondering if her son would ever forgive her for having killed his father. That's how he saw it, anyway. But she had no doubt that Siabala had already cut Kryde a deadly blow by stealing his soul.

A gift for you. That's what he'd said. *A soulless man who can only fight.*

It was Kryde's soul she'd loved the most. She didn't know how to explain it to her son, didn't know if she even knew the words needed to be understood. Or, rather, how to wrap her mouth around words her heart still couldn't quite accept. How Kryde was gone, forever. How he'd been caught protecting her. How they had taken him to toy with her.

How, in the end, Siabala's obsession with her had led to his father's death. And so she'd killed him to stop him from being a soulless slave. And she didn't regret it one bit.

Her son would expect her to feel some angst or regret at having cut him down. But she didn't. She only regretted that Kryde had used his magic to protect her and hadn't been able to protect himself.

She didn't even regret taking the oath with Siabala,

though part of her knew she should. She would be dead by now, long ago, and many more of her people would have perished. Cassara would be dead, and Shirina would have never left the Circle and would have been turned into one of his monsters.

She'd have never met Kryde, and Rojon would have never been born. That it led to that one moment where Kryde died still hurt like Eli's anger, but it wasn't regret that she felt. She did regret bringing down the Wall of Loss and falling prey to Siabala's twisted plan, but even then, she'd done the best she could under those circumstances. Seeing how Siabala manipulated so much of their lives now, still, Avarielle found herself more forgiving of her past self.

If she, at forty, couldn't predict all his machinations, and neither could Shirina nor Cassara, then how could they have been expected to do so with twenty years less experience? She'd done the best she could and would not regret that.

Her son focused on that one moment in her past, where the sword slipped in his father's chest, and she didn't know how to tell him that she didn't regret that moment. What she regretted was her inability to avoid it, and how cunning Siabala had been to ensure the moment came to pass.

She wished she could make him understand. That she could take him in her arms like she did when he was a small boy, and kiss away the pain. But he was no longer a small boy, and the world was no longer as kind. And he didn't want to be soothed right now. He wanted to be angry. All she could do was wait for that anger to pass, and not meet it with her own.

Which was damn hard, because his stubbornness, though he came by it honestly, really annoyed her.

"First we'll make sure your Circle has the help it needs," Cassara said, snapping Avarielle back to the conversation. "Then we head to help my family. It will be safe for me, Shirina. I am of no threat to Siabala, and the Larkhold Circle can see me safe."

"I don't trust them," Avarielle immediately said.

"Of course you don't," Shirina raised an eyebrow. "They're a Circle. You don't trust witches."

"I trust you. I trust your Circle." She met Shirina's eyes unflinchingly.

"It was hard earned," Shirina countered. Avarielle grinned at that.

"I can go to Massir to make sure Dayshon and Altessa are safe," Avarielle said.

"Or the Circle can simply let us know," Shirina quickly said. "They're there now and have magic. They can simply let us know."

"Do you think they've found Altessa by now?" Cassara asked, eyes wide, hoping. Pleading.

"Let's go find the Larkhold adepts and ask them," Shirina said. Anyone who didn't know Shirina well enough would think she said it without inflection. But Avarielle, and she was certain Cassara as well, sensed the ice under her tone.

"Thank you," Cassara said. "We have to get word to my brother as well, to keep Alexavier and Traina safe."

"Of course," Shirina nodded. Avarielle glanced back once at Rojon, now kneeling with his hands on the earth, as he looked down at the broken staff.

At least that would keep him busy and out of trouble for now. Silently, she followed the sorceress and the queen, to figure out their next steps, while hoping Siabala would show himself soon so she could finally end this.

2 0

Dirt crowded out the spaces between his fingers, cooling the anger that insisted on broiling in his chest. He knew this would calm him. The earth always did. It coated him, soothed him, kept him grounded. But the anger demanded attention. It forced itself into his heart, and mind.

His mother had run his father through with Graysword. And never once had she mentioned it to him. And she had not stopped wielding Graysword, despite being covered in the blood of the man she'd claimed to love.

Could you ever truly wash away blood from a blade? How could she look at it, wield it, knowing what she'd done with it? What pain she'd caused?

Had she loved her father? His mind tumbled, his heart clutching. Was his father a bad guy and she'd been too worried about Rojon to tell him?

No. His grandfather had told him so many stories of his father, too. And the way his mother spoke of him… she had loved him. He was certain of it. Enough love that to this day, she still didn't court another, or let herself be courted.

Not that she's easy to court since she scares most people. A smile popped on his lips at the thought of his mother terrifying most potential suitors. His smile began to fade almost immediately.

He loved his mother. He had so many good memories of her, even if she'd left him for half a year at a time. She loved him fiercely; he had no doubt. She'd topple the two lands if it meant saving him.

Part of that love had trickled down from his father. She'd loved him and had wished for so much more time with him. Once, as a child, when he couldn't sleep and had snuck down the stairs to listen in on his mother and grandfather chatting before the fire, he'd witnessed one of the few times his mother had been frank about her emotions, unaware he listened in.

"Growing old alone can be lonely," his grandfather had said, a tremor in his voice.

"You're not alone, you silly old man." She'd placed a hand on his and held it, though. He could see it between their chairs, the fire outlining their hands. "Besides, it's not what I meant. I just never thought I'd get old, that's all. It was always living for the day. If Kryde were still here, he'd be a nice addition." A pause. "I still miss him."

"Me, too," Kale had answered.

"He'd be crappy at keeping house." She'd tried to lighten the mood.

"But he'd be good at loving you, and Rojon."

And the silence had blanketed the rest of their evening, holding hands as they watched the fire burn low, finding comfort in each other.

She'd loved his father. He had no doubt.

She'd run him through with her blade. Part of Rojon understood part of the story simply eluded him. He trusted his mother, and knew she only had his best interests at heart, even if sometimes she might not fully understand what would help him best. But she meant well, and that went a long way. He knew that he simply needed to know the story, and he would understand. He trusted her to have done the only thing she could at that time, and that it hurt her too much to speak of it. She'd never been good at sharing her past.

But ever since he'd touched Graysword and seen that vision, it crowded out every kind thought and memory he had of his mother, and he didn't care to understand. The vision overshadowed even his love for her.

Graysword, sliding effortlessly in his father's chest, like a knife through warm butter, the magic dancing on its edges.

That was the moment he couldn't get out of his mind, focused in on just that. Not his mother's face, nor his father's. The final binding of his fate, by her blade.

The reason he'd grown up without a father.

Every time Graysword is near, it's like I lose myself in that vision. He could sense it calling to him. And he knew

Siabala had wanted him to take an oath with him, by killing Cassara.

Blood for blood. He would have had access to his powers, and they were mighty. He'd glimpsed at how it powered his mother. Kept her standing when others fell. Allowed her to heal faster. Not to mention the fires of her blade.

He would have killed Cassara. His hands would have been coated in her warm blood. He would have looked into her blue eyes, and he knew he'd only see grief there not for what he'd done, but for what he'd chosen to become.

But his mother had stepped between them and taken the blow from her own sword. He knew that he'd not connected with Siabala because of her. Just as he understood that she remained connected.

His hands had stopped moving in the earth, and he felt so helpless that it scissored his insides. He couldn't save his mother from Siabala. He couldn't stop himself from thinking about Graysword plunging in his father's chest. He couldn't stop thinking about Graysword, and the feel of the blade in his hand...

He pushed himself up, stood, and looked at the stump, where the sapling grew. He'd hoped to clear his mind to better understand it, but even working the earth failed to soothe his anger.

His gaze turned back to the piece of wood in his hand, the broken staff Shirina had kept in her study. Broken in the battle by Siabala, in the hopes of stopping the sorceress from wielding the merged strands of magic, knowing that to do so without the staff would be suicide. But she'd done it regardless. She'd wielded the magic, and fought him, and would have died if not for Cassara's magic.

As would he have. And Avarielle.

The purest magic of Graydon.

Thanks to Shirina's and his grandfather's tutelage, Rojon had learned everything he could about his magic, and the magic of Graydon. But it still felt like he knew and understood so little. He'd drawn on the magic, finally. Part of him still couldn't believe it had come to him. And he'd survived. The magic of the descendants of Elihor usually only worked to protect those they loved, leaving the wielder to be massacred by whatever they protected their loved ones from.

He swallowed hard, remembering his grandfather's death, protecting him.

His father had been captured by Siabala because his magic had protected his mother. And, when Siabala wanted Rojon to take an oath with him, something that he admitted he'd been unable to resist, Avarielle had gambled on his love for her. That it would save them.

She knew my magic would kill me. No. He physically shook his head, trying to shake out the vision of Graysword sliding into his father's chest.

No. She'd hoped it would trigger his magic and had been willing to bet on it. And she'd more than likely trusted that Shirina would find a way to save him. Not that she'd ever admit that.

What if his magic hadn't been triggered? There had always been the risk that he wouldn't have it at all. There had never been any guarantees it would ever come to him. He swallowed, mouth dry. He would have killed his mother with Graysword. Both his parents would have died by the same blade.

Why couldn't he simply get beyond that moment in time, then, of Graysword killing his father? Why did he keep falling back into the memory? A memory not even his own, but a vision possibly cobbled together by a god who felt he owned his mother's soul?

And he just might. His heart hammered in his chest. At the fear of losing her, all over again. He'd believed her dead. He'd tried grieving for her, but found he couldn't, trapped by his own fears. How did you honor someone you'd never believed could die in combat?

And then to learn she hadn't… he was mad at her for that, too. Not that she'd lived. He was grateful for that. But he was mad at her for falling. For letting him believe she was dead, even if it was completely out of her control.

No.

Sudden realization flooded him.

He was mad at himself for not trusting she might still be alive, and not going after her. He should have known she'd survived and had needed him. Except she *hadn't.* In the end, she'd saved *him.* Could he have even saved her? If he'd wielded Graysword, maybe. But then, he'd have dishonored her memory by making a bond with the darkest god.

He was mad at her. Mad at himself. Mad at Siabala… He was just angry, and he had nowhere for it to go. Like Siabala's clutches still clawed at his skin, his mind, his heart.

He was heir to Elihor, but he wasn't fully of Elihor blood. He was of Graydon's, too, thanks to his mother.

Trees fed from roots as well as the sun. Their leaves unfurled, welcoming sunshine to feed them. And from the ground, they pulled up nutrients they needed to survive. His studies, his entire chosen career path, seemed so far away now. Like they belonged to a different life. He'd chosen to go into natural architecture to help Elihor heal. More plants, which held the magic of Elihor. More buildings, which held its people. Combine the two, and you had the strongest architecture in the world.

He'd grown up in a world past the Blaze, where entire cities had been turned to scorched ruins and entire fields of Elihor's Fallen had been burned to the ground, taking the memories of entire families, of a people, with them. He'd wanted to help rebuild his world, to actively affect it, and not just watch it grow around him. He understood that his place as heir of Elihor would grant him access and opportunities not easily accessible to others. He knew that his voice would be amplified by the echo of his ancestor, her own voice a thousand years silent.

And he'd vowed to use that voice to help others. When he found that he preferred the sanctity of plants, he'd used his knowledge and voice to help people work together to accomplish greater things.

Roots. He understood the powers of roots in a way few others did, because his were known by everyone else. He pulled from those roots, from his position as a descendant of Elihor, and used it to feed the land around him.

He looked at the stump. Until today, it had no leaf with which to feed itself. All of its power, its ability to survive for a thousand years, came from its roots. Even though it had been cut for centuries, it still lived, able to produce a sapling.

"The leaves aren't feeding the tree," he mumbled. "They're a side effect of whatever is happening to the roots."

If Shirina's staff had come from this tree before, and it was Graydon's magic that fed this sapling from the roots, then it meant one thing, and one thing only. The magic of Graydon had simply been absorbed into the ground and now fed the tree that resonated so deeply with it.

Shirina would have come to the same conclusion, or perhaps was just toying on the edges of it. She needed him to confirm it, which made him feel better about all of this. It gave him purpose, and a focus. She always seemed to know exactly what would help him. Sometimes, he felt he was more like her than his own mother. Not that he'd ever tell Avarielle that.

To create another staff for Shirina, he needed to essentially figure out how to remove the leaves without harming its magic unintentionally, and then cut it from the trunk of the tree without breaking that easy flow of magic. Then, if he did it right, something he wouldn't know until Rina tried to draw magic from it, well, it should work.

Rojon knelt on the oak stump. He leaned in, focused on the sapling. Not its potential magic, but the fact that it was just a plant, with a slightly different feeding system. He needed to cut it into a viable shoot, so that it could continue to draw on the magic. Just like taking a cutting from a plant in a way that allowed it to grow roots again.

He looked at the two broken pieces of staff. At how they were cut. At the hollowed rivulets that had once held sap. He imagined they held magic, instead, and focused Shirina's abilities. Just like she'd focused his on this tree now.

After more reflection and observation, he slowly began his work, so absorbed that, for a few brief moments, he forgot about even the pull of Graysword.

The thought of speaking again with the two Larkhold adepts sandpapered the inside of Shirina's veins. Their sheer disregard for Ravenhold's experience and history, of her Circle's presence, irked her. No, it *angered* her. And she did not like feeling angered.

Avarielle and Cassara trailed her, solid presences at her back, as they headed toward the study assigned to the Larkhold witches, their so-called allies.

She used to get this angry at Avarielle, who kept her away from the old Circle as it disintegrated. As her mentor was killed for refusing to bow to Siabala. But that had been different—the warrior was never supposed to have been an ally. To fully understand the work of the Circle, and how she worked to maintain it. Avarielle Grayloft was not privy to its history and lore, and never would be.

But the Circle, any Circle, whether Ravenhold,

Larkhold, or the destroyed Stormhold, should know better than this. They should appreciate the millennia of knowledge that any Circle held, regardless of her rank. She might not be Elder, but she knew more about Ravenhold than anyone else. And she knew about Larkhold and Stormhold, too. She'd made a point not to limit her knowledge, nor her Circle's knowledge, to simply Ravenhold's point of view.

She'd strayed from established lines. She'd encouraged her adepts to refine spells. Make them better. To combine their powers and work together. And, even though she'd kept some very important ones to herself, she shared secrets, so many more than ever before. She knew Larkhold's Elders disrespected her decision to do so, believing knowledge as something to be guarded and protected, not shared. But if the Elders of Ravenhold had shared more with her, than its destruction would not have been as complete. The bridge that linked her to the Circle's past and hidden knowledge had been destroyed, leaving her stranded in ignorance.

She would have to make do with the knowledge she did possess and make use of what little powers she had. And swallow her pride when it came to asking for help from people she really disliked.

They entered the manor and the secondary study where the Larkhold witches had been asked to wait. The place was empty.

All three looked at one another and at the room around them.

"Where in Eli's armpit did they go?" Avarielle asked, annoyed.

"I'm sure they're not far," Shirina said, turning around to see two Larkhold witches entering the study. A warlock and a witch to be precise, and neither one the witch they were looking for.

Two more entered, followed by two more. And then a few more.

Suddenly, twelve witches and warlocks faced them, some moving to surround them. Avarielle growled at one, and she stayed her ground, but didn't seem impressed.

That wasn't good.

"Crimson Circle Elite Shirina," Patrile said as she stepped in. Shirina faced her, surprised she'd used her title. Unfazed, the witch continued. "The Elders of Larkhold find you guilty of failing in your duties, and wish to question you about your true intentions."

"My true intentions?" Shirina echoed the statement as a question. Avarielle took a step closer, but kept enough room to safely wield Graysword.

"That wasn't a question or an offer," the witch simply said. "You will come with us, now." Apparently considering the matter concluded, she turned to Cassara. "Your majesty, we can bring you back to Massir. To safety."

"What news of my family?" Cassara asked, though she stood her ground near Shirina. "Do you know if they're well?"

"They're safe," the witch said, eyes flickering toward

Shirina, a quick movement the sorceress did not fail to notice. She wished she had her staff, so she could defend herself. "Now we must see that *you* are safe."

"What of the rogue circle?" Shirina asked carefully. Cassara shifted beside her, impatient to get back to her family, but remaining by Shirina regardless.

"It is safe to return to Massir," the witch said. A common sidestep used by Elders. Not a lie, but not the full truth, either. Nausea clutched Shirina's stomach. Cassara had gone still. And Avarielle's hand was on Graysword's pommel, though she'd yet to draw it.

They'd all sensed the deception. Heard it in the words. Cassara was the first to speak.

"You would ally yourself with the traitors who tried to kill me, and pretend to have my family's safety at heart?" Her cold voice was accented by the soft sound of Graysword sliding from its scabbard.

"You would ally yourself with the woman who's lied to you this entire time, and kept your kingdom captive?"

Cassara did not dignify that with a response, the witch's words striking Shirina more than the queen.

"You cannot believe anything Elder Tally says," Shirina whispered, feeling the noose of Siabala's plan tightening around her neck. On all of their necks, as Larkhold's coven fell prey to the god's plans.

"You should not be so disrespectful of an Elder of your Circle," the Crimson Circle said, smug. "If you try to resist, we will use our magic to stop you. You have none, remember?"

Avarielle didn't need any further invitation. The adept had obviously not thought things through, as spells needed time. And Avarielle needed very little time to stop them, especially as they'd all gathered so closely.

The warrior dashed from Shirina's side in an instant, favoring her fists and feet over Graysword, which she'd quickly re-sheathed. Before Shirina could move, two adepts had grabbed Cassara and were pulling the queen sideways, while two others recited teleportation spells. They underestimated Cassara's willingness to fight as the queen kicked back to hit a warlock hard in the shin, her left elbow connecting with the other witch's nose. The kicked-in-the-shin warlock fell to his knees and grabbed the queen's legs, still muttering the spell. The other, bleeding from her nose, tears streaming down her face, took hold of her arms, also still uttering.

Shirina sidestepped toward her just as a spell knocked her from behind. A simple force spell, but effective against a witch who couldn't defend against it. Shirina went flying, knowing she had little time to get back up and fight back before another spell found her.

"Avarielle! Get to Cassara!" Shirina spat out as she pushed herself back up. The warrior quickly turned around, spotted the queen, and reached them just as one of the teleportation spells had ended, the second witch disentangling herself so as not to burden the other casting with her added weight. In her Circle, the two could have worked together for a stronger spell. This made Larkhold weak and gave Avarielle the seconds she needed to grab hold of the casting witch and Graysword's pommel.

She triggered Graysword's magic, undoing the adept's thread of magic. The teleportation spell exploding outward, a concussive force that shattered the nearest bookshelf, large tomes crashing down and knocking out two Larkhold witches. Shirina was slammed backwards again, but her proximity to the wall proved a blessing as she caught herself. Her friends were not so lucky, in the middle of the spell, the two flying sideways.

Avarielle grabbed Cassara and took the brunt of the blow they crashed through a window, to land in the gardens beyond.

Shirina scrambled back up to face the only still-standing witch, Kleriss, as Patrile collapsed on the ground after striking a bookshelf with bone crunching severity, books tumbling onto her.

Kleriss narrowed her eyes and began chanting. Shirina closed the gap between them and brought her fist up against the woman's chin, a sharp pain cracking down her arm but she didn't pull back, following through on the action as she brought up her knee and sunk it into the woman's gut. The Larkhold witch crumpled to the ground.

Shirina headed to the window, where Avarielle helped Cassara up. They had cuts and bruises but seemed fairly uninjured.

Before any of them could say anything, a shout caught their attention. Avarielle was gone in an instant, Cassara not far behind. Shirina ran out of the study, several of her adepts looking bewildered as they raced toward the now destroyed study.

"Do not trust Larkhold's Circle!" she shouted. "They are allied with the rogue circle!"

She bolted out of the door, three more of Larkhold's adepts holding down Rojon.

"It's for your own good, Heir of Elihor! We will keep you safe!"

Shirina closed the gap between them, noticing three things. One, Rojon's wide eyes. Two, the staff on the oak, looking finished already. Three, the teleportation spell almost completed. Her few options flooded her mind.

She could try to reach the staff and hope it would allow her to wield her magic, but Rojon might have been taken by then. Avarielle rounded the corner, but she was too far, the warrior's battle cry ringing in the air.

Rojon began to vanish, and their eyes met. Her choices dwindled to a single one.

She threw herself into Rojon, pushing him out of the Crimson Circle's grasp. The spell almost completed, the witch grabbed Shirina instead, who couldn't find her footing quickly enough to strike back.

Rojon screamed her name as the spell engulfed her.

2 2

$\mathcal{D}$ust. The entire underground smelled like dust as it danced in the shafts of sunset up ahead, filtered through the cracks of broken streets, buildings, and lives.

After some debate, they'd used an access tunnel under an old shop, one little known to even the rebels. The breadth and width of the dark-cast city terrified Altessa to her core, a discomfort nuzzled in her belly which would probably forever remain. An entire city, under her own, unknown to her. No sign of who had built it, or why it had been abandoned. And why it lurked underground.

Had it always been here? Altessa lacked the architectural context to tell and found that her historical and magical knowledge also came up short.

So, she focused on the shafts of light up ahead, where the underground city slopped downward, mimicking the same curves as Massir up above. This made her feel claustrophobic, the slope steep before her, accentuated by the darkest shadows and descending cave ceiling.

Altessa looked forward to clearing the buildings, and especially the ceiling, which blocked part of the view up ahead. That ceiling had been unbelievably high earlier and impossible to see, but now, here, she could reach its smooth surface, leaving her feeling smothered and small. Two sensations she didn't care for.

People ahead talked and shouted orders. A few moans echoed down the cave, but not many. The day had been spent helping people free, and she hoped there were more survivors than dead.

She walked faster, but Ramelia's hand whipped out, held her back, and then pushed her between two buildings. So close to her army, Altessa almost forgot herself. Almost. Then the voice cut through the quiet of the dead city, and she was glad she'd kept her peace.

"Where were you during the attack on the castle?"

"I got sidetracked chasing that princess," Ramelia quickly said. Altessa held her breath. Now that Ramelia was back with her people, would she betray her? "She's faster than she looks."

"We'll get her," the warlock said. Altessa could hear the grin in his voice.

"What happened here?" Ramelia asked. "I thought the ritual would be complete once they had the queen?"

Mom. All her worries about her mother threatened to bubble out of Altessa.

"The damn Ravenhold witch got in the way," he said.

Altessa's heart beat harder. "She'll get hers soon enough. But aside from that, who knows? The old Circle no longer has power, and Tally can rule from the throne of Massir. Imagine how it'll be once we live in that palace!"

"What did the people say?" Ramelia tried to say it lightly, but Altessa heard the strain of each syllable. The other rebel didn't seem to notice.

"They think Shirina was a rebel who attacked. That she unleashed the magic who robbed them of their queen and destroyed part of Massir. They think that Tally saved them. Refilled the wells that had been failing without Circle magic. Promised them safety. You know, stuff like that."

"Clever," Ramelia said as Altessa forced breath past the lump in her throat.

"I'm sure there's more even I don't know," he continued. "Anyway, you can get white robes now, if you want. There are some up ahead, where we're *helping* pull people out of the wreckage."

Helping. The word was said with such derision that Altessa wanted to hit him. Ramelia apparently didn't care for his tone, either.

"We *are* helping the people," she said in a threatening whisper. "We'll help save them all, from monsters and oppressors alike."

Altessa held her breath. This was it. Ramelia had shown her hand and would get them killed. If there were witches down there from Tally's Circle, what would they do when she showed up? They'd capture her. Make some excuse, take her back to Tally.

Kill her. Maybe.

She tuned back into the conversation as the two chatted back and forth, apparently no ill will found in Ramelia's fervor.

"Who else is helping there? Someone must have stepped up to help the royals," Ramelia said *royals* with such sneer that Altessa's blood grew cold.

"Well, help them how? Everyone thinks they've been saved by the Circle! There's nothing to fight. And we won't need to worry about the army—got rid of them this morning. Just a few people left to get rid of, like the royal guards, but gotta take it slow. Keep them off balance, so they don't make too much of a fuss until we can replace most of them with our own. Even Larkhold's Circle is here, and they're eating out of Tally's hands."

"Smart," Ramelia said.

Altessa didn't hear the rest of the conversation, her mind spinning with possibilities. Her father was helping them. The army was gone. The royal guards were being replaced. Her entire world, so solid and bright since her childhood, had been shattered with one decisive attack.

Ramelia slipped beside Altessa, took her hand, and made sure the princess followed her. Away from the witches. Away from the wounded and dying. Away from what she'd hoped would be her salvation. Away from the light.

Altessa didn't fight back, a strange sense of peace coming over her. No matter what she did, Tally would come after her. The noose that had tightened around her father's and mother's necks slowly tightened around hers, too. How far could she run? And for what purpose? Tally's witches were everywhere. Had she ever truly had a chance of escaping?

After about half an hour of walking in the dark, without any idea where she was, Ramelia finally whispered to her.

"I can get you out of Massir, I think. Maybe a boat or just keep walking under the city and reach the West. Something to get you out of there."

"No," Altessa said, surprised at discovering her mind made up. Every road she took to reach her home and help her people was riddled with witches. Tally's forces were everywhere. She had little reason to believe she could reach an ally before being caught. And she couldn't imagine abandoning her people. Not now. Not like this.

"Can we get under the palace, instead? Is there a way to sneak in?"

Ramelia's eyes conveyed what she thought of that plan, before the words slipped out. "Are you insane? Didn't you hear what he said?"

"I heard."

Ramelia shushed her, Altessa straining to hear whatever the rebel had just detected. She considered that maybe she pretended she'd heard something to stop Altessa from talking, but the fear in her eyes seemed real.

And, as they were too far from the faraway sunbeam to

see effectively, darkness surrounded them with threatening shadows.

"We have to move quickly," Ramelia said, using what little light she could, and no doubt familiarity with the terrain, to traverse the threatening darkness and quiet dust.

Not unlike a tomb.

Altessa looked back once where she thought she could see a tiny bit of sunbeam still, but it might have been a trick of her tired eyes. Spots in her vision to remind her of the light she'd left behind.

Altessa turned away from it, and quickly followed the rebel, before she vanished amongst the darkness around her.

23

Elder Tally didn't really want her tea, nor did she want the fresh baked bread brought to her by the palace chef. She stared with some regret at the three kinds of cheeses, one so soft the middle oozed from its rind onto the pearlescent plate. She was growing past the need for mundane things like food and water. Siabala had blessed her with life, and hope. Though she had to admit her palate missed the joy of perfect cheese on fresh bread.

But this was not a gift to be taken lightly, and she intended to repay her master accordingly.

"You did well," Tally said to Twilight, the silver woman standing near the window. From far, as she'd composed herself, she would look human. Except for her silver skin, highlighted by the rising moon, showing every piece of the naked woman. From up close, one could see flesh woven from threads, moving individually from one another, thin and sharp, and beautiful silver.

Braids gathered her long hair, but it changed as the spawn willed. She could turn into anything she desired, and never failed to amaze Tally. Not because of what she was, but because of how she'd been created. A spawn of Siabala, a creature made to kill quickly and elegantly.

Gone were the days of monsters who used claws and stank up his lands. He had been trapped with finesse and had learned from his enemies. If a hammer hadn't done the job last time, then he would use a well-honed needle. Unstitch the world they'd created in stopping him and restitch it in his image.

They would not undo Graydon and Elihor with armies, this time, especially since they'd been shoring up their defences. They would do so from within, toppling them without their even noticing.

Cassara's daughter would play into their hands. Another loose thread tied off, just like the silver threads of Twilight.

"We have a few more pieces to deal with," Tally said, sitting in the chair of the royal family's kitchen. Not the opulent one upstairs, but the one that Cassara had chosen for her family. A little princess lost in a big kingdom, too small and withdrawing to take up the space that was owed to her.

Too underserving, and painfully aware of it.

"I wish to kill them," Twilight hissed.

Tally removed her tea bag, satisfied with the dark red color of her brew. She took a long sip, closed her eyes, let the drink warm her. Soothe her. Remind her of home.

Of Siabala's Rage.

"That is an honor for Siabala himself," Tally said. The woman bristled, threads flowing like mercury. She smiled at the beautiful spawn. "But don't worry, child. You will have many others to get in your grasp. Head to Lisal Gardens. Since Larkhold failed to bring them to me, then I'll go to them myself."

Standing, she sipped and walked slowly to the window. Below her sprawled Massir, the large city the centerpiece of Siabala's new empire. People below lined up at the well, near the palace, to drink the waters gifted to them by her Circle. By Siabala. Laughter drifted up, the city releasing its tension since the attacks. Their king had spoken earlier, reassured them.

"All is well, children," she whispered, taking a long sip. She cast a smile at the sullen silver woman. "I believe you deserve a treat, as well."

At those words, sharp, silver teeth formed in Twilight's smile.

"If I were you," Avarielle hissed, "I'd talk."

The shorter Circle witch stared at her, trying to appear unafraid, but failing. Avarielle glowered over her, bruises from their combat spattering the witch's skin. She'd have a noteworthy amount more of those if she didn't talk soon. The chain of circles linking at her waist were silver, indicating she was Elite, unlike the ivory circles on other witches' dark robes. Or the black ones on Elder's robes.

Kleriss. That was her name. Not that she cared.

Avarielle shifted her weight, and the witch flinched. Her hands were bound behind her back, and she couldn't cast a spell. She had tried reciting one earlier, and Avarielle had quickly showed her that wasn't wise. All in all, twenty Crimson Cloaks from Elihor's Circle had invaded Lisal Gardens.

The witch glowered at her as Avarielle debated which

tactic to focus on next—stick or honey—when her son appeared in the doorway. He motioned with his chin to talk to her.

"Think on that," Avarielle told the witch, gagging her again before stepping out of the small study and joining Rojon. The rest of the Crimson Cloaks were being watched by Ravenhold's Circle. Avarielle hadn't been sure how the Circle adepts were going to react to Larkhold accusing Shirina of treason, but so far, she'd been pleasantly surprised.

Rojon looked grim but determined. Shirina had pushed him out of the spell, getting caught in it herself, choosing to save him. Avarielle had witnessed it all. Shirina could have gone for the staff her son had made and tried to use her magic. But the witch had done the same quick calculation Avarielle had, and it would have been too close for such a chance to be taken on something that might or might not work.

Instead, she'd thrown herself into Rojon, saving him. And getting captured.

Which meant Avarielle owed her. Again.

Bloody annoying witch.

"Let me talk to her," Rojon said. "I think she'd answer me."

Avarielle wanted Rojon to be anywhere but here. She wanted him far away and safe, where no Circle would find him, nor Siabala. She didn't want him anywhere near those witches, and she despised the fact that he was right.

He was the heir of Elihor, and Circle adepts practically swooned around him.

Plus, she saw the same determination in his eyes that shone in hers, too. Shirina had sacrificed herself to save him. They would get her back, no matter what.

"All right," she said. "But I'm coming in there with you. If she tries anything, I can't promise she'll live."

He looked like he might argue with her for a second, but then thought better of it and nodded. Avarielle followed him in, the witch looking relieved to see him. He gently removed her gag, Avarielle pleased at the blood on it.

"Are you all right, Crimson Circle Elite?" he asked. Avarielle crossed her arms. She knew what her son was doing. He was trying to make friends, so she'd talk to him. But she also knew that part of him didn't want to see this witch as the enemy. Her eyes were fully black like his, her robes familiar. The Circle of Elihor was from *his* land, and it was harder seeing an enemy when the same eyes looked back at you.

"I am." She cast a quick glance toward Avarielle who said nothing, standing back and trying bloody hard not to interfere. She had to trust that her son had a plan.

"Do you know where they took Shirina?" he asked, then added, "where they intended to take me?"

"It was for your safety, Rojon Kolder," she said, eyes darting to Avarielle.

"Ignore her," he gave her a grin. "She's just a tad overprotective. But I wouldn't try anything if I were you."

He gave a quick laugh, and she seemed relieved at his casual nature. Her son was charming, Avarielle couldn't deny that. Like his father.

That hadn't saved him, in the end.

"Please," he implored. "Can you tell me where she would be?"

She seemed torn, lowering her eyes. He needed to push her harder—Avarielle certainly would. She forced herself to stay back and let him handle the questions. She could always beat on her later, if necessary.

"If they followed the plan," she said, "she'll be in Massir by now."

Avarielle's muscles tensed. She'd hoped Shirina wouldn't be far due to the limits in teleportation. That they could get to her, still, if they were quick enough. But if she was already back in Massir, and they had no magic…

"How did they get her there so quickly?" Rojon asked, sounding genuinely curious.

"It's a trick Elder Quilsam came up with," she said, looking pleased. "One strong witch teleports two witches. Then either all three teleport, or two keep going. If it's far enough, at least one will make it, whoever is the last to use their spell. It's a teleportation chain, basically."

"Similar but not as refined as Shirina's shared magic and teleportation circles," Rojon said, and the witch looked rather annoyed. "And why were you planning on bringing me back there?" He continued before she could interject.

"To keep you safe," she said. "You and Queen Cassara, as descendants of Elihor and Graydon."

"Keep me safe from what?" Rojon asked.

"From Shirina," she practically spat out. "She planned this whole thing."

Avarielle clamped down her jaw so she wouldn't tear into the witch. Rojon was getting a lot further than she had. She trusted him to keep the course. Still, her muscles tensed, and she forced them to relax again. The scent of lilacs wafted in. Late in the season, and too sweet for the occasion, it nevertheless grounded her, helped her relax, to be better prepared to leap into action if necessary.

"What did she plan?" Rojon asked, then gave her a serious yet disarming look. When had her son learned to be so manipulative? She blamed Shirina's influence for that. "The more I understand, the better I can defend myself."

She pondered his words, glanced again at Avarielle, and spoke clearly and unapologetically. "She fabricated the story of Siabala being trapped in the Wall."

Breathe.

"We heard that already," Rojon said. "What I don't understand is why you think she did that, and why you thought I needed rescuing."

"Because she wants the magic, obviously," she said, though her voice lacked certainty. "With both the heirs to the magical lineages, she was preparing to take control of it."

"Then why did she save me from being killed by my own magic?"

"You used the magic of Elihor and lived?" Her eyes grew wide. Rojon stood taller. Avarielle forced herself to stay where she was, and to stay quiet.

"I did," he said, "to protect my mother. And I only live because Shirina managed to pull me out."

A *ah-ha!* Flashed in the witch's eyes. "No, she did that to get you in her grasp. If you were dead, she couldn't have followed through with her plan!"

"I still don't know what that plan is." Frustration tinted Rojon's words.

"It's not for me to know," she said, lowering her head slightly. "That's for the Elders to know."

"So, they tell you to come kidnap me, and you just do it?"

She flushed, flustered words tumbling out. "No! It was to save you."

"What will they do to Shirina?" He asked, the sudden question keeping her off balance. Avarielle had to admit he was doing an excellent job, lack of hitting aside.

"She'll answer to her Circle's Elder. That's not for me to decide."

Avarielle groaned, unable to stop herself. These witches really were idiots, weren't they?

"And you'd do better to distance yourself from her." The witch indicated Avarielle with a jerk of her chin. "She's done nothing but bring you grief."

"Enough," Rojon said. The witch grew silent at his

command. "Elder Tally tried to kill me," he said, "and Shirina saved me." She wanted to protest, but a sharp look from him silenced her. Avarielle was starting to enjoy the show. "You should be embarrassed to be so easily fooled by Siabala's minion." Before she could reply, he turned on his heels and left.

"He takes after me." She winked at the adept and stuck the bloody gag back in her mouth as the witch shot daggers at her with her eyes.

Satisfied the adept was secured and couldn't use her magic and escape, Avarielle followed after Rojon. It was time to form a plan.

25

"Shirina wanted us to help her Circle get the magic in order, first," Cassara said softly, leaning back into the wooden bench, leaves dancing around her. Rojon sat on another bench and Avarielle stood, too filled with energy to sit down, it seemed. "I feel like we're betraying her trust by going after her instead of trying to get the magic flowing again."

"Do you know how to get the magic flowing? Without her?" Avarielle asked. Cassara shook her head, feeling tired. So tired. Bone weary, as she had so many years ago, when everything had been falling apart and she had been powerless to stop them.

"Let's face it," Avarielle said, sounding annoyed. "I don't think Shirina herself knew how to get the magic flowing again. Without access to that bloody Elder knowledge, she can't fix this."

Cassara understood Avarielle wasn't annoyed so much

as worried. What would Tally do to Shirina? The Circle witches who had gone against Siabala back in the day had all been turned into monsters. This did not bode well for the sorceress.

"This is really annoying," Avarielle said. "First, I get captured. Then, you get captured. And you," with a jerk of the chin she pointed to Cassara and Rojon. "And now, Shirina got caught. It's like a wheel of capturing."

"They've had the upper hand this entire time," Cassara said, trying to calm her mind and find her footing. She needed to think like a queen. But all her heart wanted to do was think like a mother, and a wife, and run back to Massir to save those she loved. "How do we get ahead of them? It's like they know our every move."

"Shirina figured them out a bit before," Avarielle said, "but they've been planning this for years. Obviously they're ready for us."

"So we do the unexpected," Rojon offered, speaking up. "What would they expect you to do?"

"Go after Shirina," Avarielle answered without hesitation, taking a step forward in anticipation, shadows dancing as the day progressed toward evening. "But they didn't think they'd capture her, either. They were hoping for you and Cassara."

"Exactly," Rojon said. "They wanted to get us both there, and Shirina, and probably you, too, Mom. And now they'll expect us to mount an attack and head their way."

"I don't see that we have much choice," Avarielle

mumbled, "Shirina is annoying, but she's also our best shot at fighting back."

"What if," Rojon continued, "instead of sneaking up on them, we just show up?"

"I'm sorry?" Avarielle asked, raising an eyebrow. "Surely no son of mine is suggesting that we stroll in there?"

"I got the idea while talking with Kleriss," he ignored his mother. Cassara was caught up in Rojon's enthusiasm, and she leaned forward. "They were sent here to protect Cassara and me, so I think we can use that against Tally. She can only be so convincing of Shirina's treachery if Cassara and I are safe. The Elders of Larkhold will stop supporting her then."

"Sure, if she doesn't just immediately kill you both or cast you into some other dark fate." Avarielle quickly dismissed the idea.

"What are you thinking?" Cassara asked Rojon, ignoring Avarielle's glare.

"I'm thinking that we walk into the city's front gates. You show the rebels you're not afraid. I show Larkhold that I'm safe and well. You hold court, reunite with your family. The Circle can't attack us in plain daylight, especially if we request Larkhold's protection."

"There's no guarantee Tally won't attack in daylight," Avarielle said. "It's way too risky."

"I like it," Cassara stood up, a breeze gently blowing in the flowers around her.

"Cassara, you can't—"

"No, I think it's how we do it. It has risks, don't get me wrong, but what else do we have, if we don't have magic? We can only stand up against them. There's really no other choice."

"That's simplifying things a bit." Avarielle looked from Cassara to Rojon. "You're both kidding, right? We can't just hand you both over to Tally! That's death in a handbasket woven with stupid. It's playing right into her hands! She needs both of you!"

"Then only one of us goes," Cassara immediately said, having waited for Avarielle's objection. Seeing exactly what Cassara had done, the warrior narrowed her eyes at her.

"No," she said.

"You and Rojon can head to the West, skirt Massir, and go find whatever knowledge Shirina hoped had been decoded."

"That was a long shot, and you know it," Avarielle said. "You're not going in there."

Cassara sighed, and walked over to Avarielle, looking up into the warrior's hazel eyes. It would be easy to only see the hardness there. But Cassara knew her well enough to see the worry. The fear. The love, all hidden behind a thick layer of Westland stubbornness.

"Avarielle," she said softly, "I know you're only trying to protect me, and I will always be grateful to you for that. But this is my fight. I can't live with myself for abandoning my people. I did it once before, on the battlefield. We both did. I left Dayshon once before, to fight Siabala. This time, I want to be by his side, Avarielle. I need to go to him, and face whatever awaits us there."

Avarielle looked like she would argue, but her features softened. Then she ran her hand in her hair, further tousling her short red mane.

"I must be daft for considering this, but all right. But only if we all go together. We go, you stay visible at all times, and I stay near both of you. And then we find Shirina and get out. We'll take your family with us. Promise me that, Cassara."

"No," Cassara said. The warrior's mouth closed in a thin, stubborn line. "I'll stay with my people. This time, I won't leave them. You'll take Shirina and find a way to unfurl the magic. Take Altessa, too, and get her out of Massir. We know she can wield the magic just like I can. But I'm a queen now, Avarielle, not a princess from a small kingdom. My people need me, and I don't intend to abandon them."

Cassara waited calmly before Avarielle, waited for the storm to come. Braced herself. The warrior observed her and, instead of chewing her out, simply shook her head.

"I hate this, but I can tell when your mind is made up. And I can't think of another option, if I'm honest."

"What do I do in all of this?" Rojon asked from the sidelines.

Cassara waited for the warrior to speak, but Avarielle seemed lost in thought, her brow furrowed. In truth, she needed Rojon. It was like handing him to Tally, but Larkhold's Circle would undoubtedly protect him. Did she trust that they were powerful enough to stand against Siabala's Circle? Could she count on that?

"I can help," Rojon said, sensing her indecision.

"It's not that," Cassara said, looking into his dark eyes. She'd just met him as an adult a week ago, and already he felt like family. He *had* been her family, since the day he was born, and she'd held him as they fought Siabala. She'd used him to fight Siabala then and vowed never to put him in danger again.

And here she was, thinking again about bringing him against the demon, or at least his troops. Had her worry for her family, for her people, clouded her judgment so much that she was willing to sacrifice her best friend's son? Cold dread washed over her. Who would she be willing to become to see her loved ones safe, and why wouldn't she include Rojon in that category?

Guilt, fear, and worry all intertwined, turning her stomach.

"Are you all right?" Rojon asked.

"Honestly? I don't think I've been all right in a long time," she said, observing him more closely, as though seeing him, truly seeing him, for the first time. He did not shy away at her scrutiny. He looked like Avarielle, and she could imagine the man she had loved from his features. "I don't want to put you in danger, Rojon. You should head West and see if they've translated the texts there. Once your mom has Shirina, she'll meet you there."

"And you?" Rojon asked, taking her hand in his, his touch warm. Like her own son's, far away in Edoline. She could go to him, instead. To her son, and her youngest daughter, and her brother. She could make sure they were safe, and… and then what? Wait for Siabala to find her, and destroy them, too? Isn't that what had happened to Dayshon and Altessa, and her people? All paying the price of her actions?

"I need to make sure my family and my people are safe," she said. A counterargument flittered across Rojon's face, but Avarielle halted it by placing her hand on his shoulder, a slow grin appearing on her lips.

"What?" she asked.

"I just realized we failed to take in one very important factor into consideration."

"Which is?" Rojon asked, eager to see what they might have missed, and the potentially better path it might offer.

"Shirina herself," Avarielle said. "When the witches teleported me to Tally's underground kingdom of evil, I wacked them until I was free. Shirina wasn't knocked unconscious, and she knows how to throw a punch when needed."

"You don't think she's in Massir?" Cassara said, clutching her stomach as it twisted in her gut.

"I don't think she'd let them get her that far. Not if they need to exchange casters. She knows how to break magic. They won't expect her to be so fast."

"She's not in Massir?" Cassara's breath hitched, her heart broke, and hope blossomed in her. She wanted to go to Massir so badly. But she was so terrified of it, as well. What would she do if her family was dead? She'd lived that reality before. Could she really save them if they weren't? Would anything stop Tally or the rebels from publicly executing her?

A wave of acceptance cushioned her anxiety, smothered it. Her family still needed her. She still needed to go, to show up for her people, and her family. And she could do so alone, if need be.

She turned to Avarielle. "What do you suggest?"

"We figure out her path, which Mr. Charmer here—" she grinned at her son, who grinned back at her. They looked so alike in that moment, "—can get from the witch. Then we start making our way toward where the first stop would be. Then the second. We look for signs of a failed teleportation spell, a dead witch, or anything pointing to Shirina."

"We walk?" Rojon asked.

"We can ride," Avarielle offered. "They have horses here."

Cassara wanted to suggest that the Larkhold witches teleport them, instead. That it would be faster. But she held her peace, knowing Avarielle would never go for it, knowing that they wanted her in Massir.

Except *she* wanted to be in Massir, too. *I don't have my magic,* she wanted to scream. It should have returned, but it hadn't. For years she'd waited for the magic to return. She'd held off on calling on it, knowing it held Siabala captive. She'd felt it call to her, draw her in, beckon her to use it.

And she hadn't.

And it had changed nothing, and now she might never touch it again. She had to stand as a queen, with or without magic. And it looked like it would have to be without.

"Cassara," Avarielle said, standing in front of her. Rojon was gone, and she'd missed his departure, lost in thought. "I know you're worried about your family. And I know you want to get back to your people." She placed her hands on Cassara, helping to ground her. Like she'd done after her family had been murdered by Eloms, her younger brother taken. How lost she'd felt then. How powerless, even though she'd had magic.

"Everything is a cycle, isn't it?" Cassara said. "My family is in danger, and I don't know if I have the power to help them."

"If everything is a cycle," Avarielle reminded her gently, "then it means we'll save your family, just like we did all those years ago."

"How do you keep believing we'll win the day?" Cassara felt that her eyes should mist over, but they didn't. Cold smothered her earlier calm, instead. Numbness. Except where the warrior's hands rested on her shoulders.

"Because we're not backed into a corner yet, Cassara." Her face twisted in annoyance. "Of course, it would help if Siabala actually showed his face."

"You have no idea where he is?" Cassara ventured, a question that had been bothering her.

"You mean, can I track him with our bond?" Avarielle grimaced. "I liked it better when no one except me knew about that," she mumbled, then sighed. "I can't. No more than he can track me, as far as I can tell. I guess the magic is in Graysword only."

"You'd tell me if it was different, right? Or if you felt that something in his magic changed, and impacted you?" Cassara asked. The warrior met her eyes, unflinching.

"You'd tell me if you intended to run off and head to Massir, right?"

Cassara looked at Avarielle. The warrior's red hair had more gray in it, and crows feet lined her eyes, showing a good life. Scars ran down her arm and some on her face, but the determination there blazed unwaveringly. Avarielle wanted to keep her safe, no matter what.

And Cassara knew that her friend kept her word, always.

"I'll tell you if you tell me if your magic feels unsafe."

"Deal," Avarielle said. The warrior hugged her impulsively, and Cassara hugged her back.

"Let's head back in and see how Rojon is doing," Avarielle broke the embrace, looking in Cassara's eyes one more time, just in case a lie lurked there. Cassara met her gaze unflinchingly.

When they entered the mansion, quite a few adepts had gathered in the first study, waiting for them.

"Whatever you're planning," a young warlock with dark skin and long braids said, "we want to help. We want to help Crimson Circle Elite Shirina, and our friends still in Massir."

Others nodded, some vigorously, some more timidly. More afraid but determined.

Cassara and Avarielle shared a quick look, and Avarielle broke into a grin. Facing the determined adepts, seeing their willingness to sacrifice themselves for a cause, for a Circle, Cassara couldn't help but draw more parallels to the past, and found herself missing the sorceress even more.

And her missing magic twisted like a dagger in her stomach.

26

The witch's grasp around her lessened the second Shirina's elbow connected with her ribcage. But the teleportation spell had been completed, and the two tumbled away in a stream of light. As it dissipated, the Larkhold witch fell to her knees, winded by the blow. Shirina ignored her, knowing the use of such magic would have weakened her too much to be of much concern. Instead, she focused on what she might be landing into.

She concentrated on scent—everblooming plants that could be smelled the instant the spell began to dissipate would orient her and reveal her location. Assuming they would target one of her outposts, which they probably would. They used her network to their advantage—another tactic she'd failed to predict.

The sweet scent of lilacs greeted her, in the shadows of tall, lush maple trees. They were at the foot of the Maple

Mountains, at her outpost. Did any of her witches even still live?

Three shapes vaguely began to form in the mists. Two Orange Cloaks, one Crimson. Two black robes, one white. She bristled at that. White was Ravenhold's robes. *Her* robes. That Tally pretended to represent the very Keep and coven she'd betrayed to Siabala... Shirina focused on that traitor, first, and as soon as the spell ended, threw herself into her, black hair tumbling as she yelped.

It wasn't graceful, but she had no magic and little time. Shirina knocked down the witch, knees digging into her offending white robes, slamming the air out of her. She didn't know this witch and would have burned the robes off of her had she had her magic.

Shirina's wrists took the brunt of the blow, but she scrambled up. The two Larkhold adepts' mouths opened in surprise. The Crimson Cloak was the biggest threat, the only one able to teleport and weave communication magic. Before he could think to react, Shirina closed the gap and connected her elbow with his nose, head snapping back with a satisfying crunch before he crumpled. The Orange Circle was right beside him, and she hit her in the gut. She folded in two, and Shirina gathered her fists and hit her on the back.

Then she turned on the Crimson Cloak, and made sure he was knocked out, too. Three here, quickly dealt with. The witch who'd cast the teleportation circle had passed out, which was just as well. They conveniently had ropes, no doubt to use on Rojon and possibly Cassara.

Shirina was no master of knots, but she had enough rope to ensure many redundancies to every knot.

Once done, the first adept started writhing awake, Shirina stood and headed for the outpost. Blood marked Shirina's white robes, which annoyed her. Her knees and wrists hurt, which annoyed her even more. She was a Crimson Circle Elite of Ravenhold. Not a bloody Westland Warrior hurtling battle cries likes weapons.

Brushing down her robes, she walked into the wooden outpost, a simple building only meant to accommodate ten witches at most, and that was with bunks and room sharing. They'd failed to make much headway into the independent villages, or those under the rule of Solir. Anything north of Rashim had proved difficult to convince to trust the Circle, and so this outpost had never grown to accommodate more witches.

Shirina drew in a breath as she spotted blood near the outpost's entry. She forced her breath to blow out, hands shaking as she entered her outpost slowly, eyes taking in every detail. She needed to pay attention to her surroundings or perish rushing into a potential trap.

She hoped that not all her adepts were dead. That some had survived whatever attack had happened here. Thoughts of Shala, her second, assailed her mind, and she pushed them down, deep below, away from her grasp.

Now was not the time to falter.

She cleared the front study room, sitting room, and kitchen, where apparently Larkhold's witches had been preparing stew. Her aching fingers curled around a dirty but sharp knife, the blade comforting despite her bubbling anger at being forced into such crude actions. Next, she cleared the five bedrooms, some beds ruffled. So, they'd attacked at night, like the cowards she understood them to be. Dragged her adepts out of bed…

Focus.

Another smaller library remained at the back. It could have been converted to a bedroom, but the adepts had voted to share rooms and have more spots for books. Adepts after her own heart, which now hammered wildly in her chest, palm clammy around the blade, unused to grasping a weapon.

She turned slowly into the small study, footsteps quiet. Old books on the histories and plants of Kosel, and the creatures that lurked within, lined the walls from floor to ceiling. Shirina's chest uncoiled its fear as she found five bound, gagged, and beaten adepts. *Her* adepts.

Their eyes grew wide when they saw her. They'd been tied up for a while, the place smelling horrible, their robes soiled. Some still wore their nightshifts.

They looked hungry, and thirsty.

A quick breath calmed her shaking hands so she could safely cut their gags and bonds. Two Orange Circle, one Green, and two Blue. They'd killed the Crimson Circles she imagined, but had kept these witches alive… why? What did they intend to do with her adepts?

"Crimson Circle Elite," Ollir, one of her most advanced Orange Circles croaked out.

"Slowly," Shirina said, helping them to the kitchen

table, examining their wounds. A few mumbled apologies at their state, and she shooed their concerns away. Satisfied no wound would prove deadly, she served them some of the stew, which proved bland but edible, and water. "We don't have much time, so please listen to me as you slowly drink and eat."

She told them everything, having no time to couch the truth. About the treachery of Tally, and the new Circle under Siabala's thumb. About their missing magic. And the fact that the Wall of Loss had fallen, and Siabala was somewhere, but he was biding his time, hiding. That Larkhold had believed Tally, and decided to forego all caution and wisdom. That no one with the power to do so was even trying to stop the worst evil in the land.

Their eyes grew wider and wider.

"Pol attacked us," Ollir said between bites of stew. "We never saw it coming and couldn't defend. He killed…he killed the Crimson Circles. They tried to protect us, but his magic was…it wasn't right."

"Listen to me, Ollir. All of you," she looked to them. "Head to Rockor and seek refuge. Hide. Let no one know you're there. They'll protect you." A village founded to avoid witches, now one of their greatest allies. Her one hope in the Maple Mountains.

Shirina nodded. "Find them, and ask them to help you hide."

"We can't just abandon the Circle!" Ollir said, to sounds of agreement from her other adepts. "We can't just abandon *you*," the witch continued, green eyes flaming with determination and fierce protectiveness. Shirina's chest constricted, and then loosened. She squeezed Ollir's shoulder.

"You won't be," she said. "You will be healing and resting and staying safe. We've lost many of our brethren already," she swallowed hard, again thinking of Shala, her trusted second. "We need to maintain our ranks for when Siabala comes."

She looked at each of them in turn. The younger and older. The experienced and less so. She saw the same spark of determination in each of them.

"And Siabala *will* return. Let no one tell you differently. Be ready for when the battle calls. And—" she again looked to each in turn, "—if you find yourself unable or unwilling to come to that final battle, know that I will think no less of you." She'd told them this over and over again. She did not want to forge a Circle of warriors. She did not want the Circle to die by all heading into battle. She wanted scholars, guardians, protectors, historians, poets, gardeners… She banked the future of her Circle, on all of Graydon, on more than just warriors. Warriors existed for battle. Her Circle had been built for more than simple survival. They existed for growth. The world needed builders and poets. Thinkers and gardeners.

"When the battle call reaches you, come to me," she said.

"How will we know when you need us, if there is no magic? How will we fight?"

Shirina pondered. If she had magic, she could summon

them to her with a telepathy spell. She'd done it before, against Siabala. But there were no Crimson Circles here, and so her spell might not reach them.

The other Circles might block her spells… but it could not stop Graydon's magic, if she managed to free it. She had to believe that the magic still lurked near, and she would find it again.

"Ollir," she turned back to the Orange Cloak. Sensing Shirina's shift in tone, the gravitas, they stood straighter. The others paid more attention, eyes on their leader.

On *her*.

"Your studies as an Orange Circle adept are at an end," Shirina said. For a second, they looked defeated, short dark hair lowering with their head. Shirina smiled. "You have gained all necessary knowledge and wielded your magic admirably."

One of the first things Shirina had done after the Keep was lost, while rebuilding her Circle, was to ensure its magic and that only some traditions continued. Green, blue, yellow, and orange circles had always been gifted new cloaks by teachers, in this case, her. Crimson Circles and Elders received their cloaks from the Keep, through its followers. Or so it used to be.

Shirina knew how to gift a Crimson Cloak, bearing one herself. She sensed the magic in her adepts and knew when they were ready. Not once had the magic of Graydon refused her the gift she offered to her adepts.

It only refused her status of Elder, her cloak still unflappably crimson. Those secrets were kept from her.

But the Crimson Cloaks were not kept from her adepts.

Shirina sang the incantation needed to change the cloak, careful not to channel Elihor's magic accidentally. She could sense the magic just out of reach and chose to push aside her doubts that it was her hopes feeding that perception. No. It was much more than that. It had to be the magic, beneath her feet, trapped but still listening.

Listen to me, she pleaded with her heart. *Listen to the powers I invoke today, and gift them to Ollir.*

She sang, and they all listened, especially Ollir. The others would know the spell, but not understand its root. They wouldn't be able to grasp the finer meaning of each pitch and tone of her spell. But in Ollir's eyes, she saw the magic there, too. The witch understood, the magic becoming a part of them. Resting in their heart, their mind, and their body.

This ritual used to be private and hidden from everyone else. But that wasn't Shirina's Circle. She needed the others to see and understand the magic, now more than ever.

The orange cloak remained when Shirina was done.

"Crimson Circle Ollir," Shirina said. Ollir stood straighter. "When your cloak takes on its true color, you will know that the magic of Graydon will have been freed. Use your instincts then, follow the magic, and find me."

"Thank you, Crimson Circle Elite," Ollir's eyes shone with unspent tears. Shirina's breath caught in her throat. It meant so much to them, to be a part of the Circle. To all of them. They'd chosen this fate, whereas it had been forced on Shirina. She'd been taken from her family, forced into a life of servitude.

But these adepts, all of them, who now congratulated Ollir and hugged them... they'd come by *choice*. They'd made this their home. They'd been beaten. Hurt. Had witnessed the death of friends. But they were undefeated.

When she'd first started this Circle, Shirina had struggled with paying homage to the original, thousand-year-old coven that had trained her. And she'd fought against her guilt every time she did away with a tradition that she felt—no, *knew*—no longer served them.

Deep in her heart, she'd harbored her fear. That she'd fail. But she hadn't. She hadn't failed her adepts.

And she knew, finally fully accepted, that the death of her old Circle was the best thing that could have happened to Graydon's magic. Because her old Circle had faltered and broken without magic. But this one would fight to preserve the place they'd chosen to make their own.

"Where will you go?" Ollir asked Shirina as they left the four bound, treacherous adepts in the study and prepared to head off.

"I have to see if I can get Graydon's magic back," she said. A plan had been forming in her mind since before the magic had even vanished into the earth. A plan so simple, formed of the stones of her youth, and their roots in the earth.

"I'll find you once you've freed it," Ollir said, nodding fiercely. Resolutely.

Shirina simply nodded, and the five headed up the winding trails, toward friends and a chance to heal.

Shirina waited until she could no longer see their cloaks swirling in the fading light of the sun, and then she turned toward the north.

Toward Ravenhold.

*A*varielle scowled at the cloud cover which delayed their departure until dawn, lest one of their horses break a leg in the pitch dark and slow them down even more. With her hand on Graysword, she focused back on doing a final walk around the Lisal Gardens. Rojon and Cassara were already in bed, the only battle she felt like she'd won today.

Her son had argued, but she'd pointed out that she'd slept last, and she needed him sharp in the morning. His expansive yawn had won her the argument.

Cassara had looked ready to fall over, so she'd just nodded and headed off to take the bed Shirina had occupied while healing this morning. Avarielle was worried about Cassara, and hated feeling like she couldn't help her friend. She'd watched her, since meeting her so many years ago, take blow after blow and rise again. Forcing herself back up.

She'd watched her be willing to die in the battle against Siabala, willing to leave her magic within the Wall of Loss to keep the world safe. But they'd saved her. And Cassara had lived to become the young queen of a large kingdom. To become a legend, even: the one who'd stopped Siabala. To bear three children. To help rebuild after the war.

And, every time Avarielle saw her, every time she visited, she saw her shrink a little bit more under the weight of responsibility. She'd shrugged it off well, of course, being Cassara. But Avarielle could tell her friend suffered and didn't know how to address it.

Avarielle wasn't the kind of friend who knew how to fix anything except by beating on it, so she'd tried to distract her friend with bow and battle training. With jokes and stories. With just being there as often as she could. It was her role to protect her, yes, but Avarielle wasn't clear on how to protect her soul. How to help it out of the dark pits she fell in after each of her children were born. How to pull her away from the despair that flittered across her face, when she played her flute in the gardens, eyes closed and shedding tears, as though she still sought the comfort of the sea.

In a kingdom she'd given up to gather an army. To fight back the Eloms killing Avarielle's people, because she felt she owed Avarielle.

She hadn't. Avarielle wished she could have made that clearer to her. And now, knowing Cassara had stepped into a life she'd never wanted in order to save the

Westlanders, Avarielle would always owe her. And she'd never be able to repay her, because she only knew how to fight monsters she could see. The darkness crushing her friend? That, she had no idea how to fight. All she could do was stand with her.

Her people rising against her—well, *some* of her people, idiots all—had crushed the queen's spirit. And the uncertainty about Altessa's or Dayshon's fates ate at her soul. Cassara wanted to go home, but Avarielle couldn't let her, no matter how much she fought. Because Avarielle knew exactly what Cassara was doing. The same thing she'd tried to do twenty years ago when she'd decided to fight Siabala.

Cassara was planning on letting it all go. On giving her life for those she loved. And she loved so many that it made Avarielle's head spin.

The warrior looked around the perimeter. The Lisal Gardens were quiet, the night still and dark around them. She could see fine in the dark, another gift of Siabala, but this stillness bothered her. Because she knew an attack was coming, if not now, then soon.

Just like she knew it was coming for Cassara. And she wasn't sure the queen would fight back, tired from years of fighting, of living a life she hadn't really wanted. Of making peace with it, or trying to make peace, anyway. Of convincing herself and others that she was fine. But Avarielle could see the cracks in her friend. Cracks forming since the day she'd lost her family in Edoline in an Elom attack. The day that Avarielle had met her, the young, innocent, stubborn princess of a small kingdom.

And the one person who could stop Siabala from returning.

Had she ever planned on coming back from the final battle? Avarielle asked herself that question every time those cracks resurfaced. And every time, the answer was too painful to speak aloud.

Avarielle sighed and placed her hand on Graysword's pommel, wishing her friend's malaise was as easy to dispel as monsters. She knew how to fight those. She didn't know how to fight demons of the soul.

She stopped, looked toward the horizon. She couldn't see it, that far and beyond the Maple Mountains, but she could sense the location of the Bloody Mountains. Of Siabala's Rage. Her left arm ached, where Siabala had pushed his magic inside of her, cracking the bones, almost pulverising them. The limb had never felt right since then, and she was okay with that.

It reminded her of the monster who'd killed Kryde. Who'd hurt Cassara. Who'd tried to break her.

For a second, she thought she could sense him, on the horizon, laughing, the sound resonating in the never-quite-healed scars of her bones.

"I know you're still out there," she hissed into the dark. "When I find you, this time, I'll end you."

The darkness seemed denser, and a breeze picked up the leaves, turning them over like a long, pitched laugh.

Avarielle's eyes narrowed and, hand still firmly on

Graysword, continued patrolling the Circle outpost, and making sure the adepts in charge of watches had not fallen asleep.

It was dark, they were exhausted, and so this would be the perfect night for an attack.

2 8

The attack came at dawn.

When the witches were just changing shifts, yawning. When Avarielle and Rojon had finished saddling the horses in the traditional Graydon way of using full saddles, unlike Elihor's simpler blankets.

A scream pierced the quiet morning, abruptly cut off.

"Cassara," Avarielle said, the queen not yet with them.

"I'll get her," Rojon offered, grabbing his sword, his gaze flickering for just a second to Graysword.

"You need to protect the horses so we can get out of here," Avarielle said. "I'll get Cassara."

He looked about to argue but she shot him a look making it clear she expected no argument. The scream had come from the other side of the Gardens, but Avarielle couldn't count on them not being surrounded.

"Be careful," she told her son, and he nodded. She hated leaving him in the stables, but she needed to get

Cassara. She'd trained her son. She had to trust that his training, not to mention his bloodline, would see him safe.

Avarielle took off across the Gardens, skirting the trees and keeping low. A green-cloaked witch cowered near a bush, eyes wide. Avarielle hadn't missed seeing children fear for their lives. And lose them.

She grabbed her by the upper arm and practically dragged her up. "Keep up and give me space to move if I need it," Avarielle whispered. The adept nodded, but still looked terrified and shaking. Avarielle freed Graysword, the blade warm in her hands already, dark magic surrounding them.

The blade's power slipped into her blood, energized her, and increased her senses and speed. The Green Circle kept up as Avarielle crouched and ran toward the mansion. A scream to the right and Avarielle turned to see a Crimson Circle with a slashed throat gurgling on their blood. The young adept screamed, and Avarielle threw her back as tendrils lowered from the branches of the tree, sharp and deadly.

The green cloak and white robes tumbled into some bushes, and Avarielle jumped back, swinging Graysword at the tendrils. It struck like steel on steel, and the tendrils started wrapping around the blade, pulling it, and Avarielle, up.

Holding on to the pommel, she ran up the side of the tree, using the creature's strength against it as she leapt, activated her full magic, and yanked down. The creature shrieked, tendrils collapsing to the ground and turning into smoke. Without waiting to see what else the creature could do, Avarielle yanked the Green Circle back to her feet and ran for the manor, trusting her instincts to lead her to Cassara.

Kleriss struggled against the bonds the Ravenhold witches had so effectively trapped her with, to no avail. She felt like she was on a slope, slipping backward, unable to catch her footing. She'd been surprised to be asked to lead a mission here, with Patrile. And she wished she could be anywhere but here.

"You will not be harmed if you cooperate," the heir of Graydon, Queen Cassara, told them. "If you try to use your magic, you will be injured." Three Crimson Circle adepts stood behind her, robes white in the increasing morning light.

Kleriss mumbled, indicating she'd like to speak. The queen nodded to one of the adepts, who removed her gag. It was good to breathe easily, and she was tired of tasting her own blood on the wet and soiled fabric.

"We only came here to protect you," she said, meaning every word. "I don't understand why you refuse our assistance, Queen Cassara."

"Protecting me would mean working *with* me to see me safe," the queen said, silver streaking her blond hair, only adding to her presence. "You treated me like a bag of potatoes you could simply haul out of here at your own whim. You never asked if I needed, or wanted, protection. I do not, but I would appreciate your help, instead."

"You simply don't understand—"

"No," the queen interrupted her. "I understand perfectly well, Crimson Circle Kleriss. You are following orders, without thinking them through." The queen's voice softened. "That's a dangerous thing to do, when you have so much power."

"It's Crimson Circle Elite," Kleriss corrected her. "The Elders of Larkhold only want what's best for Graydon," Kleriss said, though her voice lost some of its strength. She had to admit that, with Shirina gone, the threat to the heirs of Graydon and Elihor seemed minimal. Plus, Ravenhold's adepts no longer had their magic, making them not much of a threat at all. Even if they were good with knots.

"The Elders of Larkhold have allied themselves with a rogue Circle faction that tried to injure Rojon and kill me," she said, calmly. Kleriss admired the queen's calm, as anger bubbled within her, though she was no longer sure at what, or who.

"But the Elder—"

"Betrayed Ravenhold twenty years ago and allied herself with Siabala," Cassara said. "So your choice is clear. You decide to believe someone because of the color of their cloak, or you choose to believe them based on what they've shown you they're willing to do. Words or actions, Crimson Circle Elite." She bit off the title and gazed unflinchingly at Kleriss, who fiercely wished she hadn't led this expedition. Well, with Patrile, who stayed sullen and silent, staring daggers at her.

"The Elders know what's best." The words sounded weak.

"Do you know why I'm still talking to you?" The queen asked after a moment of reflection.

Kleriss shook her head. There was really no reason for the queen to give her the time of day. She'd done nothing to ingratiate herself, and Kleriss was bound and effectively useless. As useless as a Ravenhold adept without their magic.

"Because my family is in your Circle's hands," she said softly, blue eyes made of steel. "And I have no one else to implore to help them except you. And if your Circle is now under Siabala, you deserve the chance to break free, before it consumes you."

Before Kleriss could do or say anything, a scream ripped through the gardens, quickly cut short.

The queen looked to the window, eyes wide, and then focused back on Kleriss.

"Words, or actions, Crimson Circle Elite. Are you willing to help us survive, or will you just blindly follow orders?"

Another scream. The other Larkhold adepts writhed in their bonds, trying to break free. If they remained bound, they would all die.

"I'll help," Kleriss said, uncertain if she'd just lied.

∿

"Barricade yourselves in the study and watch out for monsters," Avarielle said, stepping over a dead creature—some type of long-tooth cat covered in dark fur that cut like knives—and two dead witches, leaving the stunned Green Circle with a few of her peers. Two of them had short swords and looked like they knew how to use them. Avarielle guessed ex-soldiers from the way they held themselves.

Good. She'd never been more glad that Shirina had welcomed anyone to her Circle.

They did as asked, and Avarielle followed her instincts to the back of the mansion, to the secondary library up the stairs, where the Larkhold adepts were being kept. She took the wooden stairs two at a time, about halfway up when the window atop imploded inward, a four-legged beast which looked like a lynx mixed with an octopus, launching itself at her. Avarielle ducked and swung, taking out two of its tendrils as fires licked the edge of her blade, greedy for blood.

Shadows exploded from the severed pieces, but the beast wasn't done, landing awkwardly on the steps and turning around, snarling and leaping without hesitation.

Avarielle threw herself up the stairs, not liking the battleground of the uneven steps. She didn't quite make it, needing to turn around and defend herself before reaching the top stair. But she let the movement carry her, turning Graysword on the creature as she fell back on the top landing. She cut through the creature, shadows licking the usual white flames of her blade. Red instead of white.

Red fire on Graysword. That was new, and she'd worry about it later. As long as there were fires, she would wield them.

Avarielle launched herself back up and ran down the corridor, just as the ceiling collapsed above her, smashing on her back as something large crashed through the roof. Crushed by the debris, she fell on her stomach, using her muscles to try to contract out and breathe, but the breath had been blown out of her.

A talon landed near her head, piercing through the debris. Avarielle focused on the little air she had left, tightened her grip on Graysword and struck backward with it, its fires pummeling into whatever tried to crush her. The monster shrieked and stank the whole place up with burnt feathers. The weight on her back lessened as it withdrew, and Avarielle dragged herself out from under the debris.

Red feathers fell from the hole, glistening with silver blood, but the creature itself was gone.

Avarielle didn't linger to figure out what it had been or where it had gone, focused on her goal. Get Cassara, and get out with Rojon. She hated leaving the adepts to fend for themselves, but she'd learned long ago that, sometimes, you just couldn't save everyone.

With any luck, the attack would stop once they'd figured out that Cassara and Rojon were gone.

She turned the corner, white fires smashing into a tentacled creature, vanishing into smoke and shadows.

The adepts were loose! Avarielle grabbed Graysword,

ready to cut them down. Cassara stood among them, spotted the warrior, and quickly called to her.

"They're helping us, Avarielle."

Avarielle reached in and snatched Cassara away from them, hard, pulling the queen behind her.

"It's fine," she said, but Avarielle shot her a look. She had no doubt that Cassara was willing to risk being snatched away to Massir. Avarielle wasn't willing to lose her. She could count on Shirina to fight her way out of a teleportation spell, but Cassara was desperate to see her family, and might be willing to be stupid about it.

"Stay behind me," she growled.

"Where are these monsters coming from?" One of the annoying witches leading this hunt—Kleriss—said.

"Where do you think, stupid witch?" Avarielle growled again.

"We didn't send them," she said. "We have no such creatures in Elihor."

"I've lived there for twenty years so I know, you idiot. That's not what I was implying."

The witch started stuttering something and Avarielle ignored her, turning to Cassara. "Rojon is waiting. We have to go."

"But Shirina's adepts…" Cassara's voice died off, knowing that there was nothing they could do. She turned to the Larkhold Adepts. "Protect them. Don't bring them to Massir. If you have any doubt at all that Elder Tally is allied with Siabala, do yourselves a favor and don't betray your brethren from Graydon's coven."

"And do yourselves another favor," Avarielle eyed the lead witch. "Don't follow us."

She grabbed Cassara by the arm and dragged her down the stairs. She heard the witch give a few orders, all of them focused on protecting the Lisal Gardens. Then a crash, and flames shot down the stairs.

Their problem, not hers. Cassara wisely kept any doubts she had about saving them to herself.

They cleared the mansion, to come face-to-face with a feathered creature with large dark purple and red wings, silver talons, and silver blood dribbling down its side.

Avarielle didn't hesitate, letting go of Cassara as she charged forward.

"Get to Rojon in the stables!" She instructed, the queen hesitating for only a split second before following her orders. The creature turned its head and glanced at the queen, as though intending to pursue. Avarielle stepped before the escaping queen.

"I'm your problem, not her," she growled, calling forth the magic of Graysword. The red flames licked the edges of the white ones—red flames reflected in the strange creature's large, dark eyes.

Without hesitation, Avarielle attacked.

The horses shuffled nervously behind him. If they hadn't been secured, Rojon feared they would have bolted. As it was, he wasn't sure they'd be able to ride them.

He held his sword before him, debating whether to stay in the safety of the stables to protect the horses, or to step out and have a look at the surroundings, to see if he could figure out what was attacking. He heard noises from the direction of the mansion, mostly.

Screams, crashing, the breaking of glass.

His mother had trained him for this, but being surrounded by monsters was different than training in the fields by his house. Last time battle had found him, in his village, he'd frozen, and his grandfather had paid the price.

If I had Graysword... The thought was whisked from his mind as an adept stumbled in, orange cloak sliced open, blood dribbling down the white robes. The whites of Graydon eyes amplified her terror as their eyes locked. She barely had time to scream before whisps of silver wire tangled her neck and yanked back, her body flopping to the ground, her dark-haired head flying backwards, jets of red blood darkening the wires.

The horses reared and kicked up, buckling the entire rear wall in their panic.

The threads of silver united and from the shadows of the ceiling a figure descended, the threads settling on her head, long silver hair floating around her, ready to strike. Her skin was pure silver, her eyes hollow. Red blood dripped from the deadly silver strands.

Her voice froze his blood, like liquid silver in his veins.

"Hello, Rojon Grayloft," she said, taking a step toward

him, her legs unnaturally long and made from the same silver coils. "I've been looking forward to meeting you."

He remembered the short sword held loosely in his grip as strands of her hair approached to caress his face. The blade felt uncertain and clunky as he struck down at her. The silver strands wrapped around it and absorbed the metal, the pommel falling uselessly to the ground.

"Don't worry," she said. He found that he couldn't move, uncertain if it was her voice or his fear holding him captive. Or maybe both. "You'll be of use in the new world."

A scream bubbled up his throat but remained trapped there, and all he could do was watch as strands of silver reached for him, wrapped around his hands and torso, and pulled him up like she intended to carry him away.

"Rojon!" Cassara screamed, striking the creature with a rake. The silver woman smiled, head spinning as her body remained facing Rojon, her hair cutting into him where she held him captive.

"How pleasantly convenient," the creature said, silver hair scrambling toward Cassara. Unlike Rojon, the queen did not freeze, throwing herself to the side as she slammed the rake at the woman's head. She missed, but bought herself time and rolled aside, behind a stall wall.

Her gambit to find safety failed as the silver hair simply pierced through the wood as though it didn't exist. Rojon heard Cassara struggling, the woman's cold, empty silver eyes narrowing in pleasure.

"I promised to deliver you alive, Cassara Edoline," she said, "but I never said I'd bring you in one piece."

Cassara screamed, and a jet of red blood flew from behind the stall. Like the adept's head.

No. He would not lose her. Not like this, not so easily.

"Leave her alone," Rojon screamed, shedding her hold on him, wanting, *needing,* to protect Cassara. His hands... no, all of him, his entire body grew warm, hot, *burning...* He screamed, and magic pulsed out of him, slamming into the creature. For a second she looked surprised, and then it was her turn to scream as the silver strands turned dark with magic, with *his* magic, which consumed the attacking strands, but left the others, inert ones alone. Without the hair supporting him, he collapsed to his knees, magic exploding out of him, pushing the creature away from Cassara and away from him.

The silver creature looked at him with interest and surprise, skittering back up as another wave of his magic exploded out of him. He couldn't stop it. He didn't know how, seeing his magic wrap around the stall where Cassara remained, hidden from him, willing her to be okay, not to die like his grandfather had because he'd failed to act.

The magic deserted him and he collapsed to his knees, arms wrapped around his abdomen. Everything hurt. Ice filled his veins, coiled around his heart, kept him trapped on the ground. He was so cold, and so alone.

The silver woman walked toward him, looking amused and annoyed as her body grew slimmer, like a wood post, and more silver streaked down from her head, thinning her torso in favor of shifting the silver to her attacking hair. The strands began to grow, and she ignored where the queen lay fallen outside of Rojon's view, walking toward him.

Still, he couldn't move, the ice holding him captive from within. *At least my magic worked.* It shimmered around Cassara, still. He couldn't see her, but he could see his magic, protecting where the queen lay, hopefully not dying. It had abandoned him. Saved her but abandoned him.

Like my father before me. Dying, but saving those I love.

"Don't worry, I won't kill you," the woman cooed and cocked her head sideways. "You're still needed."

Rojon gritted his teeth and looked up, breath misting before him. Why was he so cold?

"Siabala will warm you," she said, laughter like metal on metal. He tried to focus on her, but found breathing hard, and he curled back in on himself, willing his magic to protect him. Or to keep protecting Cassara, if he was lost.

A familiar battle cry, seeming so distant yet beckoning him to look up, eyes blinking, trying to focus on what he was seeing: Graysword sticking out of the woman's chest. Silver eyes filled with surprise as white fires bathed her body. Tinted with red, reflecting in the creature's eyes, who smiled as she jumped up, not caring that Graysword cleaved her in two, her body in pieces but still interconnected by those silver strands as she vanished into the surrounding forest.

His mother giving chase, screaming something back. But he couldn't make it out, focused on how the red magic made her hair even more red. On how cold he was. On how warm those red flames would feel on his tired skin…

And then Cassara knelt before him, took his shoulders in her hands.

"We're safe, Rojon. We're safe," she said it over and over again as he choked on his magic, and slowly the words turned from sound into meaning, and he understood.

They were safe. They were all safe.

He let go of the need for magic. The ice vanished, and it left him feeling empty, hollow. He folded into Cassara, who held him as he drifted into darkness.

29

$\mathcal{A}$varielle crossed her arms, tallying the situation, trying to contain the multitude of emotions pummeling her. The flying monster with talons and the silver cutting creature had both managed to escape. The Larkhold witches were free. One of the horses had escaped, the other too spooked to carry anyone. They only had one left, which wouldn't exactly get Cassara and Avarielle far. Rojon's magic had knocked him out.

And there was no way Avarielle was leaving either Cassara or her son with those treacherous witches.

Ten of Shirina's adepts had been killed, mostly Crimson Circles. At least the Larkhold witches seemed humane enough to stop lording over them and were actually helping the wounded. Not that the warrior trusted them, but right now, they had no choice but to accept the help.

Had Siabala predicted them helping their sister coven,

or had that been a surprise? Because no matter what they did, he was always a step ahead. Maybe ten steps.

And Avarielle hated every moment of it. She hated feeling so helpless to save her friends and family. And she hated that she couldn't go after Shirina, to make sure the blasted sorceress wasn't still captured, or wounded. And she hated that she hated it.

She wished Cassara hadn't freed the Larkhold adepts, but they'd dealt with three of the monsters and saved a number of Shirina's witches. Avarielle just really wished she wasn't here, in this moment, with impossible choices tumbling down around them.

And no easy means of escape, or clear path to victory.

"He'll be all right," Cassara said, having tucked Rojon in like he was a child, and not a full-grown man. His strained features didn't make Avarielle think of Rojon as a child. It reminded her of his father, when pain wracked his body. And it hurt her how hard it was for her to go to him, letting the queen tend to him, instead. And so she did the only thing she knew how: watch over him, and stand guard. Avarielle took her place before the door and had no intention of moving.

"I got knocked out pretty good when I used my magic, too," Cassara said. There was a fondness in her voice at the memory, then regret flittered across her features.

"How did he activate his magic?"

"I got hurt," she said, touching her arm where the garment was mangled and cut. "He did it to save me. He healed me."

Avarielle looked at her sleeping son. His features had loosened, and he looked so peaceful. Spent. He'd used his magic to protect Cassara, and he'd healed her, too.

"Did his magic only protect you?" the warrior asked softly.

"He protected himself, too. At least, at first. I heard the monster scream, so he hurt her." Cassara looked back at Rojon, seated near him. "His magic doesn't act like his family's before him. It might be because of your bloodline. He's not fully from Elihor."

He'd saved himself, because his mother hadn't been able to. Because her magic wasn't enough. And Rojon's magic wasn't enough to save them, either. And without Shirina's Circle…

"We need more magic," Avarielle said, hating that she didn't feel like she could protect her family. But she'd been trained to survey and understand the battlefield, and that included knowing her own abilities. She was good. Great, even. But she wasn't enough.

And she hated that, too.

"I wish I had my magic," Cassara said, looking up to Avarielle, hands turning to fists on her lap. "Avarielle, why didn't my magic come back? Where do you think Graydon's magic went?"

"I'm not sure," Avarielle said, then rallied, for the sake of her friend, who looked more and more crestfallen. "But I know three things. One, it might not be such a bad thing that the magic vanished for now, so that the two strands of magic don't get mixed and then no one except Siabala's adepts could use their magic." That's what had happened the last time the Wall had fallen, and it hadn't gone well for either Circle and most adepts.

"Two," she said before Cassara could speak, "they targeted Crimson Circles, meaning they don't anticipate the magic to stay away forever. It's gone, or inaccessible, but not destroyed." Hope lit Cassara's eyes.

"And three, I know that our best chance of figuring out exactly where the magic is, and how to set it free, lies with Shirina."

The hope that lit Cassara's eyes evaporated as quickly as it had sparked to life.

"We don't know where she is," Cassara whispered. "It all feels so hopeless."

"It feels hopeless because we're cut off from so much," Avarielle said. "But we have allies and friends out there. We just have to connect with them again and find a path. It's hard to feel confident in our path when fog covers it, which is what we're facing now. So, let's go with what we know." She twisted her features. "I sound like Shirina."

"You do," Cassara said, then rallied. "We know Shirina would not allow herself to be taken all the way to Massir without fighting back. And the first stop was at the base of the Maple Mountains, to the north, where only three other Larkhold adepts waited."

"Shirina would have been ready to attack, and they wouldn't have been ready for a crazed witch flinging herself at them."

"You paint a flattering portrait of Shirina."

"I know." A slight grin played on Avarielle's lips, feeling more relaxed. Trying to convince Cassara there was hope forced her to find it and make it her own. "So, if we assume that the Larkhold witch spoke truth to Rojon and she escaped there, where would she go?"

"She'd check on her adepts," Cassara said. "She's at her outpost, after all, and knows she has traitors in her midst." Cassara's hand protectively moved over Rojon, sleeping peacefully under the blanket. Avarielle smiled and spoke more softly so as not to disturb her son.

"She needs magic, and so does her Circle," Avarielle continued. "She knows that Siabala wants you and Rojon to finish whatever insane plan he has, and she can't protect either of you without magic. And her Circle is painfully vulnerable without it."

"Right," Cassara said. "So, where does she go for magic?" Realization crossed her face. "Wait. Not for magic. For answers."

Avarielle followed her string of thoughts. "For the chance to become an Elder."

"She needs the hidden knowledge of Elders to bring back the magic, and she knows it," Cassara continued. "She said herself there were only two ways to gain it. One, is from an Elder, which we know of at least one survivor of Ravenhold's old coven."

Avarielle grimaced. "I'd like to slice her. Again." It would have been nice if Tally had stayed dead.

"Or," Cassara continued, meeting Avarielle's eyes, "she'd go to Ravenhold."

"The keep is underwater," Avarielle said. "It plunged into the sea. She can't get to it." A pause as the two friends looked at each other. "Can she?"

"Without magic?" Cassara followed with the question. "I don't know, but would she be more likely to try that than to try to get on Tally's good side?"

"Does Tally have a good side?" Avarielle mumbled. "No, she'd never try with that witch. She knows that the only way Tally would give her the secrets would be if Shirina swore allegiance to Siabala. Something she'd never do."

"To Ravenhold, then?" Cassara asked, agreeing.

Before Avarielle could answer, a knock came at the door.

30

The red-headed, mean-eyed warrior of Graydon opened the door, and Kleriss did her best to keep her chin up and not show how intimidated she felt. She'd seen the warrior face the flying, taloned creature and draw silver blood from it before it had withdrawn, no doubt terrified for its life. The warrior's movements had been seamless, self-assured, and unhesitant.

Then she'd seen her throw herself against a monster, walk over a dead witch, and run to help her friends. Kleriss had heard stories of Avarielle Grayloft, both good and bad, but she'd never known just how terrifying being in the presence of the warrior would be.

The warrior blocked the entrance to the room, making it clear that she wouldn't get to either the heir of Graydon or of Elihor easily. She emanated power, tall and athletic, her armor and skin stamped with the scars of battle. Many battles.

"May I come in?" Kleriss asked politely, not quite sure how to get past the warrior. She'd be cut down before she got off a spell, and she honestly just wanted to talk. Behind her, two of Graydon's Crimson Circles and one Blue Circle stayed at her heel. Larkhold's adepts had stayed behind, even Patrile, who seemed vexed that Kleriss had received the message, and not her.

"She got a message from the Elder." The Blue Circle, an older woman with a no-nonsense attitude, elaborated for Kleriss. "And she wanted to tell you what it was."

Avarielle nodded at the adept, her eyes never leaving Kleriss, who tried to ignore the nervous sweat running down her back.

"We can keep an eye on Rojon," the adept offered. "We'll let you know if we need help," she added for good measure. The woman might be thin and frail looking, but Kleriss knew she could hold her own. When her adepts had gone to help the magicless coven of Graydon, they'd found her hitting a monster with a large wooden chair, protecting her wounded sisters.

Even the Crimson Circles did not question her, even though she vastly under-ranked them. This Circle was so different from her own that it left her head spinning.

The warrior nodded again. "We'll just be outside this door," Avarielle said to the adept. "I'm trusting you to make sure he stays where he should."

"With my life," the older adept said, and all three adepts slipped in. Queen Cassara stepped out. Kleriss lowered her chin, a sign of respect. The queen had trusted them to protect the adepts of Graydon and not betray them. That was not something Kleriss would easily dismiss out of hand. She didn't care that she was queen of the biggest kingdom in Graydon, but the fact that she was heir to Graydon warranted her respect.

Even if he was the Great Betrayer, having turned against Elihor in her final moments, according to their land's myths. But that did not undo a lifetime of love.

The door closed and the warrior assumed her post before it, crossing her arms.

"What message?" Queen Cassara asked, staying near the warrior.

Kleriss forced herself to meet the queen's white-coddled eyes, the blue throwing her off, the small black pupil entirely too little black for such a wide area. Too much went on in Graydon eyes. So many different parts, all trying to convey different emotions. She trusted the eyes of Elihor, fully dark and hiding nothing.

Graydon eyes were just too shifty for her liking.

"Elder Rale informed us that Shirina had escaped, as you'd theorized," she said. She had pondered the ramifications of sharing the Elder's message. But it bothered her, still, and she didn't know how to interpret any of it. She wished the heir of Elihor was awake and could advise, but he'd been knocked out by his magic.

The magic of Elihor.

It was the same magic she wielded, but his was so pure. So raw.

And he'd lived. Never in their history had any heir of

Elihor survived channeling the protective magic. Yet he had. By all accounts, twice.

"What else did he say?" The queen pushed. "He wouldn't have just sent a message stating that."

Kleriss wished she'd have just ignored receiving the message and not decided to speak to them. Maybe just teleport away, except that would mean potentially leaving the heir of Elihor without protection. And the damn Graydon adepts had seen her receiving the message, the flicker of recognition in their eyes.

She could have lied. But she wasn't confident in her abilities to fool both the queen and the warrior. She feared it wouldn't end well if she failed. And she'd already lost two adepts during the last battle. She'd never lost anyone under her command before, anger and guilt churning her insides.

Who had attacked them, and why? That bothered her. And the message's timing bothered her even more.

"He said, and please keep in mind that I am just relaying the information…he said that we needed to get the heirs of Elihor and Graydon to Massir. For their safety." The final message sounded weak.

"You're being awfully honest." The warrior didn't move a single muscle, but Kleriss flinched.

"Those were your earlier orders." Queen Cassara pointed out, though her voice held no harshness. "What changed? Why do you look so disturbed by them, when you'd been so willing to carry them out earlier?"

"Because of the timing of it," Kleriss said. Mumbled,

even. She took a deep breath, met the queen's eyes. "It came right after the attack ended."

"You didn't have to tell us that part, and I appreciate your honesty," Cassara said, and Kleriss suspected the queen simply wanted to make sure the warrior took note of it. Showing the Circle Elite how to slowly win the warrior's trust, something Kleriss doubted was even possible.

"I am a Crimson Circle Elite of Larkhold," she said, the words giving her strength. "My job is to protect the Wall of Loss. To protect Elihor. And to protect the heirs of Elihor."

"How do you intend to protect him?" The warrior kept her voice soft, which made it all the more terrifying.

"By telling you what you need to know to protect him," she honestly said. "Because I don't know what's happening, but I know enough to know that bringing Rojon to Massir might be a terrible idea."

"Might be?" The warrior's eyebrows shot up.

Kleriss flushed, and then just became annoyed. "Look, I'm not from Graydon, and I don't really understand how things work here. I want to go home. And I don't want the heir of Elihor to die." She paused, hesitated. Then sighed. There was no point in holding back. "And I don't want Larkhold to fall at Siabala's whims like Ravenhold did two decades ago."

"Do you think your Elders are compromised?" The queen gently asked as the warrior studied her and gauged her honesty.

"I don't think so," she said. "At least, I hope not. I asked him why bring them to Massir though, and perhaps that Larkhold, although further, might be a better solution."

"And?" the queen pressed.

"He said that the Circle of Ravenhold had a strong presence in Massir and would keep him safe there. And that he would be there as well, with several other Elders. It seems the Circles are converging in your city, your Majesty."

The queen paled, lips forming a line.

"What of her husband and daughter?" Avarielle asked, as though to spare the queen, her voice softer.

"King Dayshon is with Elder Rale," she said.

"Are you sure Dayshon is all right?" the queen asked, her voice so soft Kleriss barely heard.

"As far as I know," she said. "But I don't know a lot. I could ask, maybe Elder Quilsam instead of Rale, but…"

"That might raise their suspicions," Cassara said. "Any news of my daughter?"

"I'm sorry, I don't know."

"Even if Dayshon is under the Circle's hold, he can take care of himself," Avarielle said. "He's no stranger to politics and has a good head and an even temper. Tally might be maintaining her front with him, too."

"He won't fall for it," the queen said. It was like the two women from Graydon had forgotten Kleriss was there, quickly conferring with each other. Kleriss was like that with her best friend, who was still in Larkhold, she hoped. She found herself missing the keep even more. "He knows about Tally," Cassara said. "I told him everything. Everything I could," she relented.

"What couldn't you tell him?" Kleriss asked, then wanted to hit herself as two sharp sets of all-too-white eyes focused back on her. "I want to help," she said. "But I don't know how."

Avarielle clamped her mouth shut, but the queen shrugged. "I'm not sure that it matters anymore. The Wall of Loss was rebuilt using my magic only, so my death would have released Siabala. Except the Wall fell, Siabala hasn't made himself known, and I don't have my magic back."

The warrior gauged Kleriss's reaction, as though debating if cutting her down now was the right thing to do. Kleriss ignored her, looking down at the ground. She hadn't been taught to question. She'd been taught to follow what Elders asked of her. To do their bidding and trust that their greater connection with Elihor's magic and Larkhold gave them knowledge, wisdom, and insight inaccessible to her.

But she'd always questioned. She'd always demanded explanations. When she'd made Elite, her mentor, Elder Rachalt had winked at her. *Questions are good. It's all about how you ask them that matters, Crimson Circle Elite.*

Elder Rachalt had been the one to select her for this mission. Amongst all the other witches in Massir, she'd selected *her.* The one Circle Elite who questioned everything.

"Out with it," the warrior growled. Kleriss jumped out

of her reverie and flushed. She wasn't good at this. At keeping her face inert and not showing her emotions. She loved books, and mysteries. She'd joined Larkhold to make a difference and help her land regrow. Her parents had both died in Siabala's final attacks, and eventually she'd wanted a home. She wasn't much older than the warrior's son, born in the heat of battle.

"It's just…" What was she doing? Should she be helping them? But why shouldn't she be? The heir's mother, even if she was generally disliked for having the misfortune of being born from Graydon? And the heir of Graydon, even if her ancestor had betrayed Elihor? They'd both been strong allies to Elihor, helping it grow and sharing resources and knowledge freely.

"You're not betraying Larkhold by speaking with us, Kleriss," Queen Cassara said, as though reading her mind. "Whatever you're thinking, share with us. You already mentioned that you feared Siabala might take over Larkhold. Why, when Elder Tally is telling you that he's not a threat?"

Kleriss met the queen's eyes and found warmth there. Her strange Graydon eyes seemed more familiar already, and less frightening.

"Your magic didn't come back but the Wall that held Siabala vanished." She focused on her, ignoring the warrior's mumbling about them having just said that. "So, what if Siabala, or at least the greater part of him, is still trapped in it? And they just moved him?"

It sounded ridiculous to her ears, but the warrior and

the queen shared another quick look.

"If they simply moved the wall, and it didn't fall," the queen said, "then why would all of Graydon's magic be gone?"

"It doesn't make sense, I know," the Crimson Circle Elite said, not able to make her theory work.

"It does if the magic is responding to something else, or *someone* else," Avarielle said, looking to Cassara. "Could you have done this?"

The queen flushed. "Moved all of the magic of Graydon? No. I haven't used my magic in years."

"They melted your amulet," Avarielle said. "It went into the earth, mixed with Siabala's magic."

"Which amulet?" Kleriss asked. This time, it was the warrior who answered her.

"The amulet of the heirs of Graydon. A sun nested in a half moon."

"The amulet of Elihor," Kleriss whispered. "That's where it's been this whole time."

Cassara nodded. "It was in my family's keeping."

"Why would you have Elihor's necklace?" Kleriss asked. "Why would Graydon have it, when he was the one to gift it to Elihor in the first place?"

"It was used to bring down the Wall of Loss," the warrior said, apparently deciding she was worthy of some confidence. "It was activated with magic from Elihor, and Graydon, and brought it down."

The three stayed silent for some time, then Kleriss shook her head, annoyed. "I don't know how to make sense of any of this. It's like we're missing a piece of the puzzle."

Avarielle eyed Cassara. "Shirina suspected the magic had slipped into the ground. But she doesn't know how, or how to get it back."

"Tally knows," Cassara said. "She's the one who's orchestrating all of this on Siabala's behalf."

"You're sure she's with Siabala?" Kleriss asked, then wanted to kick herself.

"We're sure," the queen said. "She tried to kill me. She hurt Rojon. And she wore his red robes. We need to figure out what she knows."

"The only way to do that is to get her to talk," Kleriss said, "but Elders are impossible to make talk." Avarielle's lips quirked at that. Perhaps Kleriss was getting a tad too liberal sharing with them. But, then again, all of her questions led her in one direction only. "Shirina will need to become an Elder."

The adept forced herself to meet both sets of strange eyes. "Her only recourse is Ravenhold. That's her only path to find out what is happening. And if I can figure it out, you can be certain the Elders will, as well."

Avarielle glowered and the queen grew even more pale.

Kleriss held her peace, wishing she could reach out to Elder Rachalt and ask her counsel. But the Elder had sent her here, and she had to trust that she had had an ulterior motive in doing so. Elders usually did.

And that worried Kleriss most of all.

31

The last time she'd travelled to Ravenhold, before it collapsed into the sea, she'd teleported. Not just because it was the quickest means of transportation available to her—the roads to travel to the keep were treacherous, and only used by merchants bringing supplies. These wagons, pulled by sure-footed oxen, had tackled the winding mountain roads to Ravenhold when the weather promised to be welcoming for at least a few days. The journey was dangerous enough without ice or rain.

As she walked across a large, rocky field, Shirina wondered what had happened to those merchants, and nearby farmers, without the need to cross to Ravenhold. Had they moved somewhere closer to one of the large cities? She'd been walking all night and most of the morning, with a few breaks to let her body rest, and she hadn't encountered one farm or village. There were no tell-tale smoke plumes on the horizon. No scent of food or humanity.

She'd have to stop soon and find a place to sleep. Her body hurt from too much magic, not enough rest, and too much hitting people.

She missed her magic. She missed her adepts. She even missed that bloody warrior. Her boots were comfortable, and her feet used to walking, but she wasn't twenty-five anymore. And she hadn't exactly been walking everywhere. She's set up teleportation circles for a good reason.

A gentle breeze caressed the tall grasses around her, and she headed for a copse of purple-leafed trees surrounded by stony outcroppings. She could find shade there and enjoy a meal. She'd traveled light, carrying only water and food. She had everything she needed, and hoped the journey wasn't in vain. It would take her two more days, at least, to reach where the keep used to be, and then… well, she'd figure something out.

She'd come here, once, looking for knowledge. She'd stood in the library during the last moments of the keep, and remembered the books, the precious, irreplaceable knowledge consumed by the destruction of Ravenhold.

Standing on the stone bridge over rough waters that had once led to the keep, now leading nowhere, she'd retreated from the cliff.

But she hadn't really tried to reach Ravenhold, too busy rebuilding a Circle outside of the keep. She'd just wanted to confirm that it was truly gone. Part of her had been relieved the keep hadn't returned, though she'd be hard pressed to admit it. But the thought of using the cold keep as her Circle's center, away from the life and gentleness of the Lisal Gardens... She couldn't wrap her mind around that possibility, nor her heart.

This time, as the world slowly crumbled around her, so insidious that most people weren't even aware of it yet, she sought the keep out of despair, hoping her need would drive her search. Of course, reaching Ravenhold meant going underwater. A feat impossible even with magic, needing air to vocalize her spell. But the keep *had* been magic, and perhaps... She sighed, reached the shadows of the trees and large rocks. A cozy oasis on the mountainside.

I should be heading back to Avarielle and Cassara, she thought, then dismissed the idea. It was her heart talking, seeking comfort in familiarity, but that's not what Shirina needed. What she wanted was irrelevant.

What she needed was to uncover the secrets of Ravenhold and hope they would level the battleground. Shirina had been the last person to leave Ravenhold before it had fallen to Siabala's magic. Perhaps the keep would allow her safe access, now that despair fueled her movements. And, if not, she hoped what Carsyn had revealed to Avarielle might prove handy. Perhaps access to the keep didn't rely on her going underwater, but instead on finding the right path. And one of those underground chambers might exist there.

She had a faint memory of being in one as a Green

Circle, a time long ago when she'd been terrified of the witches who'd taken her from her home. She'd been so embroiled in missing her family and grieving that every memory from that time was tainted with fear and a blurring of details.

But perhaps if she was in the area of Ravenhold, more memories would be triggered, and a path would reveal itself.

It was worth trying. It was the only idea she had left to try, to reach Elder status without compromising herself.

She would reach none of these things unless she rested first. Shirina settled in the copse's tallest tree's shadow, near several large boulders, and sat cross legged. She wished she had grabbed the staff Rojon had made for her. It might have allowed her access to the magic.

Something she desperately craved.

"This isn't the first time I don't have my magic," she reminded herself, her voice soft as it joined breeze-licked leaves.

"No, but I fear this time shall be more permanent."

Shirina scrambled up, dropped her waterskin, and ignored it as liquid soaked the ground at her feet.

Elder Tally appeared from behind the tree. Another Elder, wearing Ravenhold's robes, stepped over the rocks. She recognized him as the warlock Vangle, dark hair wild around his head, framing his pale and stretched face. He'd attacked the palace and been quite difficult to beat, when she did have magic.

A teleportation spell shimmered, and two Elders from

Larkhold appeared. For a brief moment, Shirina felt hope. Then they nodded to Tally, and her stomach plummeted. They'd come to help the treacherous Elder. She hoped they hadn't allied themselves to Siabala.

Not yet, anyway. She had no doubt Tally had asked these two Elders' help simply to sway them to her cause. She'd found the weak links within Elihor's Keep, and intended to exploit them.

The steep rocks to Shirina's back offered no escape, and the four Elders before her blocked any path of escape. Not that she believed escape was even a possibility.

She focused on Tally and Vangle.

"You have no right to wear those robes." She turned to the Larkhold Elders, Kush and Rale, if she remembered correctly. "And you should be ashamed to have allied yourselves with someone who follows Siabala."

"You have no right to speak to anyone that way," Tally stepped forward. "You betrayed Ravenhold. You imprisoned us in Siabala's Rage!"

Shirina ignored her tantrum as a deep calm came over her. She had no way to escape. No magic to aid her. No allies in sight. All she had left was her wit and cutting remarks.

She intended to deploy both with impunity.

"You look very good for someone who was stuck in a dungeon for twenty years, Tally. Did it come with a spa?"

The Elder moved faster than Shirina would have believed possible and struck her across the jaw, hard. Shirina's head snapped back. She caught herself on the rocks behind her and managed to remain standing. A small victory.

The Larkhold Elders looked uncomfortable with the display of violence. Shirina knew them, in a way that Tally did not. They were kinder than Ravenhold Elders. Some would say weaker. She was not among them, though she wished they believed her.

If they allied themselves with Siabala, they would quickly need to get comfortable, and deeply familiar, with violence.

"Will you kill me now, Tally? Is that what your master wishes?"

"Do not be disrespectful of your Elder." Kush approached her, his white hair perfectly sideswept, making Vangle's look even more messy. "You have lied to us, Shirina." The lack of title stung, the insult broiling at her core.

"I have not." She stood her ground, looked at him calmly. "Tally is the traitor in Ravenhold, not me."

"Ravenhold no longer stands," Tally said. "Is that where you're headed?"

Shirina met the Elder's eyes but said nothing.

"Foolish child," Tally tsk-tsked, and Shirina wanted to hit her so badly her hands shook. The disrespect, the constant need to prove herself, being tossed aside... she could take it—*had* taken it—but not from Tally. "Ravenhold is gone."

"I was there when it vanished," Shirina said. "And you were not. You were busy doing Siabala's bidding."

Magic lanced her mind and she fell back against the rock behind her, the tang of iron filling her mouth. Tally intended to kill her.

"It is as I said," Tally spoke to Elder Rale, white hair glowing in the day. "She has never shown any respect to the Elders and needs to pay for her crimes."

"Graydon's magic is gone," Shirina said, blood dribbling down her chin. "How are you using it on me? How did you teleport here?"

Tally's eyes narrowed. "That is Elder knowledge, child. Something that you will never know."

"I am not your child." Shirina spat blood out at her, satisfied to hit the woman's white robes. "Your robes are red, like Siabala. Not white."

Vangle hit her, hard, her head bouncing off the stone. This time, she slipped down, stars exploding before her eyes. They were going to kill her with their fists. Like a gang in an alleyway instead of the greatest wielders of magic in Graydon.

"I think you'll agree, Elder Tally—" Kush, to his credit, stepped before her to stop another incoming blow, "—that she's suffered enough. Leave her without her magic. Without allies, and without a coven. That is punishment enough. We have greater concerns to worry about than this petulant child."

I'm a forty-five-year-old witch who built her own Circle from scratch, you old fool! Shirina's head spun too hard to form the words. She would be happy enough to be left alone, though she was no longer certain that she could walk all the way to Ravenhold. She'd figure it out if she lived.

She focused on the scent of grass beneath her. On the steadiness of the ground. On keeping her eyes closed, hoping the world stopped spinning. And on not giving Tally the satisfaction of throwing up all over herself.

"Elder Kush," Tally said. She really hated the sound of her voice. "She imprisoned us for twenty years. I'm sure you'll understand if we are less than sympathetic to her pain."

"Of course," the Elder relented, and said no more. Shirina forced her eyes open, looked up at Tally, the light like daggers in her brain.

"Elder Kush, Elder Rale," Shirina tried to reason with the Larkhold Elders. "I plead with you not to listen to her. At least to consider she may be lying."

"I have," the Elder said, "and I found her story much more believable than yours, Shirina. I am sorry, but your lies must end. I was there when the Wall fell. There was absolutely no sign of Siabala. No sign of him at all." He sighed. "I wish you hadn't wasted twenty years for all of us. Think of how far we could be by now in rebuilding Graydon and Elihor, had we not been spending resources on a threat that didn't even exist. I'm disappointed in you."

I don't care. Shirina didn't bother voicing the words. He'd always been pleased that Larkhold was the biggest Circle, and now, with only Elihor's magic traveling the air... Shirina closed her eyes slowly again. She was tired, and in pain, and the world wouldn't stop spinning.

She'd tried her best, but it hadn't been enough. She hoped that Cassara and Avarielle would succeed where she had failed.

"Now the real work must begin—rebuilding Ravenhold to its former glory."

"I suspect most of her adepts won't be worth saving," Tally said casually. "We can't have witches using magic randomly. We'll cull those who don't fall in line."

Shirina's stomach twisted violently. She would kill her witches. Undo all of her work. All of *their* work.

"Tally, don't," she found herself saying, willing to beg not for her life, but for the lives of her witches. She'd taken humiliation before. She'd grown tempered by it, and had learned to stand in it, when necessary.

Now, if begging an Elder would spare her witches… she would do it. Pride would not stand in the way of her adepts' lives. Not after they'd trusted her with them.

"Please don't." She managed to open her eyes, still on her knees like the supplicant she was, and looked up to face the victory in Tally's eyes.

"Begging, Shirina? You would have never become an Elder."

"Maybe not," Shirina said. "But I would never bow to Siabala, either."

"You poor child, clinging to this fantasy so…" Tally cooed, actually *cooed*. "Well, if Ravenhold is truly where you want to go…"

Vangle pulled Shirina up, holding her hands behind her back. The sudden movement made her head spin even more, but she managed to focus on Tally's hateful face.

"Don't fret, Shirina." Her cold hand touched the side of her face. She could smell the sulfur on the woman's robes. She could smell Siabala's Rage, because she had been there and would never forget its burning stench. "If you really want to go to Ravenhold, then who am I to deny you." A flash of a smile.

"Goodbye, Shirina. I'll make sure to pass along your regrets."

Before she could answer, a teleportation spell carried her away as Vangle held her hands behind her and she choked on the smothering sulfur, Siabala's magic strong. Too strong. She forced her eyes open, forced herself to look at the land around her as he took her over mountains, toward the sea.

Much further and more easily than one of her spells could take her.

How strong had Siabala's magic already grown?

Trapped in the spell, she could see the magic feeding it below. Red cracks lined Graydon, where once light magic should have glowed. Not hovering in the air, just beneath the surface, as though it waited. Fed its disciples and waited to be free. On the horizon, there was no sign of her own source powers. It was gone. Graydon's magic was gone, slowly being replaced by Siabala's.

How do they not see? She wanted to scream, but couldn't risk breathing in the dark magic, like a cloud over Graydon, brewing up a storm.

And then they arrived, on the stone bridge that had once led to Ravenhold, on the precipice at the very edge of Graydon. The sea crashed below, angry waves furling and unfurling on the cliffside. Somewhere beneath the waters lay Ravenhold's final resting place.

She'd hoped maybe, just maybe, she could find a secret entrance. A place where Elders had hidden knowledge. Faced with the unforgiven waves and the undeniable power of nature, Shirina now understood she'd been holding on to foolish hope and had wasted energy she could have better used elsewhere. Maybe helped Altessa, or her witches, or perhaps warned people. Helped some to safety, before Siabala's attack.

"Don't be sad, Shirina," Vangle said over the sound of the surf, the taste of sulfur replaced by salt spray. "Look on the bright side. At least you won't be around for the grand finale. And your friends and witches won't live long enough to miss you."

He leaned in, warm breath on her ear. "Your Massir witches are dead, including Shala. Everything you've built is gone and destroyed. Your life is meaningless."

Before she could fully grasp his words and answer, he pushed her over the edge, her body hopelessly heavy. She reached for her magic, desperate to stop her fall, but Graydon did not answer her call anymore than it had before.

A spray of cold water and she met, swept down by a wave as she tumbled below, into the lurking dark.

3 2

Without enough horses, their choices dwindled.

"I used to just walk everywhere," Avarielle grumbled, arms crossed as she stared out the window of Shirina's study, distressingly empty without the sorceress. "That was plenty good enough for me."

"Sure," Rojon said, "if you want to get there after everyone is dead, let's do that."

Cassara sighed. "Rojon is right, Avarielle. We need to move more quickly. This isn't like it was twenty years ago. We have more options, now."

"Trusting those witches with our lives shouldn't exactly be top of the list," Avarielle said. "Did you miss the part where they were going to teleport you to Massir? Kidnap you?"

"Well, things have changed." Cassara smoothed out her

pants, the new clothing a gift from the Circle. Shirina's Circle. Thank goodness she kept well-stocked stores.

Cassara would have to thank her. She bit her lip, an old habit that had been returning of late. She'd worked hard to stop doing so once she'd become Queen of Rashim.

"Avarielle, what if Tally has already caught up to Shirina?"

"They won't have." Avarielle brushed off her concerns. "And, even if they have, she'll talk her way out of it or hit them with a rock. Shirina might be all fancy magic talk, but she can throw a punch."

"I know," Cassara said. "But they'll want her dead."

"She's not dead," Avarielle said with such certainty that Cassara stared at her. "You thought I was dead and I wasn't, right? Shirina is at least as stubborn as I am, so she's fine." Her lip quirked slightly. "She might be more stubborn than me, but don't tell her I said that. She's insufferable enough as-is."

Cassara wished she could possess Avarielle's certainty. Tally would want Shirina dead. Out of her way, and never to return. Unless…

"Siabala will want revenge on the three of us," she said. "He'll want to see us suffer."

Avarielle nodded and sat in the chair across from Cassara. Light filtered in through the windows into Shirina's study, blanketing her sturdy oak desk and faded carpet. The day was beautiful, the sun warm, and it all felt so wrong.

"That's what I figure," Avarielle said. She hesitated, but Cassara knew what the warrior was thinking, because she'd been thinking it herself.

"That's why he went after Massir," she said softly. "And my family."

Avarielle leaned back in the chair and sighed. "That's what I think, but don't feel bad. It's not your fault. He's an evil god."

"I wish we could have killed him," Cassara whispered, looking into her old friend's eyes. Avarielle said nothing, simply met her eyes. Steady, unflappable, and willing to still do what needed to be done.

What they'd tried to do twenty years ago.

"If we go to Massir," Rojon said, standing near his mother, "won't he just do that, then? Kill Dayshon before you?"

Another smile pulled at Avarielle's lips. "Good thinking," she said. "He wants you to suffer, Cassara. More than any of us, I imagine. It's your magic that trapped him."

"It's your blade that killed his body," Cassara countered.

"But I haven't kept him imprisoned for twenty years, helpless. My blade couldn't stop his soul." She looked thoughtful. "But your magic could. What if this is about you? And don't go taking this personally. Again, he's an evil god."

"It feels personal," Cassara said, but she held her chin

up as she answered this time. Avarielle grinned at the sight, before growing somber again.

"What if, now that the Wall is down, he wants to make you suffer. Even if he has Shirina, which again I seriously doubt, what if he's waiting for you to show up to kill her before you?"

"You've given this some thought," Cassara said, trying to make light of the situation.

"I don't want him to win," Avarielle whispered. "I don't want to lose you, or Rojon, or Altessa, or even Shirina. To do that, we have to try to think like him. And I think he's a petty tyrant looking for revenge on the person he holds responsible for his downfall above any other. The woman who gave up her magic to stop him."

Cassara swallowed hard. "I never wanted any of this."

"I know," Avarielle leaned over and took Cassara's hand in hers. "I was there, remember?" A quick motion of her chin toward Rojon. "Even though I'd just given birth to that one over there." She focused back on Cassara. "We can't assign him more power than he already has over us. If you walk into Massir, you're playing into his hands. Let me go alone, and you head to the Southern Coalition. Find allies."

"I can go with you, mom," Rojon said. "I can watch your back."

Where Graysword is currently sheathed. No chance of Avarielle allowing that.

"I think you should go with Cassara to the Southern

Coalition. The witches will lend credibility to Cassara's words, not that you need it." Cassara nodded. She'd worked at freeing the coalition and had helped it rebuild. She was well-respected there, and she was fairly certain they would come to Massir's aid. Her defenses hadn't just relied on walls, but on allies, too. "And the witches will stay in line if they have the heir of Elihor watching your back."

Rojon looked thoughtful, and then nodded, probably sensing as she did that Avarielle had made up her mind.

"And what if Shirina is in Ravenhold?"

"She'll find her way to us, Cassara. We'll all meet again in Massir."

Cassara nodded but couldn't help but bite her lip again. Avarielle walking into Massir still felt like giving Siabala exactly what he wanted.

Everyone finally seemed on board, so Avarielle moved quickly to get supplies ready and threaten the witches with terrible fates if something happened to her son or Cassara. They seemed muted, and untethered. Avarielle remembered what Shirina had been like when she'd lost her link with Ravenhold. She'd been adrift, and bitchy about it.

These witches didn't seem as fiery as Shirina, which might be to their advantage. Less moaning to listen to.

After getting everyone else to scramble, the warrior soothed her worries by checking the perimeter again, this time including the skies. Once she'd made sure everyone and everything was safe and working toward one goal, she decided to make sure *she* was ready. Stepping just to the edge of the mansion, in a fairly open area of the gardens, where she wouldn't accidentally trim the gardens with her blade, she pulled out Graysword, examined it, testing the familiar weapon with her hands, warming up her muscles. She hoped she hadn't been wrong about Shirina. If she'd died protecting her son... she didn't even want to think about how much she'd owe her and the Circle.

She's fine. Shirina was too stubborn to die. She'd proven that over and over again. The warrior couldn't afford to believe differently. They would need Circle magic. If Larkhold was all they had for now, so be it. But she would feel better if Shirina's Circle had its magic backing them up, too.

How things have changed. She shook her head and smiled, moving Graysword in a graceful arc. Once, she would have done anything to get rid of the witch. She'd wanted the Circle to die. And it had, leaving Graydon dangerously vulnerable.

Shirina would see to a greater Circle. A stronger one. She just needed her magic, and Avarielle needed her to figure herself out and get back here so they could stop Siabala before he made himself known.

Her feet fell into the familiar rhythms of dance, moving quickly and without effort, Graysword a part of the music of her mind, moving seamlessly. She'd loved dancing and had incorporated all of her training into sword fighting. In the West, the dances weren't choreographed. You followed the music as quickly as you could, followed your dance partner and let yourself be followed, all very useful traits when handling a blade.

Her steps faltered as darkness crushed her happy childhood memories, but she pushed through them, forcing her feet to keep moving, to stay smooth, to focus on movement and speed. Memories could destroy her just as quickly as the present during a battle, and she'd learned to let them wash over her, embrace them, dance with them.

An Elom attack. Her brother, dead. Graysword beckoning her to use her magic. *Take the oath, Grayloft.* Her blade sliding into her dance teacher's chest, effortlessly. Wide eyes of surprise. Shock. Betrayal.

Falling to the ground, fresh blood burned off the blade as white flames flared to life. Laughter in her mind… She pulled herself back to the now. To the smell of earth, plant, and life. To the sound of the leaves in the trees, a sound that took her a long time to get used to once she'd exiled herself away from her people.

Her steps slowed, calmed. Her heart beat hard in her chest, but not uncomfortably. A thin layer of sweat coated her, her clothing sticky. Feet hip-wide apart, she held up Graysword and examined its blade, and its lack of chips or damage despite countless bone-shattering battles. How it still looked like it had just been forged. The red jewel in the center of the pommel flawless.

What are you up to, Siabala? She wished she could track him. Feel him, and what he was up to. Sometimes, she thought she could. Flashes of insight, or intuition. She didn't know how to explain it, and so never had. The only person who could maybe help her would be Shirina. Maybe once she'd be back, they could work together with Graysword to see if they could use his magic against him.

She smiled sadly. Shirina had been after her and Graysword when they'd met. Now, she would hand the sorceress her sword willingly, knowing the witch would respect her wishes.

They'd both come a long way.

A shadow caught her attention. Rojon stood near the edge of the mansion, staring at the sword, oblivious to anything else. Avarielle quickly sheathed it. He blinked, snapping free of Graysword's hold.

Her heart beat faster and ached. Her son had touched the magic of Graysword. He had not taken an oath, but Siabala's hold on him grew every day. She needed him away from her, even though she wanted nothing more than to keep him safe. She needed him away from Graysword, and she needed to wield the blade to fight Siabala.

She couldn't stay with him, but she had to believe he would be safe with Cassara. They would keep each other safe.

"Are you ready?" Avarielle asked. The witches had been

working with Cassara to look over maps and plan how close they could safely teleport. There were several teleportation circles within the Coalition, but all of them were too far to reach in one jump. They'd go to Kosel, and ask Kaden's daughter for help, with her crazy fast lizard. And Avarielle would head up the Maple Mountains, to reach Massir.

It wasn't a great plan, but it was a plan, and she was itching to take the fight to Siabala, or to his minions, should he fail to reveal himself.

"We are," Rojon said, standing before her. He'd found pieces of armor and made them work, leather covering his torso, a metal plate on his right breast and shoulder. A long sword hung from his hip, something obviously Rashim-forged, based on its intricately designed pommel.

"Shirina doesn't mess around, does she," Avarielle said, pulling on his armor to test it. It was sturdy and would protect him should he need it. Which hopefully he wouldn't.

"Looks like she was preparing for war," Rojon said with a smile, then dropped it as he realized that she *had* been. "And yes, we're ready to go when you are."

"Perfect." She shifted to move, but stilled when he didn't move, hesitating. Knowing her son at times needed a bit more space to turn his thoughts into words, she waited him out, even though she wanted nothing more than to get him away from Graysword.

"I want to take the oath, Mom," he whispered.

Avarielle stared at him, mouth slightly open, eyes wide,

terror like an angry snake in her gut. Seeing her reaction, Rojon quickly elaborated.

"The oath to protect the descendants of Graydon."

Avarielle started to shake her head, but he took her hand in a surprisingly effective and controlled gesture. It grounded her and linked them. Forced her to pay attention to whatever would come out of his mouth next.

"I can feel it in me, and I know you know Siabala is trying to get to me, Mom." Her heart broke all over again. "You're getting me away from you so I'm away from Graysword." His voice lost some of its strength. "I think that's wise, although I want nothing more than to go with you and fight by your side."

"Me, too," Avarielle said softly, not trusting her voice not to break if she tried to speak more loudly.

"I've been thinking about it, and figure the oath to protect the descendants of Graydon is a way to keep us away from Siabala, right?"

His hand slipped from hers, and Avarielle took a deep breath. She didn't want to talk of cursed bloodlines with her son. But time was cascading away from her, and it no longer mattered what she wanted. What mattered was what her son needed. What he would need to keep moving forward.

"Our bloodline took the oath with Siabala originally to be his assassins, Rojon." He looked at her unflinchingly, and she found it hard to see her young boy in this man's calculating eyes. She wanted him to need her to make everything better again. To need her to coddle and hold him and keep him safe.

Which she was, in her own way. Not by soothing his fears away, but by keeping him informed. When had her son become a warrior? When had this edge begin to harden around him?

"Specifically, to kill Elihor." Avarielle finished. Rojon didn't look away. Didn't even look shocked. "That's what your grandfather told me, and Siabala confirmed it. That's why Graysword's magic hurts you, Rojon." Although it hadn't done nearly as much damage as she'd thought it would, which only added to her worry.

"Graylofts killed Elihor?" Rojon asked, wonder in his voice. "I thought she'd thrown herself into the sea to stop Siabala from gaining her powers?"

"No one is sure what happened to her, except maybe Siabala, and we won't be asking him." Avarielle sighed. "But we didn't kill Elihor, at least not as far as I know. The oath to protect Graydon's descendants...I guess it might be a countermeasure?"

"If I were Elihor," he said softly, eyes looking less hard as he thought about his ancestor, "and I stopped an assassin from killing me, or helped them break free of Siabala's control, I would make use of them to keep those I loved safe, regardless of whether or not I knew this curse was hereditary."

Avarielle smiled at her son. "I love that about you, Rojon," she said. "Your ability to put yourself into other people's shoes. To imagine what their lives are like. To see beyond what your eyes tell you. That's how you managed to turn plants into buildings and understand the needs of people. Your heart is your greatest strength." She placed a hand on his cheek, needing him to hear her. "I don't want you to lose that to an oath that would need you to focus all your energies on being a warrior, Rojon. You're more than that. You're more than *me*."

Rojon's eyes widened, and he took her hand in his. "Mom, *you're* more than a warrior. No, let me finish." She held her peace, the words to tell him off sticking in her mouth. "You made a home for us in a land you didn't know. You grieved dad in your own way. You're a terrible cook—" a quick grin, "—but you made sure we had plenty to eat. You took care of Kale in his old days," he paused, swallowed hard as his eyes misted over. In those tears, she saw her little boy again. "Mom, you're a good friend to a queen and a sorceress. An aunt to various children I haven't even met. A protector of more than just a bloodline, but a people. You're a strategist when you need to be, a healer at other times. You're a dancer, and sometimes I'd get up before dawn broke just to watch you dance the sunrise into existence, with such grace that it made me think you weren't really of this world."

"Rojon—"

"Mom, you're not just a warrior. You're amazing, and I don't feel trapped into taking this oath. I *want* to, because I know what you don't want me to become. I know you know that I'm drawn to Graysword, and you've faced Siabala. If you couldn't kill him, nobody could." He took a deep breath. "So, let me protect Cassara. I've always been an heir to Elihor. Let me be an heir to Grayloft, too. I want to take the oath, mom. Not because of Siabala. Because of *you.*"

Avarielle swallowed hard, looking at her little boy, and the man he'd become. She'd been trying so hard to make sure he'd have all the options available to him that she'd never considered he might *want* to follow in her footsteps.

To honor her name. To be a Grayloft, with all of its pain and demands.

And beauty, too. She'd met Cassara because of this oath. She'd been given purpose. Otherwise, she might have fallen prey to Siabala. Become the monster he desperately wanted her to become.

This oath had saved her. Her bloodline had saved her.

"Siabala is the curse," he said, "but our bloodline isn't."

She swallowed again, fighting to push the words past the lump in her throat.

"I guess I wanted you to get to be more like your dad than like me," she said with a sad smile.

"You told me he was a great warrior."

"He was. But he was a poet, too. And had the gentlest of souls..."

"And I will be all of those things, still. Why do you insist on pushing me away when all I want is to honor you, Mom? I'm proud to be your son."

Another deep breath.

"I did run your father through with Graysword. But he was already dead, Rojon. Siabala had stolen his soul." He went to say something, but it was her turn to hold up her hand. She needed to finish telling him the truth. All of it. "Siabala turned him into a puppet for me, Rojon. Thinking it would...thinking it was what I wanted. I didn't even know I was pregnant."

She'd never imagined telling her son this. Never. Part of her never believed she'd have to.

"I figured out I was pregnant because of that blow. It activated Graysword's magic, and I thought...maybe... maybe he was still alive. But he wasn't. And I felt the magic attacking you..."

"You did what you had to do. It was an impossible choice. One baby versus the world."

"I was willing to sacrifice you. To let you die before being born. Elihor's last descendant, too, like I was finishing Siabala's work for him." She flinched at the realization. "I didn't think I'd survive, to be honest. If not for Shirina's magic, you would be dead."

"If not for my mother, I wouldn't be the man I am today."

She laughed, trying to dismiss her growing emotions. "Okay, this is too much for me." She sought out his eyes. "Do you feel better? You were so angry, and you have reason to be, Rojon. It's dangerous going into battle angry. Trust me on this. You need a clear head."

"Honestly? I feel better since I used the magic. Now I feel it more than Siabala's pull. But..." His eyes almost twitched to Graysword's pommel, and she could see him forcing them back to hers.

"Elihor's magic will keep you safe," she said. "You've proven that already. Trust that it can protect you."

"I have no idea how to wield it."

"Shirina taught you everything she could about it. You're now in uncharted territory. You need to make your own path. Something I know you can do, Rojon."

"I do," he said. "But I need an anchor. Away from Siabala." The last words were spoken with regret. Away from Siabala. Away from Graysword. Away from her.

"Kneel, Rojon." The words but a whisper, like she couldn't believe they tumbled from her lips, even as she felt their necessity. He knelt and looked up at her, hands resting on his knee. She freed Graysword from its scabbard. This oath was meaningless, in a way. It did not bind with magic, unlike her oath with Siabala. It was no curse, nor boon. It was a focus, like a sword in battle.

And focus was sometimes all that was needed. Her son had asked her to trust him. Who was she to tell him what his path should be when she'd always encouraged him to follow his own?

"Descendant of Grayloft," she spoke softly. This was not an oath to shout. This was an oath to let fall on your heart. To allow it to guide you. Her father had made her take it when she was a child, terrified of the war that had seen her mother dead. Of the monsters that would soon destroy him, too. And then her brother.

This was an oath for whispers. For the gentle moments that kept a family together; for traditions repeated late at night, in blanketing darkness. For the blood that bound, not the blood that tore families apart.

"Do you swear, by sword, by bow, by heart and soul, to always protect the sacred lineage of the sorcerer Graydon? To see to their safety above your own? To put all aside to protect them from the darkness of Siabala?"

Siabala. She'd taken the oath differently. *To protect them from the darkness of Elihor and Siabala.*

But she knew better now and would only pass down what she knew to be true.

The world had changed. And so must oaths and traditions.

"I do," Rojon said.

Avarielle had had to cut her thumb on the blade to seal the oath. At the time, she'd believed it to be not only painful, but a symbol. Now, she wondered if more magic might exist in the simple act. But would it bind her to his oath, or further to Siabala?

I wasn't bound to him until I killed my mentor.

It had maybe helped save her. She was willing to change things to reflect the new realities she understood. But she was also willing to accept that she didn't have all the answers. And that she wasn't willing to risk her son's blood on Graysword. Not knowing the blade had been forged by Siabala. Not after everything she'd been through.

She sheathed the blade again, and Rojon stood.

"I'm proud of you," she said, meaning it. "Remember, this is not an oath to give up everything for."

"I know, Mom," he smiled at her, and hugged her tight. "Thank you for trusting me." He whispered in her ear.

She held him back, wishing she could keep him safe forever, but trusting that he would do the best he could, no matter what. She'd done her best at protecting him by encouraging him to follow his own path.

She just hoped that path would lead him away from Siabala, even if it meant taking him away from her, too.

33

"I hate this," Avarielle told Cassara, low enough that others couldn't overhear. The witches were getting ready outside, taking one more look at maps and studying the topography before teleporting. They should be able to find Kosel's outpost, but the more prepared they were, the better.

"Me going to the Southern Coalition was your idea," Cassara said, even though she knew exactly what the warrior meant. "So was bringing Rojon."

"I know, and I still think it's brilliant." She shot Cassara a quick grin. "But I hate that I won't be there to protect you." She hesitated, glanced at her son.

"What is it?" Cassara asked, looking at him. He seemed to have recovered fine. Better than she had after using her magic. He seemed more energetic and focused than before, in fact. She hoped she'd get to help him hone his magical skills while they travelled. Only because she couldn't access her magic hardly meant that she didn't remember how to use it.

It would take more than two decades to forget its warmth within her, filling her, making her whole.

"He took the oath to protect the descendants of Graydon," Avarielle said, sounding annoyed and proud. "He…he wanted to."

Cassara smiled. "I'm not surprised, Avarielle. He's proud of you."

"It's a big oath." Avarielle crossed her arms. "You lot can't stay out of trouble!"

Cassara continued without skipping a beat. "And your 'lot' is so stubborn that he wouldn't let you stop him anyway."

The two friends exchanged a glance and burst out laughing. A couple of witches stopped working and glanced at them, before resuming their whispered consultations. Rojon just shook his head, a smile on his lips.

"I missed this," Cassara said.

"Us being clever?"

"Laughing," she said, then focused on the warrior. "Thanks for always having my back, Avarielle."

"Same to you," Avarielle said, returning the hug.

"Don't worry," Cassara whispered in her ear. "I'll make sure Rojon is safe." They broke their embrace and Cassara grimaced. "The Southern Coalition is really boring."

"Just make sure you *both* stay safe."

"And you, too."

"I will," Avarielle said. "When Shirina comes back, and she will, I can't let her live down the fact that she was teleported away."

"She saved Rojon."

"She saved Rojon," Avarielle repeated with a grimace. "She'll never let *me* live it down."

"You'll never let yourself forget it," Cassara said with a gentle smile. "I'll miss you."

A familiar lump formed in her throat. Painful yet welcome, reminding her that she loved her friend dearly. Then the lump morphed, at it always did, into fear gripping her chest—fear she'd lose someone else she loved. That everything and everyone she cared for would be swept away in the tides of Siabala.

A strong hand gripped her shoulder.

"I'll see you soon," Avarielle said, forcing some of Cassara's fears away with her strength. "That's a promise."

Cassara nodded and the two went to join the witches, though her breath still felt shallow and a stone had settled in her stomach.

3 4

———

Altessa followed Ramelia down the dark corridors beneath the city of Massir, the dread of ages filling her bones, a chill gripping them that she could not dispel. They'd reached utter darkness, so much higher than the filtering sunbeams, and Ramelia had grudgingly lit a torch. The ceilings were lower here, and the structures closely knit, sometimes barely leaving them enough room to squeeze by. Her breath felt too loud, her mind squeezed by the proximity of large, immovable, flanking stone.

Shadows danced around them, though not the dust of earlier—yesterday?—even the torchlight still and not flickering, as though it understood these shadows could not, would not, be dispelled. They'd rested, a fitful, smothering sleep that left her more weary. Time seemed eternal in this place, and she found that she had no idea if it was day or night.

The torch itself was unlike anything Altessa had ever seen. The handle was thinner and finer, and seemed to be made of stone. The wick burned something that must have been at its center, but no material Altessa knew. The strangeness in usually such a simple and known item set the surrounding city even further apart from Altessa's life.

She forced herself to keep pace with Ramelia, while focusing on the city around her. Not on the smooth stones, nor the impossibly rounded buildings, but on the small imperfections. On a scratch in a wall, near a door, perhaps a measure of a child's height. Surely children had once lived here.

She tried to find these imperfections, these signs of life, but found so little that the exercise left her feeling even more anchorless. There was no furniture in the homes. Only the stone remained. No wood, no fabric, no decoration, no toy nor discarded weapon… nothing.

Just stone buildings, like mushrooms growing on a tree trunk, beneath old, damp bark. And nothing else.

What if the people here were so different that they needed none of these things? What if they'd been beings of magic, and had somehow vanished into light? Or shadows? What if each shadow held a piece of their spirit, and they waited to swarm them, only a strange torch keeping them at bay?

Stop.

She pulled her coat closer and held the large scratchy faded red scarf more tightly against her neck. Everything was damp. Her bones ached, her muscles were on fire and, after what might have been hours of walking in dark corridors with looming buildings at the edges of the light that frightened her to her core, Altessa found herself feeling frazzled, a sensation she found entirely distasteful.

She looked to the back of Ramelia's head. The rebel seemed perfectly fine. But Altessa's feet ached in the too small boots. Her thighs chafed with the uncomfortable, rough material. And her hair felt like someone had slathered oil in it. She needed to bathe and change into something entirely more comfortable.

Busy considering all the ills currently befalling her, she didn't pay enough attention and tripped on a stone. She landed, hard, on her side, her pants ripping below her knee. Ramelia didn't stop, even though she'd heard her fall.

"Come on, princess," she whispered. "Gotta save yourself, because nobody else will."

Her face burning, Altessa pushed herself back up and scurried to catch up to the rebel, though she hated every moment of it.

Altessa had convinced her to get her beneath the castle, doubling and tripling down on her stubbornness. The rebel had given in but had been angry. Much angrier than Altessa had believed she would be. She'd thought she'd be pleased to be done with babysitting her, but the rebel hadn't spoken a word to her since.

Using the underground city to travel Massir had been Ramelia's idea, saying she knew the passages well enough to get her where she needed to be. She wished her mother was here. She'd know what to do, and she'd tell her to stay safe.

She wanted a safety net, but it was gone.

My mother fought Siabala when she was two years younger than me. She reminded herself again, though it didn't exactly help her feel braver. All it did was make her feel more inadequate.

They climbed a passageway, round structures rising around them, the lower cave expanding outward again. This was the third time, and the third village, or neighbourhood, they'd crossed. All under her city, beneath even the sewer and water systems, lurking and ready to swallow them.

Like beneath the West.

Water trickled somewhere in the distance. Twenty years ago, the waterways of Graydon had vanished beneath ground. Massir would be without water entirely if not for Circle magic. Tally had given her people water again… the darkness turned to smothering hopelessness. She'd planned for everything, the Elder. Hand on smooth stone she walked on, a thin layer of moisture covering her fingers, the cold infiltrated her skin. Winter settling in her bones.

Did all of Graydon sit atop an ancient metropolis made of stone? What had happened to its people? What else lurked down here?

Wrapping her arms around her middle to save whatever warmth remained, she followed Ramelia who ducked inside a building, torchlight quickly vanishing.

Altessa placed a hand on the side of the structure, and received a shock. Her face grew hot, and she removed her hand, looking at it.

What had just happened?

"Come on, princess," Ramelia said, sounding impatient.

Altessa followed in silence, trusting that her guide would show her the way, trusting that she would figure out what to do once they'd reached their destination.

"We're near," Ramelia whispered, despite being the one who'd insisted no one else came here. But in the vast catacombs of the ancient city, Altessa wondered if even the steel-nerved rebel feared the whispers of ghosts.

"How do I get up there?" Altessa asked, crossing between buildings which hid the high ceiling from her. Stone nooks had been built in the walls of this structure, at arm level, but she had no idea why.

That's what bothered her most about this city. Its *emptiness*. If Massir were abandoned overnight, things would be left behind. Maybe this place simply hadn't been abandoned overnight? If not, then where had they gone?

She shivered, wrapped her arms around herself again.

"There," Ramelia pointed up once they'd cleared the building. A staircase hugged the edge of the dome that covered this part of the city, leading to a door. Avarielle had told her stories of the city beneath her lands, and how they'd accessed it via such a door. She'd found the stories fascinating. Riveting, even. Now, they simply terrified her.

The stairs looked unsafe, without railing, though the

stairs themselves seemed evenly and clearly chiseled. The rebel walked toward them.

"I don't know where that door goes, exactly," Ramelia said.

"Have you never gone up there?" Altessa asked as they both stopped, looking up. It seemed impossibly far, and so easy to stumble from.

"Never had reason to," the rebel shrugged. But Ramelia had admitted to exploring these caves out of sheer curiosity. Altessa wasn't fooled. "I'd much prefer you going another way, too," she said. "But this is beneath the palace." A pause. "Tally probably knows of it, too. This is frustrating," she growled, keeping her voice low. "I don't know why you're insisting on going there. They're just going to kill you." A scowl. "I don't know why I bothered saving you, if all you're going to do is run right back to the palace."

"I need to get help," she said, "and maybe find my father."

"If we go through that way," Ramelia pointed further in the darkness, beyond where Altessa's eyes could see, "I think we can actually reach the city beneath the West. I think it's all connected."

Altessa looked toward the place coated in darkness, unable to spot any corridor or passage.

"I need to get my father," she said, walking resolutely toward the stairs.

"He's probably dead." At the look Altessa gave her,

Ramelia relented. "Or under such tight watch that you won't get close to him. This isn't a good plan, Altessa."

A tint of despair lined Ramelia's voice, and it was the first time she called Altessa solely by her first name. That made the princess pause, and she met the rebel's eyes. Were she in the palace, she would have put her in her place. Told her that she knew what she was doing because she was the princess and knew her way. But here, lost and alone, she didn't know how to be a royal. She'd only been a princess in court, and even then, she knew her mother and father were lax in their demands of her. That they, having felt the crushing weight of demands as they tried to save, and then rebuild, their land, had taken a different approach with her.

That even though she would have traditionally been married off and her younger brother heir to the throne, she was heir, and could marry whoever she pleased. *If* she pleased.

Her mother had made sure she knew the ways of the court, but also that she knew the ways of magic thanks to Shirina, and the ways of battle and the world, thanks to Avarielle. She hadn't excelled at either, never feeling very motivated to push herself, and regretted not applying herself more to her lessons, even if they'd seemed pointless at the time. She'd been surrounded by strong women all her life, and now wondered if any of their strength graced her, too.

Because right now, she didn't feel strong at all.

She met the rebel's eyes. The woman had risked

everything to save her. And had only wanted to save Massir, even if she'd decided the royal family was the enemy. She didn't agree with her tactics, nor her logic. She hated feeling like she was a terrible person because the rebel hated her family.

Regardless, she thought she could trust Ramelia's heart. She wanted what was best for Massir. Her Massir was just very different from Altessa's.

"Say he's dead—" Altessa swallowed hard at the surge of emotion, "—then there is no king on the throne. My mother is missing, and possibly dead as well." Her voice cracked, but she pressed on. "What happens then?"

Ramelia opened her mouth to say something, an annoying quirk on the side of her mouth. Altessa cut her off.

"Someone else takes power, Ramelia. Someone always tries to take power. And I know you want it to be the people, but it won't be."

"Elder Tally will take it," Ramelia crossed her arms. "So, what? She represents the people." The last part was spoken with little conviction.

"Elder Tally represents Siabala," Altessa said, keeping her voice gentle. "We cannot let Siabala take control of Massir. Of all of Rashim. And from here, Graydon."

A sharp laugh flew from Ramelia's lips and echoed bitterly in the city. "And what, you'll stop him? You, all by yourself?"

Altessa flushed red, with anger and embarrassment. "I'm the heir to the throne," she said, and held up her hand to stop Ramelia's obvious retort. "I can at least rally the troops. Right now, they don't even know that they're in a snake's den."

"You'll sacrifice yourself for your kingdom? How noble." The sneer in Ramelia's voice was like a slap across Altessa face.

"What else can I do?" Her own words echoed weakly back to her. She forced her voice to be lower. "Unless you think you can get us more help from other magic users?"

Ramlia shook her head, looking just as angry. "They were desperate people, *princess.* Tally saved them. Saved *me.* You don't betray those who offer you life."

"Then why did you?" Altessa asked softly, wondering what she would do if Ramelia decided to go back to Tally. She had nothing to offer the rebel, and no longer any magic to protect herself with.

"Because… Because it wasn't the right way to go about this. But it doesn't mean I'd use my magic against Tally and the others."

Altessa stood very quietly before Ramelia, like cold water had coated her and, in her lack of options and allies, her mind came into sharp focus. She had no allies she could trust to help her, not even Ramelia, though she'd gotten her this far. Chances were that both her parents were dead, and the king issuing these orders was some kind of fake or illusion. Her siblings were hopefully safe in Edoline, but there was no guarantee that Tally hadn't seen to their deaths, too.

The longer she waited, the deeper the Circle's clutches —no, *Siabala's* clutches—dug into Massir.

She had no magic. For a brief moment, she'd touched the glory of Graydon's powers, and it had deserted her just as quickly.

All she had was a throne she would probably never rule from.

And a people to inspire.

She wondered if this was what her mom had felt going up against Siabala. She'd never mentioned that she had no plans of coming back, but Altessa had understood, once she'd grown older. Her mother was kind, gentle, and loving. With a sadness that permeated every movement, something Altessa had only seen once she was old enough to understand true heartbreak.

She'd tried to ask her mom about it, once. All she'd done was smile and say that someday she might understand. But hopefully she wouldn't.

She'd given up everything for her people. For Graydon. Her freedom, her power. Her magic.

And it hadn't returned.

Would Altessa be brave enough to give up everything for her throne, too? For her people? To face off against Siabala? And accept that she might not return?

"I don't want to die," Altessa said slowly. She pulled her eyes away from the door crowded in shadows, down the narrow stone staircase, and found Ramelia's eyes. "But I don't want to live with abandoning my people, either."

There it was. Her choice, as ugly as it was. What she

could and couldn't live with. It sounded stupid to her own ears, and she was surprised when Ramelia studied her instead of immediately mocking her.

"You don't know what you can live with until you have to," she said softly. "You'd be surprised just how much one heart can bear, princess."

Altessa's resolve dwindled without the clear road. She tried to imagine her life down both paths. One, she would try to find a quick ally in the city before the Circle caught her. Or she'd try to convince allies in nearby cities. Before the Circle caught her. She could go West and speak to Avarielle's people.

But the Circle had all the magic. And Builder Hilar had been killed so easily, when she'd gone to him for help. Because of her.

Nothing I do will matter.

She was insignificant. Her only power was that throne, which she would probably never reach.

But maybe, just maybe, the attempt was what mattered. Maybe by trying to do the right thing, she would inspire others to do the same. Maybe, just maybe, she'd find the help she needed. Maybe her father was still alive and...

Ramelia shook her head.

"You're going in there, aren't you?"

Altessa realized that the rebel was right. She'd known it before Altessa herself knew it.

"I have to," she said. "You're right, it's probably suicide. But imagine if it's not. It's worth the risk."

"I should have never bothered saving you," the rebel muttered, though she sounded more regretful than angry.

"Thank you for buying me the time, and lending me the courage, to do what must be done," she answered. Ramelia just looked at her, struggling with what to say.

Then she handed her the torch and turned on her heel.

"If you're going to kill yourself, princess, it doesn't mean I have to watch."

And she was gone, leaving Altessa alone with only shadows and doubts.

Altessa.

Her mother's older sister had been named Altessa, by their mother, the grandmother the princess of Massir had never met. It meant child of light in old Edoline.

Each step on the stairs felt like a century, a risk of falling, a chance of reaching her goal, so far away.

Edoline had once been a matriarchy. When her grandmother had died, so young, it had turned into a patriarchy. Her aunt Altessa should have ruled Edoline. Instead, she was shipped off to marry a promising suitor.

The rough wall was cold under her hand, but was her only guide, the only thing grounding her away from the growing precipice to her right.

Her grandmother had died from her daughter's—from Cassara's—magic. Too young to know how to wield it, the scar haunted her mother to this day.

The torchlight shook in the unsteady hold of her right hand, the shadows dancing dizzyingly quick on the wall and ceiling, shadows scrambling around her as she tried to calm her mind.

Her aunt Altessa had become queen of Edoline after her father's death. And then her husband's death. But it had been under Circle control, then, and she'd had few allies to rely on. She'd sent for help.

Her breath sounded too loud, too raspy, too forced, her fear escaping with each lungful, with each exhale.

Help had come, but too late. And the young queen of Edoline, her aunt, her namesake, had died fighting to protect her people. By Siabala's hand.

Altessa reached the top of the stairs, and crumpled in the landing near the door, gathering her legs against herself, making herself small so the landing felt bigger, safer. The torch lay on the stone, burning, casting its strange shadows.

She wanted to close her eyes, to center herself, but she was too afraid the shadows would throw her off the edge, to the rounded rooftops in the sea of darkness below.

She trembled to her feet, grabbed the torch, and pushed on the door. It budged, moved inward, away from the terrifying city, the shadows, and the doubts. The fear that history would only repeat itself, and that for Altessa, dying by Siabala's hand was the only legacy she would leave behind.

～

Below in the city, eyes watched the heir of Graydon vanish into the door. Legs scurried silently, too quiet for human ears to hear, and went to report to their master what they'd seen.

All except one pair of eyes, unaware of the others. Ramelia had forced herself to breathe as she'd watched Altessa's slow progress up the stairs. She'd feared the door was locked, and the princess would have to come back down. She'd desperately hoped she would.

Except then she'd vanished, taking the light with her.

Ramelia took a few breaths in the protective dark, lit her last torch, and headed back into the city.

Bring the heirs to Kosel, Quilsam finished his instructions to his Crimson Circle, then settled back down before Elder Tally, in one of the palace's gilded libraries, tall bookshelves filled with old tomes and volumes. A place of comfort for those who'd dedicated their lives to learning.

"Will she do it?" Elder Tally asked, looking annoyed. Quilsam did not care for the Elder of Ravenhold, but she had earned her rank, as he had earned his, and was worthy of consideration. That she was impatient to see this over with did not surprise him. In her shoes, he might very well have felt the same.

Her tactics were coarse, but undoubtedly fueled by her shame and fear: never before had a coven been taken over by a traitor. Elders Rale and Trulia trusted her, and Elder Rachalt couldn't be reached, probably too busy in her studies. As next in seniority, it fell to him to contact the witches afield in Graydon, something he grew increasingly annoyed at wasting so much energy on. Spells came at a cost, no matter how widespread Elihor's magic currently was.

"She will," he assured her. He had trained her himself and knew where her loyalties lied.

"They are separating," he informed her, relaying the information that she'd given him. "The heirs of Graydon and Elihor are heading to the Southern Coalition via Kosel. The Grayloft is coming this way."

"I have no doubt that the Grayloft will come to us," Tally said, though she still seemed pleased to hear it. "But we need to secure the other two. Particularly the Heir of Graydon. Queen Cassara needs to retake her rightful place by her king."

Quilsam glanced at King Dayshon, sitting on a plush chair in a corner, looking at nothing in particular and seeming content. The king had not been what Quilsam had expected, but Tally assured him the rebel attack had rattled him. Now, under her protection, he was safe.

And they could all breathe more easily. The breeze shifted the fabric before the open windows, and Quilsam forced his eyes to focus on Tally.

"We need to bring Rojon back to Elihor for safety," the Elder said. "To Larkhold." Part of him felt pleased that he could call the heir by his first name, instead of his title. He was young, but also had been raised by one of Graydon. He even had her red hair, a color not found in Elihor.

The gravitas and respect that had accompanied the Kolders, even Kale Kolder, did not extend to Rojon Kolder. But his bloodline did, and despite his mother's lineage, he would respect him for his position. Pay homage to Elihor, and do his duty.

A duty that was, however, on the cusp of change.

"Have you considered what our duties look like now that here is no more Wall of Loss, Elder Tally?" He stood and looked out the window at the palace repairs, and further down below where at the edge of the city a piece of it had caved in. It was just as well that Larkhold was here to lend their magic and expertise.

"I have," Elder Tally said, voice soft and reflective. Having an Elder from another coven to exchange ideas with was invaluable in helping circles grow and maintain their sacred duties. Especially in these turbulent times. The breeze furled the fabric before the large windows, and he found himself counting the panels before it. He pulled his eyes back to Tally, who impassively observed him.

"What conclusions have you reached?" He asked when she didn't offer.

"No conclusions yet, Elder Quilsam, just curiosity. I suppose we will see how things fall."

"Wise, Elder Tally." He paused. "What of the traitor Shirina?"

His eyes flickered toward a crimson panel of fabric before the window.

"She was dealt with by Elder Vangle. She will not bother us anymore."

Quilsam nodded and looked back to the window. Past the crimson, orange, and yellow cloaks, some burned, others covered in blood. Ignored the blue and green ones. Focused on the light beyond them.

When the Wall of Loss had risen a thousand years ago, it had cut off Ravenhold from the other two keeps, save for a few messages able to get across. Ravenhold had grown much harder than the other two keeps, showing little mercy to others, or themselves.

She'd killed Shirina's followers. He didn't know how many. Or who they'd been. He tried not to count the cloaks on display.

Tally was harsh, but she'd survived, and he was certain they would learn from working with the Elders of his Keep. Given time, a once precious commodity now made widely available as Siabala was no longer of concern. After a thousand years of keeping watch, this reprieve was long overdue.

"When will your adepts be in Kosel with the heirs?" She asked.

"Imminently," he answered.

"Good," she replied, smiling. "Then this soon shall come to an end."

Shivers clung to the base of Elder Quilsam's skull, but he shrugged them aside and left to focus on his studies. To await the arrival of Rojon Kolder.

Without the Wall of Loss, Larkhold's duty had to be to preserve Elihor's thinning bloodline.

Graydon's problems were not, could never become, his own. Still, as he left the room, his eyes went to the line of cloaks, lazily dancing in the wind, a testament to what happened to those who crossed the last remaining Elder of Ravenhold's old covenant.

Altessa heard the tail-end of the exchange from where she hid in the partition in the wall. She had spent a lifetime figuring out how to get in and out of the palace. How to remain undetected within it. And she'd heard enough. The heirs were returning, which meant Rojon and her mother were coming here. She'd have to be ready to help them as soon as they arrived.

Her heart caught in her throat, hammered in her ears, and she forced her breath to relax, lest she reveal herself. Her mother would be returning. And Rojon. Straight into a trap, she had no doubt of that, no matter what the Elder of Larkhold believed.

Did he believe Tally? He'd hesitated. She was certain he'd heard him hesitate, and a whispered threat at the end.

She had no plan but had her instincts. And she could use a powerful ally. Wasn't that why she'd returned to the castle in the first place? Altessa moved quietly and quickly in the family's second floor, toward the Elder, the corridor empty of guards where once a few would have been around. She slipped into the study after him, gently closed the door. The old man's completely dark eyes looked lost for a second, his mouth moving. Then he blinked, saw her.

"Princess Altessa," he said, recognizing her no doubt from the various royal portraits, even if she looked a mess right now.

"Elder Quilsam," she said, having heard Elder Tally speak his name. If he was surprised that she knew it, he did not show it.

"I am glad to see you are safe," he said. "We should alert your father of your return."

"My father is all right?" The weight that had pressed against her chest lifted, releasing some worry. She'd heard them mention him but hadn't been able to see into the room.

"He is, quite," he said. "He is with Elder Tally now." Altessa began shaking her head before she'd even realized it.

"Elder Quilsam," she said. "I've come to implore you to help rid my kingdom of these rebels."

"That is not for my Circle to do," he said. "But I'm certain Ravenhold's Circle will assist you."

"Shirina was taken by them," she said, her voice growing soft.

"Shirina fooled you all," he answered, looking like a grandfather offering bad news to a child. Altessa stood straighter, more regally. She would not be spoken down to in her own palace. Nor would she be lied to.

"Shirina did not lie to us and has been nothing but good and loyal to my family."

Don't justify yourself. It feeds their fire. Her mother's lessons came back, too late.

"Shirina is a master manipulator, who imprisoned her Circle's Elders in Siabala's Rage, and ensured the Wall stayed up, trapping them. The only reason they're free now is because the Wall fell."

"That is not true," she said, though she could see in his passive features that she wasn't getting through. She chose another tactic. "Why does Elder Tally want Rojon and my mother?"

"To ensure their safety," he said. "We will take Rojon back to Larkhold to ensure his, and Ravenhold will take over the safety of you and your mother, until we're certain that Shirina's Circle is well broken."

"Elder Tally follows Siabala," Altessa said, lack of conviction in her voice. She hadn't been ready to argue for aid against Elder Tally. She'd assumed they'd know, and that Shirina would be respected... *Never assume you know the battlefield until you step in it,* her father would have said.

Another lesson she'd forgotten.

"Another lie by Shirina," he said, shaking his head. "You won't have to worry about her anymore. Her Circle has dealt with her."

It felt like being punched in the stomach, and she

hadn't been ready. She wobbled but managed to remain standing.

Shirina was gone. The kind sorceress who'd taught her magic. Who'd watched over her mom silently during her dark moods. Who'd been there when Altessa had almost lost herself in magic. With both her and Avarielle gone… Altessa felt numb. How could she fight Siabala when those who'd once defeated them were so effortlessly destroyed?

The Elder seemed to ponder something, his eyes moving and his lips whispering something.

"I had my doubts too," he admitted, hands clasped behind his back. "But, princess, the more evidence I look for of Shirina's treachery, the more I find. And the more I look for Siabala, the less I find. Even my witches see nothing in Siabala's Rage, as I just had them go look and they've reported back."

"I'm glad to hear of it." Altessa jumped as Elder Tally stood in the doorway. "Princess Altessa, I assume." She lowered her chin respectfully.

"Daughter." Dayshon walked unsteadily toward her, his smile wooden.

"Dad?" She asked, seeking recognition in his eyes but finding none.

"Altessa," he said, each syllable given the same weight, clunky. He gathered her in his arms, and she held him back awkwardly. It felt like her father, but it didn't. "I'm glad you're okay," he said as she withdrew from his embrace.

"I'm glad you're okay, too," she said, heart sinking.

"I'm Elder Tally," the Elder said. "Of Ravenhold."

The Elder's sharp eyes sought hers out. How much had she heard of her conversation with Elder Quilsam? Was her father under a spell? What did she plan to do?

"Well met," she simply said, wishing her father would step in and take over the awkward conversation. To kick them out of their home and lead their people. But Dayshon remained silent.

"It has been my pleasure to watch over your family," she said, the smile not reaching her eyes. "We will keep you under our protection, as per the king's request."

Dayshon smiled, unwavering.

"Thank you," Altessa mumbled. "Perhaps I'll help my father to his quarters." *Address him, not them.* "Father, you seem exhausted, and I am, too. Perhaps we should catch up?"

"Of course, daughter," he said, and suddenly she found herself less eager to try to figure out how to snap her father out of whatever had been done to him.

"We will meet again soon," Elder Tally said. "I'll be near, if you need me."

Altessa mumbled another thank you and walked Dayshon back toward their family wing, painfully down the stairs, each of Dayshon's steps lacking his usual practiced grace. If his legs hurt, he didn't show it. Wherever she looked, she only saw Tally's Circle adepts, or guards she didn't know. No familiar faces remained, save a maid who quickly looked away. Maybe one of the guards, though she couldn't tell from this distance.

Only strangers, and the seemingly empty body of her father. He walked crooked, like he'd been wearing his prosthetics too long.

I don't know what's wrong with him, or how to help him.

Altessa walked beside her father in their home, wishing that she'd stayed down in the dark city, risk being lost there forever, than to feel such emptiness.

Such helplessness.

*E*lder Tally excused herself from Elder Quilsam's study after some chitchat. The Elder suspected something, but Altessa's ravings only seemed to convince him further of her truth. If the Larkhold Elder could have considered that the young princess might not have been ranting imaginings, things might have turned out differently. Especially for him, as she would have killed him without hesitation.

But that proved unnecessary as he seemed unwilling to trust a young woman over an Elder, even if the princess was also a descendant of Graydon. And so Quilsam still seemed to be of use.

For now.

"Elder Tally," Vangle said as he fell in step beside her. He looked sharp in the black cloak. All in all, she'd already initiated eleven new Elders into Ravenhold. This would solidify their ranks and allow them to cast larger spells against any incoming attack.

Not that she expected much resistance. Shirina's witches, those who remained, couldn't pull on their magic. Neither could the Heirs of Graydon. The Heir of Elihor had survived longer than anticipated. Massir's army had been sent away, most of its royal guards destroyed. And Avarielle Grayloft was no longer of concern, though she'd yet to realize it.

Like a great gaming board, she'd moved her pieces perfectly for the final attack.

"Did you take care of her?" Tally asked. She'd wanted to kill Shirina herself but didn't want to give the witch the honor of sullying herself with her blood.

"I have," Vangle said, a smile on his lips.

That smile worried her. She'd wanted him to teleport her high above Graydon and blast her with magic and disintegrate her body, her ashes falling on her adepts below like dark snow… but Vangle at times wrongly believed that his ideas bore more merit than hers.

Fool.

"How?"

"I threw her in the water. She never came back up."

That did not dissipate her worries.

"Where?"

"Where Ravenhold once stood." Another smug smile. "It was symbolic."

Could the keep and Shirina find each other? Tally

wasn't sure. The Keep was gone, she was fairly certain. But she'd never dived underwater to find out.

Chances were that Shirina was dead. But Tally had once taken that chance with her, and it had undone her. She wouldn't make that mistake again.

"Go back there," she said. "And bring me her body."

"From the water?" He asked. Tally turned her head slightly toward him.

He flinched.

"Yes, Elder."

And he was gone. He would learn that listening was a better skill than thinking.

If not, she would gladly get rid of him, too.

38

Her dead mentor, Elder Tanja stood before Shirina, a crinkle of laughter in the corner of her eyes.

Where am I? Shirina thought, before memories from twenty years ago crowded her mind, as though they happened moments, not years, past.

Her mentor had saved her. First, by making sure she was no longer in Ravenhold when Siabala's clutches had cut deep into the Circle. She'd sent her after the Grayloft, on the near impossible quest of capturing Avarielle alive. While her magic did not work on her.

While Shirina was gone, Tanja had been turned into a monster by Siabala. And, even then, she'd tried to save Shirina from the infection that had taken a hold of her. The dark magic of Elihor writhing within her. She'd seen her mentor shredded to pieces by the dark magic.

"You're dead," Shirina told her mentor. Her hair, dark brown streaked with white, was pulled back into a tight bun, as it had been in life. Her piercing eyes focused on Shirina, an eyebrow slowly rising. As it had for so many years, pushing her pupil to think, to see beyond the obvious.

"Am I?" Tanja asked, voice soft, like a dream.

"I saw you die," Shirina said, surprised by the lump in her throat.

"You have grown weak," Tanja said, eyebrow fully raised now.

"Perhaps," Shirina acknowledged. By old Circle standards, she was. She explained things to her adepts. She had allies. She'd learned to admit when she was wrong. And she'd learned to apologize and take judgment for the Circle's ills.

"If having allies makes me weak, then so be it," she said, not bothering to deny what her mentor—her mentor's apparition, or whatever this was—already seemed aware of. "I'm here because I wish to save Graydon. To do so, I need to become an Elder."

"You have grown weak," Tanja repeated.

"I have learned humility," Shirina countered, "and my attachments make me stronger. You yourself saved Kale Kolder from Siabala." She'd found him in her office, locked in the dark, where no one could reach him. Except for her, the one person she trusted not to fall prey to Siabala.

"It is not your attachments that make you weak," Tanja said. "It is your inability to become an Elder."

"I agree," Shirina said, trying to temper her annoyance. Whatever was happening, perhaps a fever dream as she drowned, reminded her of what she did not miss about the Circle.

"You cannot become an Elder when you are weak."

"This is ridiculous," Shirina said. "If I cannot become an Elder, simply tell me so that I may find another way to save Graydon." Once, she would have never spoken to her mentor this way. But Shirina had grown. Also, her mentor was dead, and Shirina wondered if she might also be passing into the Afterfate. She hoped her Afterfate would not be filled with Elder riddles onto eternity. Better to stay alive, were that the case.

"How would you save Graydon without being Elder?" Her mentor asked. "If you do not know the secrets of its magic, how will you save it?"

"I'm not sure," she said. "Becoming Elder seems the next logical step." She paused, studied her mentor. "Why would you not wish to make me Elder? Have I not shown my commitment to the Circle? To its ways?"

"You have broken so many ways, Shirina," Tanja said, shaking her head slowly, in the eternal darkness surrounding them. "How are we to trust that you'll make the best decisions for Graydon?"

It was her turn to raise an eyebrow. "You made Tally an Elder."

Perhaps I am simply drowning, Shirina thought.

"And she remains one to this day."

"No," Shirina said. "She worships at the altar of Siabala."

"And which altar do you worship at, Crimson Circle Elite Shirina? Madeline Monlie?"

Before she could answer, images flashed before her. Of herself as a small child, playing with her older brother. Bright tulips in the spring lining the walkway to her home. The scent of roses in the summer. Her mother's apple pies cooling on the windowsill. Memories she'd tried to keep buried deep within, of her life before the Harvest that had given her a new name and taken her away from her home. From her family. From everyone she'd loved.

Gone, now.

She was a young witch in Ravenhold, fighting for control and to understand her powers. Tanja taking her under her tutelage, helping her grow her powers, the scent of peppermint in her study, the puff of magic she'd yet to understand.

Gone.

Standing with the witches that remained from Ravenhold's fall, awaiting Siabala's attack, when the magic was mixed. Calling to them to help, knowing she had no choice, but that the battle would see them dead.

Gone. Gone. Gone.

Ravenhold trembling around her, the magical lights frantically dancing, shepherding her toward the exit. The books—oh how it hurt to see again—the books vanishing into dust, knowledge never to be recaptured. The Keep crumbling in the distance, its emptiness still echoing in her heart.

Gone, and never to return.

"At which altar do you worship, Shirina?" The words echoed around her, and Shirina realized she was on her knees, tears running down her cheeks. She could feel her mother's touch on her face. Could smell the death of the battlefield. The scent of tulips leading her home. The charred flesh. Memories that should have never intermingled did, leaving her nauseated and weak.

"I want to stop so many from dying," she whispered. "I need to stop Siabala from destroying all that's been rebuilt."

"You mean all that *you've* built."

A deep breath and she sat back on her feet, looked up to her mentor, refusing to hide her tear-streaked face.

"Perhaps," she said. "But it's part of a greater network. Of all of Graydon together, like a web of magic."

"But you have no magic," Tanja said. "The magic is gone."

"I need it back." Why was Tanja making it so difficult to claim her powers? Why wasn't she helping her?

"At which altar do you worship, Crimson Circle Elite Shirina?"

"I don't know what you want from me," Shirina said, throat filling with acid.

"Do you want the magic, or the cloak?"

That got her attention. "You mean I don't need to become an Elder to restore Graydon's magic? You can restore the magic without making me an Elder?"

"I can teach you how to access it," Tanja said. "I can show you where it hides."

"It holds Siabala captive."

"Does it?"

"Where is he, then?"

Tanja remained passive, looking at her. Shirina really, really hadn't missed this.

"I know you're dead," Shirina snapped, "but can't you make yourself at least remotely useful?"

"At which altar do you worship, Shirina?"

"I don't have time for this," Shirina said. "Just give me access to the magic. Being Elder isn't as important as having magic back."

With her words, Tanja stepped back, the great petrified oak tree that used to stand in the center of Ravenhold appearing behind her. She held up her hand. Bark crinkled down, collapsed on itself, absorbing branches as it turned into a single, perfect staff, glowing between the two witches.

"You worship at the altar of magic," Tanja said. In that moment, Shirina saw her mentor's spirit in those eyes— the depth of knowledge, the slight grin that said *someday, you'll know better.*

Then she was gone, the familiar aching grief clutching her heart. Focusing on the next steps, Shirina wrapped her fingers around the smooth, polished staff.

A deep breath to calm herself turned to ruin as water rushed into her, choking her, crushing her, the calming lights vanishing, leaving her underwater in the dark, with no idea in which direction to kick to reach the surface.

If she even could.

ojon's hand rested on his sword, ready to draw it if needed. Cassara held a bow, a quiver of arrows at her waist. Avarielle hated this, so much. She wanted to go with them, wanting to protect them so much it hurt. But she needed to be in Massir more, to see that Dayshon and Altessa were safe.

And, with any luck, to find that wretched witch Tally. She'd do more than slice her neck this time. She'd cut her whole head off.

Let's see you heal from that, witch. Cassara would find help for her kingdom, and Avarielle would clear the road for her.

"Ready?" Kleriss asked Avarielle. The Crimson Circle Elite had offered to take Avarielle part of the way before seeing if she could find and aid Shirina. Chances were that she was already headed toward Ravenhold. Kleriss would follow, teleport that way once she'd regained her strength, and help Shirina get there faster.

Avarielle would continue to Massir on foot. Not a short journey, but she saved at least a day with the witch's help.

Which was the only reason she was willing to trust her.

"Ready," Avarielle replied, keeping a hand on Graysword. The witch tracked her movement but said nothing.

The warrior nodded to Cassara and Rojon. "See you in a few days."

"We'll be there. In a week at most." Cassara said, looking resolute. Avarielle had no doubt that Cassara could convince the Southern Coalition to give her the help she needed. It was just a matter of making sure Massir still stood by the time Cassara arrived.

The spell began to form around Cassara and Rojon, a shimmer of pearlescent darkness ensnaring her loved ones. Kleriss began chanting, the words different than the ones Shirina's witches used, but cast to a similar cadence and rhythm. Avarielle stood near her, hoping they weren't dooming themselves by trusting these witches.

The familiar shimmer of a spell surrounded them, the ground progressively getting further away as they shot upward in the sky. The land stretched beneath them, beautiful and beckoning, though she still missed the sands of her homeland. Alert for the slightest sign of treachery, Avarielle noticed immediately when the spell began to buckle and Kleriss's cadence changed. Where the warrior had expected the Maple Mountains beneath her, the pines of Kosel began to loom.

She took hold of Graysword, ready to call on her magic, but the witch's hand came on her shoulder, squeezing it.

In her dark eyes, Avarielle saw a plea to trust her as she continued reciting her spell, unable to speak. Battling against her growing dislike of Larkhold's Circle, Avarielle stayed her hand and did not call upon her magic.

Graydon was still unfamiliar to Kleriss, a land she'd read about but could only now visit. She'd been, once, to the ruins in the West. But never this far, and never this lost.

Just yesterday, Elder Quilsam had asked them to retrieve the heirs. She respected the Elders. She'd joined because her uncle had been an Elder, though he preferred to stay in Larkhold. She'd been pleased to be asked to join Elder Quilsam in Graydon—a welcomed chance to prove that she hadn't just become Elite because her uncle had been an Elder.

Larkhold had long ago grown as quiet as the other two keeps, no longer choosing its own adepts. Only Elders did that, now. Which, Kleriss admitted, could lead to a thinning of the magical potential, as political and blood alliances were selected over studies and magic.

Kleriss called on her magical sight to observe the land

beneath her. The magic of Elihor danced thickly in the air, a ripple revealing the two teleportation spells of her sister witches heading to the thick forest country known as Kosel. She glanced toward their planned landing, and her breath caught. Red threads pulsated amidst the pine trees, waiting for the adepts. She forced her drying mouth to continue reciting her spell, fighting the crushing fear that begged her to scream a useless warning.

She saw dark threads, too. A strong beacon of Elihor's magic, representing maybe an Elder or two. But so much red.

Siabala's magic. Her breath caught in her throat, heart pounding in her throat. They were waiting for the heirs. Had Larkhold Elders allied themselves with Siabala? Had Shirina been telling the truth all along?

Without thinking, she began the dangerous maneuver of turning her spell toward them. The warrior wouldn't want her son and her friend to be trapped, of that she was certain, and Kleriss was duty-bound to protect the heir of Elihor. She couldn't afford to break the cadence of her spell to warn the warrior. She'd already be pushing beyond the boundaries of her energy and abilities by redirecting them, much further than usual.

I just need to get the warrior close enough.

Avarielle sensed the shift, her hand on her sword. Red flickers began to link her hand to her sword, and Kleriss's eyes grew wide. If the warrior called on her magic now, they'd both tumble to the ground and die. She'd been aiming up in the mountains. They were too high, and too fast.

She placed a hand on the warrior's arm, implored her to trust her as she kept chanting, fatigue beginning to trap her in her own mind.

I can do this. Her thoughts spun like an off-kilter windmill caught in a hurricane. Could she warn the others? Were they, too, using the Sight to see the land around them? Would they know what they were heading into? Or would they fall prey to Siabala's rage?

White-coddled hazel eyes met hers and Kleriss sensed as though her worth was being weighed, something that had never truly happened, not even when she'd become Elite. She'd always felt like she'd been gifted the rank not because of her skills, but because of her relative.

So, when the warrior stopped pulling on her magic, deciding to trust her, Kleriss found herself boosted, energized. A test of worth, and she'd been found worthy.

The two teleportation lines were reaching Kosel, and she wasn't far behind.

She had to tell the warrior where to go as soon as they arrived, but she wasn't sure she'd live long enough. Her heart hammered her chest, sweat poured down her back, ice gripped her spine. She was overexerting and knew it.

I must protect the heir of Elihor.

The warrior's hand found her shoulder and squeezed. And Kleriss found that she had the strength to go a bit further.

Vangle stood at the end of the bridge, enjoying the breeze of the ocean and the way his cloak billowed behind him. Black, like the Elders, the highest rank in Ravenhold.

He'd always envied Shirina her crimson cloak, though he hadn't been able to join her Circle. Too much learning and Tally understood him better. He'd wanted a crimson cloak when Tally had reclaimed her Circle, but Tally had insisted he was worthy of being an Elder.

He smirked. A rank that Shirina could never aspire to.

The water below him was dark, quiet save for the surf striking the rocks.

The Keep, which he'd never even seen with his own eyes, taken down by Siabala decades ago, was nowhere in sight. He respected Tally, but the old witch could really be paranoid sometimes.

Knowing that she'd never let this go, he used the Sight to make sure he couldn't spot any magic down there. The old witch could always tell the lie on his lips, and he didn't want to feed her paranoia and anger.

They might both be Elders, but he knew full well who was in charge.

He relaxed his eyes, letting the world shift, blurring at the edges, before becoming sharper, revealing the strands of magic. Traditional adepts of Ravenhold saw the light of Graydon dancing all around them when they did this, and the other strands of magic, as well. He could, too, but a green mist clouded his sight. A side effect of Tally's magical sharing. A small price to pay.

He blinked, looked down. Blinked again.

Did he see light?

Another blink as he focused more on his spell, and the light grew brighter beneath the waves.

It's been hours, he thought frantically. No one could survive that long underwater. Witches couldn't cast underwater. He'd thought long and hard about how to kill witches, and that was definitely a trustworthy method. Spells needed words. Words needed air.

Simple, effective, deadly.

The light grew, and he took an involuntary step back as the water's surface rippled and exploded upward, a column of water filled with strands of magic shooting into the sky, toward the south. The magic continued, but the water did not, scooping the warlock backward and choking him.

Vangle recovered and growled, annoyed at the mud on his robes. He glanced up.

A teleportation spell.

He swore, cast his own teleportation spell, and followed.

Graydon spread below her, its magic hidden, but so many other threads still visible to her. The magic of Elihor. That of Siabala, spreading from the Bloody Mountains into

Elihor and Graydon.

Green flames smothering the sprawling city beneath Massir, like a plague, a monster waiting in the dark. Red magic licked its edges, threatening to claw its way up and destroy all in its path.

Shirina held the staff gifted to her by Ravenhold, filtering magic through it. She was careful to avoid the magic of Siabala and only pull on the strands from Elihor, uncertain how they might affect the gift from Ravenhold.

Despite all the colors below, her eyes sought the familiar. She sought the magic of Graydon. When she failed to find it, she sought her friends.

Them, she managed to find, caught in webs of teleportation cast by adepts of Elihor, heading toward Kosel. Red light waited for them. More teleportation spells streamed their way, both red and green, like they were heading to the heart of a deadly bloom.

Shirina pulled on the threads of magic, demanding that they carry her faster than she'd ever gone before… and found that they answered. She feared tapping her energy out, but the magic channeled through the staff didn't seem to draw her energy like magic usually did.

Like it absorbed the shock, instead of demanding that her bones bear it.

Cassara and Rojon arrived in Kosel, flares of red light shining as spells were cast.

No.

She pushed faster, catching up to a teleportation beam heading toward them, though the caster was losing strength. Shirina could look into it, could see her, as though walking up beside her casually on the streets.

In the spell stood Crimson Circle Elite Kleriss of Larkhold, Avarielle beside her, one hand on Graysword's pommel, the other on the witch's shoulder. She looked toward Kosel, perhaps not able to see all that Shirina could, but sensing the danger ahead.

They wouldn't make it, the witch's lifeforce dwindling as her body was ripped to shreds by the very magic it filtered.

Trusting in her magic and her instincts, trusting in the Circle and Ravenhold, Shirina did the once impossible and stepped into the other adept's teleportation circle.

Avarielle's eyes grew wide as Shirina suddenly appeared, holding an obsidian staff, her robes and cloak wet, her once raven hair even more streaked with white.

The sight was so strange that Avarielle didn't back away from her.

"She's about to pass out," Shirina told Avarielle, as though simply telling her the weather was lovely today. "I need you to knock her out before she kills herself."

Avarielle found that she had a lot of questions. Primary among those was how Shirina had just walked into the teleportation spell. Not far behind that question were other important ones, like where she'd gotten the staff from, and how she could use her magic again. Perhaps more important was whether or not they'd plummet to their deaths if the witch passed out, though it seemed fairly safe to assume that Shirina, not being a lover of theatrics, wouldn't have gone to such lengths to simply see them dead.

She shrugged aside all questions, blood pulsing with the battle call.

She hit the witch in the back of the neck and instinctively reached for her to soften the blow, but found that they weren't falling. Shirina's magic held them up, even though her lips weren't moving. The magic flowed from the staff, and she wielded it effortlessly, though Shirina's cloak was still crimson. She was no Elder yet but had obviously tapped into some form of knowledge.

"Where do you want us?" Shirina asked, waving her hand and showing her strands of magic waiting for them up ahead. Avarielle blinked, seeing what an adept saw with the Sight for the first time.

It was breathtaking. And very useful.

"Red for Siabala?" She asked. Shirina nodded, the land growing closer. So much closer.

"Behind the line of red," Avarielle said, letting go of Kleriss, assuming Shirina would take care of her. She pulled Graysword free. "And make sure to move out of my way."

Before Shirina could answer, land resolidified under Avarielle, and she leapt forward without hesitation, screaming as she cleaved the nearest adept, white dress covered in blood, black cloak slashed in two.

She turned, managed to take out two Crimson Circles before they'd even realized what was happening.

Then Shirina screamed a warning, and the ground exploded outward, sending her flying toward the sorceress.

She pulled on the strength of Graysword, reoriented herself and landed on her feet, pushing herself back up even as the body of an adept flew beside her.

She needed to find the others and get out of there.

Fast.

40

The teleportation spell—whisps of dark magic Cassara couldn't see but could imagine—vanished, and Cassara's blood turned cold at the sight of five Elders—both white and black robes but all dark cloaks—and ten Crimson Circles, dark robes and red cloaks, facing them.

The Crimson Circle who'd brought her here took a step back, as though to stop her from escaping.

Rojon appeared, and he shared a quick look with Cassara. She shook her head slightly. They couldn't win this battle. Not with only a bow and a sword.

"Queen Cassara," an Elder wearing a Larkhold robe said. "I am Elder Kush, here to bring you back to your husband, King Dayshon. He's very worried about you."

Cassara's breath threatened to engulf her as emotions surged through her. Relief. Hope.

Mistrust. Fear.

She wanted to simply take their word for it and let them take her back home to her husband. But every fiber fought against it, so strongly that it twisted her gut with nausea. Grief bubbled within her at the thought of being offered such an easy and convenient way home yet being unable to take it.

"I thank you for your consideration." Her own measured voice surprised her. "But I do believe that Rojon and I intended to walk. It's a beautiful day, after all."

One of the other Elders stepped forward. As did Elder Kush.

"I'm sure you understand why we must be quick in this," he said. "Your husband has ordered us to bring you back to him."

"And, as we rule equally—" the back of her neck prickled in anticipation, "—my orders count just as equally. And I am ordering you to leave."

The Elder's smile twisted. Rojon took a step toward her, shadowed by the Crimson Circle at his back.

"We just want to bring you back safely to Elihor, Rojon Kolder," the Crimson Circle behind him said. "We mean you no harm. Only safety, as the last heir of Elihor."

Rojon growled beside Cassara, a move so like Avarielle that it made her feel better.

"My *name,*" he said, "is Rojon Grayloft."

He unsheathed his sword.

"Don't be a fool," Elder Kush scoffed. The prickling at the back of Cassara's neck grew more intense, and adrenaline flooded her body.

A scream and commotion behind the Elder, followed by the familiar battlecry of Avarielle. Even as Cassara was relieved, the sensation grew worse, heart hammering with her need to move.

"Rojon!" she screamed, needing to warn him of the danger, but uncertain what the danger was and so how to react.

She saw the flash of light from Graysword, and then the ground beneath her buckled. Without thought, she threw herself toward Rojon, who'd knocked down a witch with his elbow. She wanted to pull him away, keep him safe. The ground near her exploded outward before she reached him, earth and grass raining on them, several large trees teetering away. Cassara fell to her knees, the earth tipping as it slowly fell, toward the newly formed maw, ready to swallow her.

"Stay back!" Cassara screamed as she tried to catch herself, but the ground tipped faster and faster. Quick-footed, Rojon closed the gap between them and grabbed her arm, but couldn't recover from the slanted ground and slipped down with her, sideways. Her fingers reached for the edge of the maw, trying desperately to avoid falling in, but the earth was slippery and damp, and offered no purchase.

Shirina felt a surge from below, a strange coiling of magic and blood, dark and dangerous. She cried a warning, but too late. She tried to contain the explosion, but it knocked her back in a whirl of red cloak and white robes as she clutched her staff, unwilling to be without power again.

Before she struck a very large tree, Avarielle caught her, absorbed the blow from the tree and cushioned Shirina. Without missing a beat, the warrior leapt back to her feet, dragging Shirina unceremoniously along.

Red strands of energy crept up to where they'd just been standing, flowing outward and slamming back down. The strands of magic from Elihor were sucked into it, converted into something different and dark, then burned bright red.

Siabala's magic was consuming Elihor's magic!

A dark-robed Crimson Circle moved her hands in unison with her lips, finger flicking their way in what Shirina recognized as a sleep spell. But the strands of red slipped in her. Her eyes grew wide, fingers still outstretched to cast her spell… and she burst into flames from within.

"Don't use your magic, Larkhold adepts!" She said it so fiercely, with such command, that two chanting witches stopped. A third completed her spell, only to explode into flames.

The red shoots of power devoured the magic of Larkhold, though it seemed unable to expand beyond where it currently was, tethered to something below this newly formed chasm.

"The Elders should unfortunately be fine, since they're using the magic of Siabala," Shirina said. She glanced at

Graysword, the usually white strands of magic turning red in the growing mists.

"I'm fine," Avarielle said. "My magic is from Siabala, remember?"

Shirina nodded, though she hated the look of the red flames on the warrior's sword. They used to be white. Was that a sign of his growing dominion? A worry for later. She pulled her gaze away.

"Cassara and Rojon are down there." She pointed at the new crevasse.

"Then that's where we go," Avarielle said, just as another Elder teleported in front of them.

"You're supposed to be dead," Elder Vangle spat out.

"Go," Shirina told the warrior, taking a step back as she carefully welcomed only the magic of Elihor in her staff. She absorbed it and slammed into the Elder. He was ready for the blow and didn't go flying back, but that was fine. She'd just wanted to buy Avarielle time to get by him, which the warrior did, running over two smoldering witches and jumping into the pit after Cassara and Rojon.

"Why does Siabala want the heirs of Elihor and Graydon?" Shirina asked Vangle conversationally. Two more Elders stepped up beside him. She faced the only three Elders remaining up here, or that she could see. Well, that she could see still alive. One was dead, cleaved by Avarielle before he'd even realized she was there. Two were missing, and possibly down the hole.

She focused on the threat right in font of her.

"For revenge, of course," one of the Elders hissed. A

Crimson Circle of Larkhold's eyes grew wide at the mention of Siabala, and the Elder's lack of denying it. So the adepts of Larkhold weren't aware of Tally's ties, then, or refused to believe them to be true. There was hope yet.

Before Shirina could say anything, the Elder twisted his wrist toward the adept, and she collapsed. Maybe dead. Maybe not. There was no time to check, and Shirina had to focus on the immediate threat before her or she'd be next.

The staff pulsated in her hand, wanting her to draw more magic. Greedy for it. But she held it at bay, fearful of accidentally drawing Siabala's magic and being tainted by it.

Elder Vangle's eyes half-closed then snapped open, lips muttering. He didn't seem pleased with whatever message he'd just received. "Elder Tally wants to deal with you herself," he said. "Join us, and convince your witches to join us. She'll reestablish their power. Gift back your magic."

"I seem to have no problem with my magic," Shirina said, holding the staff more tightly. If she lost it, she was as good as dead.

"But your adepts back in Massir... so many of them. Most are already dead, but you could still save a few of them."

Shirina's anger flared to life, her magic responding before she could think of what spell to wield against them. The staff sucked in all of Elihor's nearby magic, morphing it into strands of fire which slammed into the Elders, without needing her to voice a spell. The assault took them by surprise, offering them no time to cast any defensive spells. Legs tumbled in cloaks as they were thrown back. Even Shirina stumbled backward, pushed by the strength of her own spell.

She clutched the staff like a lifeline, collapsing to the ground and stopping near the still unconscious Crimson Circle Elite from Larkhold, the one who'd teleported Avarielle.

Pushing herself up, she looked at the angry strands of magic. The staff still pulsated in her hands, the magic and staff responding to her emotions, reflecting her state of mind. She needed to figure out how to master this new means of casting spells, fast.

It would be a trial by literal fire. She had no time to practice, and there were Elders in the gaping maw that held her friends, red magic streaming out of it, brimming with strength, keeping Elihor's magic at bay.

With no choice but to follow, Shirina collected as much of Elihor's magic as she could in the staff and hoped it would prove enough. To save her friends and win this battle, she needed to face the magic of Siabala himself.

41

ojon tested his left leg, hand against the stone wall beside him. It hurt, like he'd sprained part of his ankle, but he could still stand on it. It would slow him down, which was less than ideal. He'd also lost his sword in the fall, and a gash on his forehead at his hairline burned like Elihor's anger.

But worse than that, he felt off. Physical pain aside, something gnawed at his gut, and he couldn't quite grasp what it was.

Had he broken a rib? His mother had told him about all the various injuries she'd suffered, which were many, and the pain that accompanied them, and how to move beyond it, in case he ever needed to. This didn't feel like a broken rib. Or a strained back.

It felt like deep pressure trying to crowd out his thoughts and heart. Trying to take control of something within him.

No. Not of *something.* Of him. He could feel the pressure crushing his brain, strands of red magic going into his nostrils every time he breathed. The magic was so thick that he could see without the Sight, just like everyone could see the magic of the Wall of Loss when the sun was just right and the day clear enough.

"No," he whispered and fell backward as his legs gave out. A splash of pale yellow caught his eye.

"Cassara," he muttered. *I took an oath to protect her.* He pushed himself toward the queen, who lay motionless on the ground. He growled at the red mist. "I took no oath to serve you."

The pressure increased, like laughter in his mind. He reached Cassara. Felt her warm hand, pushed hair off her face. She blinked, disoriented. And she took hold of his arm and pulled herself to a seated position. Her presence, her touch, grounded him.

"Are you all right?" he asked, the queen covered in dust.

"I am," she winced. "Well, I will be. You?"

"I am," he said, standing and helping her up. Uncertain on her feet, she held onto both his arms for a few moments and steadied herself.

"Where do we go?" She looked at the sky above. They'd fallen quite a ways, with no obvious path up.

Rojon looked around. Large boulders and pieces of crumbled earth and trees lay crashed around them. A red mist permeated the darkness beyond them, where there seemed to be more passageways leading deeper beneath Kosel.

"We shouldn't go in there," Cassara whispered. "This is Siabala's domain." Her voice held no hint of a doubt.

Red flames lashed toward them, curling and angry. Rojon instinctively moved to shield Cassara, but they never struck. His mother stepped before them, absorbing the blow with Graysword. She turned toward them.

"We have to go," she snapped. "Quickly!"

"Can we go back up?" Cassara asked, eyes darting toward the red glow of the caves.

"Not enough time, too many witches," Avarielle said. "Always too many witches."

The warrior grabbed the two and pushed them deeper into the cavern, and they silently made their way down, careful not to trip and fall as red mist hid their steps, rippling not away from them, but toward them as they walked deeper beneath Graydon.

And deeper into Siabala's mists.

Shirina used the magic stored in her staff to teleport down to the crashed, crumpled pieces of what had once been her outpost in Kosel. Red mist danced distractedly on the ground, covering everything from sight.

Red, like Siabala's magic.

Shirina couldn't sense any of Siabala's adepts, hidden in shadows. But she could sense a couple of Larkhold's injured on the ground. She headed to them, quickly and carefully.

She met a Crimson Circle, a young warlock with a broken leg.

"Don't use your magic," she said as he spotted her and his eyes grew wide. "You'll only absorb Siabala's magic. And he will kill you."

"I saw Astal burn alive," he said, his voice a panicked pitch.

"I can heal your leg," she said. "And you have to find your way out of here without magic and send news to your Elders once you're away from here. Do you understand?"

"They just burned alive," he said. Shirina added her old Circle edge to her voice.

"Do you understand, Crimson Circle?"

That snapped him back. "Yes, Crimson Circle Elite. I understand."

"Good. Now, run," she said, gently filtering enough magic to heal his leg. His relief at the lack of pain turned to surprise at her using magic.

"You used Siabala's magic." He scrambled away from her. "The Elders were right!"

Shirina stood up and watched him running back in the gloomy mist. She could have explained herself to him. She should have.

Now he'd uselessly spread more rumors about her.

What does it matter what they think?

She had more immediate concerns, and so she turned

to follow the slight trail leading deeper into the mists, trusting she'd find her friends, or an enemy.

And she tried really hard not to regret using some of her magic on the panicked Crimson Circle who now decried her a traitor.

42

Red light permeated everything, danced around them, making Cassara dizzy. Beside her, Rojon seemed as uncomfortable as her. She'd given him her bow, which she'd miraculously managed not to let go of. Not because she thought he was a better shot than her, but because she thought he needed something to hold on to. Something to make him feel more grounded, now that he'd lost his sword.

Her hand went up to near her neck, where her mother's amulet, *her* amulet, had rested for so many years. It was as gone as her magic, melted by Tally. She hadn't had time to grieve its loss, the last thing she still had from her mother.

But here, trapped underground and surrounded by Siabala's magic, Cassara grieved it. And missed its power, her fear curling in her stomach. Avarielle walked before them, hair reflecting the red glow of magic, the warrior seemingly confident of where she was headed, Graysword clutched in her hand. Red mist danced up and down the blade.

Her stomach churned. They'd had a plan, but it had all gone wrong. They should have never trusted the Circle witches. But what choice did they have?

"This way," Avarielle whispered back, making sure they still followed her.

"How do you know where we're going?" Rojon asked, voice calm but thin.

"I'm guessing." She shot a quick grin back their way. "It's better than waiting to face off with an Elder. Though I'd love to cut another one in two."

Cassara looked around, feeling like they were being followed. Like in every shadow lurked monsters and deadly Circle Elders. But nothing moved out of the mist.

"Do you think they're following?" Cassara whispered. They'd been walking for some time. Maybe up to an hour? Cassara had lost track of time, but she felt the crushing weight of Siabala gain strength over them. Like the deeper they headed into the caves, the more they played into his hands.

"Mom," Rojon said, his voice sounding hollow. "This doesn't feel right."

"I agree," Cassara said, looking to Rojon. His face was drawn, his eyes tired—like she imagined she must look, too. His red hair didn't reflect the magic like his mother's. Rather, it turned it dull orange. Siabala's powers wanted to be let in, offering to fill the void left behind by her missing powers. She couldn't stop all of it and it snaked within her, making her queasy.

No. It made her feel like she was contracting. Closing in on herself. And it hurt.

Avarielle stopped, dropping her annoyed look as she studied them. She glanced down at Graysword and sheathed her sword.

"I'm sorry," she said. "I don't know what I was thinking. Of course, Siabala's magic would hurt you two more than anyone else." She paused, looked back the way they'd come. "I was hoping we'd see another way up, but maybe we can double back and with any luck, Shirina's dealt with all the Elders."

"Shirina's back?" Cassara felt the stone in her stomach lessen, the snake uncoiling a bit.

"And she has magic," Avarielle frowned. "A lot of magic. I'm sure there's an interesting story in there somewhere. Let's go back and see if we can connect with her."

Avarielle had taken two steps when laughter drifted from the mist leading back to the exit. She unsheathed Graysword again, and both Graylofts stepped in front of Cassara.

"Relax." An Elder stepped out, black cloak on black robes, the shades different enough that he didn't just become a dark blur. "I just want to talk."

"You're from Larkhold," Rojon said. "Why would you ally yourself with Siabala, Elder Kush?"

"I am not, Heir of Elihor." The Elder bowed his head

slightly. Rojon didn't seem affected by the reverence. "I am simply trying to ensure that you and the heir of Graydon are safe."

"If Siabala isn't back," Cassara asked, "then from what do we need protecting?"

The Elder hesitated for a moment, then he sighed. "From the Circle," he said, "though it pains me to say it. Shirina has fooled you all so thoroughly that we can't risk her getting her hands on any of you. Whatever her plans are, they're certainly deadly."

"You don't really believe that, do you?" Cassara asked. "She worked with you to keep Elihor safe. She helped us fight Siabala!"

"She created bracers to filter out the magic of Graydon and Elihor and shared this with no one else. Why would she have created such a thing, if not to be more powerful than the rest of us?"

"She was testing them out," Avarielle said through gritted teeth. "Making sure they were safe to use. She's just the right amount of stupid and curious to test them on herself and no one else."

"You saw her magic out there," the Elder persisted. "She's more powerful. What deal did she make with Siabala to gain such power?"

"She would never make a deal with Siabala," Cassara said, wanting to find the words that would convince him, doubting any such words existed. "She put everything on the line to stop him once. She will do so again."

"She fooled you all. Queen Cassara, I mean no disrespect, but perhaps your desire to explain your friend's actions and behaviors has clouded your judgment."

"I doubt that," Cassara said softly, the rumbling of Siabala's magic growing in her stomach, threatening to make her ill. "I was there when she fought Siabala. Where were you?"

The Elder looked down at her, though she didn't feel intimidated by him.

"Siabala destroyed Ravenhold from within, Elder," Cassara continued. "I doubt that Larkhold is above falling prey to him, as well."

"I would listen to her," Shirina stepped out of the red mist, near the Elder. He shifted sideways, hands stiff at his side. "In all of our interactions, Elder Kush, you have always weighed fact versus opinion expertly. Please use the same vigilance here as you would in your magical studies."

"I know that Ravenhold now has Elders," he paused, as though uncertain how to address Shirina. She looked calm and collected before the Elder, her robes white despite the red mist, her cloak standing out, crimson defying Siabala's red magic.

She gripped a dark staff the color of an Elder's cloak. If Shirina had found Ravenhold, she had certainly not found the title of Elder.

"If you judge an organization simply by its highest rank and not its mission," Shirina calmly said, "you are showing how elite your thinking has become. And that's exactly what Siabala will use against you."

"I would bring you to Elder Tally and we can all discuss this together," the Elder offered. "She seems only concerned with the safety of the heirs, and of Massir itself."

"She is holding my family captive," Cassara said, feeling numb. The nausea was making her salivate, and she felt unsteady on her feet.

"They are safe, and I've spoken with your husband myself, Queen Cassara. And your daughter, Altessa, has returned and is now with him."

"Altessa is safe." The ensuing relief flooded her mind and left her feeling lightheaded. Red overwhelmed her sight, nausea slammed her throat. She was about to pass out.

"Shirina," Cassara croaked out, not having meant to utter the name. But the sorceress went to her, unhesitant. A quick glance at Avarielle, and she took hold of Cassara and Rojon.

And with power Cassara had never seen Shirina wield, not even in their most desperate times, the sorceress wove dark strands of teleportation and pulled them out of the red mists.

Pakana hadn't been in the bar for a few days, and she admitted to missing it dearly. But the staff would handle things until she felt comfortable leaving the house again. Well, not the house, but her father, Kaden.

Carsyn had been gone for almost a week, and his loss had snuffed out Kaden's strength. He wandered around the house without purpose. Sometimes she'd find him on the porch, just staring at the woods, for hours at a time.

He used to sit there with Carsyn, the two grumping and making fun of each other. It felt like a lifetime ago. Carsyn's death had blanketed their house with silence, and Pakana didn't know how to let the air back in.

And so she sat with her father, even if in silence, so that he wouldn't be alone.

Kaden sat up, and Pakana lowered the book she was reading to ask him if he needed anything. He looked ahead, mouth open, and gasped. Pakana followed his gaze and gasped herself as a white-robed witch with a crimson cloak appeared, holding up a blond-haired woman and a younger man with completely dark eyes and red hair.

Pakana had never met Queen Cassara, but she'd heard so many stories of her and of the sorceress Shirina that she knew them for who they were. And knew the young man could only be Avarielle's son, Rojon. He held himself like she did.

"Kaden," Shirina said, voice crisp. "Help us." Cassara fell to her knees and, not something that Pakana expected she'd see a queen do—especially not one she'd idolized as perfect since she was a child—threw up, gasping for air.

Rojon also fell to his knees, gulping in deep breaths.

Kaden moved toward them, but Pakana reached them first.

"Clean air and water, and a bit of food, but not too quickly," Shirina instructed her. She looked to Kaden. "I'll get Avarielle, and I'll be back." She turned to Rojon. "Don't use your magic."

Then back to Kaden. "We might be followed. I'm sorry."

"Go," he instructed her, his voice sharp and his eyes clear for the first time in days as he rubbed Cassara's back gently. Like he used to do to Pakana when she was just a little girl and didn't feel well.

"I'll get water," Pakana said, running back into the house.

It took her just moments, but by the time she returned, the sorceress was gone, a strange tang of the sea clinging to the air.

43

The Elder stood calmly, hands clasped casually before him. Avarielle's body practically vibrated with anticipation, from her toes and hair all the way to the tip of Graysword, which she held before her. She could cut him down if she had to, and she really wanted to.

"Where did she take them?" The Elder asked, looking concerned. "Are you not at all concerned for their well being? He's your son!"

Avarielle took a deep breath, shuddering at the scent of sulfur. It smelled like Siabala's Rage. Where she'd been held, tortured. Where he'd tried to break her.

Her left arm suddenly stung where he'd shattered it again and again, but the pain was gone as quickly as it had come. A trick of the mind. A memory turned physical.

"You should turn around and walk out of here," Avarielle said. "This place isn't for you."

"All I wanted to do was help your son," the Elder said. Avarielle gripped Graysword more tightly.

"Stay away from him. He's not yours to worry about."

The Elder cocked his head, examined her. Seemed to decide she wasn't worth worrying about and took a step back. Two other Elders stepped forward, wearing white robes.

Avarielle had quickly memorized the topography immediately around her, trained to observe and remember her surroundings, especially when battle was imminent. As battle always tended to be imminent in her life, old habits died hard.

So, she knew that she had few places to hide, and the only escape route further down the cave, toward Siabala. That probably wouldn't be the best course of action. She was looking forward to settling her score with him, but she had faced him before and knew she couldn't stop him alone.

"Shouldn't your robes be red?" Avarielle asked the two Elders. She remembered one of them from the ritual with Tally. "You—" she indicated him with her chin, "—tried to hurt my son and kill Cassara. Don't think you're walking out of here alive."

"You hurt the heir of Elihor?" Elder Kush asked Tally, as though finally deciding Avarielle was worth listening to.

"We only do what is necessary for Lord Siabala to return to us," Elder Vangle said. Behind him, the other Elder slammed fires into the Larkhold Elder. He tried to summon defenses, but his skin burned from within, and he collapsed, unable to contain his fires.

Vangle's lips quirked up. Before whatever words lingered on his lips escaped, Avarielle had closed the gap between them. Her blade met flesh, cut, satisfying. But instead of bleeding, the Elder simply exhaled red mist.

Not one to easily give up, she used her own momentum to swing back and strike the Elder in the mid-section. Again, no blood. Only red mist.

Siabala's magic.

"Siabala keeps us whole," he said. "You of all people should understand that."

"Except you can die," the other Elder said, flames flying towards her. She brought up her sword, took the brunt of the magic with it, pushed back but still standing. Her sword, which would usually dispel the magic, glowed fierce red, as though absorbing the power.

"Perfect," the Elder whispered. Avarielle screamed and leapt forward, swinging down on the second Elder, cleaving him firmly in two from head to groin, red mist cascading around his two broken pieces.

"Heal from that." She turned to kill Elder Vangle. A wave of energy crashed into her, and she knelt to keep from flying back, planting Graysword into the ground and holding on to it, muscles straining as rocks and debris hit her.

The energy turned to flames, hurling toward her… and dissipating.

"Enough of this," Shirina said, appearing beside

Avarielle, striking the Elder in the chest, red mists exploding outward. "You do not deserve to wear the robes of Ravenhold." White fires curled around him, and the stench of burning flesh filled the cave.

"Are you all right?" Shirina asked.

Avarielle stood up, pulled Graysword out of the ground, and dusted herself off.

"I am," she said. "Are Rojon and Cassara safe?"

"They are," Shirina said, though she didn't offer where. Avarielle understood her caution. It felt like the walls had ears, and something, or someone, kept watch on them.

"Great," Avarielle said. "Can you teleport us to them?"

"I used my stored magic to save you," Shirina said. "I don't dare use any of Siabala's magic."

"Save me?" Avarielle said. "You helped, at best. But I would have been fine."

"It looked like saving to me," the sorceress said as they began walking back. "You were on your knees and about to be flambéed."

"Hardly," Avarielle scoffed.

"And," Shirina continued as though Avarielle hadn't spoken at all. "That's two that you owe me. Today alone."

"I'm willing to owe you for saving Rojon yesterday," Avarielle said seriously.

"I wasn't even referring to that, but you owe me for that, too." Shirina was enjoying this, even though her face betrayed no emotion and she kept her voice at a whisper. "I was referring to saving you from the teleportation spell."

"That was hardly saving me," Avarielle countered. "You grabbed me mid-teleportation and threw me into battle."

Shirina pondered for half a beat. "You're right," she said. "You owe me for that, too."

"For throwing me into battle?"

"Yes," Shirina simply said.

Avarielle smiled. "You're right. That was fun."

"I know." Shirina gave her a thin smile. Avarielle looked at Shirina's staff and raised an eyebrow. The sorceress shook her head slightly, indicating she didn't want to talk about it here.

Again, Avarielle understood, though she was curious.

The two walked in silence back up the cave, keeping an eye out for intruders.

Once outside, the only adepts left were dead ones. Avarielle looked for Kleriss, but there was no sign that she'd ever been there.

"What are the chances she teleported herself away?" Avarielle asked Shirina. She'd tried to save her son. She had no doubt of that. For that alone, she wanted to ensure the witch's safety.

Shirina's look was the only answer she needed.

Avarielle clutched Graysword's pommel more tightly, the jewel glowing red under her hand.

44

assara watched the tea steep. She remembered being young and feeling useless. At sixteen, having so much to contribute, no one interested in hearing her thoughts. Her ideas of how to support her people, and her land. How she'd been dismissed out of hand and promised to a powerful prince in marriage.

Then she'd discovered her power. Her magic. And everything had changed. She could fight back against the Eloms, could protect people from terrifying monsters, and even stop Siabala himself.

In the end, she'd given up that power. And taken up a throne.

Tea bag out, she placed it in the sink, then examined the unevenly thrown ceramic mug with a chip near the handle.

The powers of the throne weren't the same as her magic. Her magic was hers alone and could be unleashed as she saw fit. The throne was something the people gave her. If she didn't do well, they could dethrone her by uprising.

Something she'd always known, but never imagined would happen. She'd been a good queen or had tried to be. But she had too many chips, many more than this mug. In the end, she'd broken.

When the rebels had risen against her, when everything had started crumbling around her, she'd realized that she was still that young girl leaving her homeland, her Edoline, and its orchards and courtyards, and prayed that someday she could return.

She hadn't wanted the large kingdom, nor its responsibilities.

But her family needed her, and for them, she would go. She wanted to love her people, and part of her did. But the burden of being queen was more than she cared to handle.

It would be easier if I didn't care what anyone thought. Except she always had. Worried about what others thought of her. How they'd react to her policies. She'd wanted to sit at the table with them, not on a throne above them.

She'd fought against the court and its traditions. Against only supporting the already rich and help the poor, as well.

She'd tried but failed.

Not at everything.

But at so many things. Even when faced with deadly danger, her magic had failed to return. She'd thought maybe it would return when things got desperate, but now…

"Do you intend to drink that tea before it gets cold?" Kaden asked from the door of his home, right off the tidy kitchen.

Cassara flushed and picked up the mug.

"Just lost in thought, Kaden," she said, and smiled at him. He looked the same, but older. Well past eighty, the lines and scars on his skin had grown deeper, but his eyes had only grown warmer. He walked more slowly, and his back was more curved, but he still emanated the same strength he had as a Royal Protector of Edoline.

"This place is lovely." Her smile faltered. "I'm sorry I never visited."

"You're queen of the biggest kingdom in Graydon, Cassara. I don't expect house calls." He paused. "And neither did Carsyn."

Cassara hadn't managed to cry for Carsyn, yet. The weariness extended through her entire body, filling her soul. She was numb, too numb to cry for a man who had once been such an important part of her life.

That should have made her angry. But it just made her more tired.

"Come sit on the porch with me," he said, extending his arm and inviting her to step outside. She did, and sat on a reclining wooden chair. Kaden placed a blanket across her knees. Perfect for the cool weather of the evening.

Above them, the tall pines of Kosel sang in the evening

breeze, the stars slowly appearing in the sky as the sun vanished.

"Avarielle and Shirina should be here, soon," Cassara said, to fill the silence. Then she found she wasn't really interested in filling that silence. Shirina had her magic back, and Avarielle had Graysword. She was worried for her friends but knew they could handle themselves. Part of her hated that she could be of no use to them.

Rojon and Pakana weren't far, hanging out with her large lizard Rolly, dark scales shining in the fading sun at it bathed happily near the two young adults. Rojon had taken an immediate interest in nearby mushrooms after she'd assured him she was fine, and that they were safe. Still, he wore Carsyn's old sword around his waist, ready to pull it out as needed.

Kaden made a non-committal sound to her statement and looked out toward the trees. She knew that deep within them, Carsyn was buried. No markers in Kosel. Lives here were marked with laughter and memories, not with stone and chiseled names. In Edoline, he would have been buried in the royal crypt. But here... here, he returned to the nature he loved.

"When Carsyn and I were in the Westland Wars," Kaden started, as though continuing a conversation and not just filling in the silence, "we did things we regret, as you know." She did know. Carsyn had made peace before dying, and that was a gift she couldn't thank Avarielle enough for. But she didn't, because it wasn't her place to.

That had been between her and Carsyn.

"Then we found purpose in Edoline," he smiled at her, "and keeping an eye on the youngest princess of Edoline. And she was full of bad ideas!"

She gave a soft laugh. "They weren't all that bad."

"They were." He gave her a sideways look. "Sneaking out by your brother's bedroom window?"

"I didn't think you knew about that!" This time, laughter bubbled easily out of her.

"Oh, we knew. But if you knew we knew, you'd have found a new route that we'd have to then figure out."

She shook her head, smiled. A breeze ruffled the trees more strongly, and she looked up, letting the breeze pick up her freshly cleaned hair.

"Then we failed Edoline," Kaden said. "And our king died, and our princess was shipped away."

"You did not fail Edoline," Cassara said, some of her numbness lifting at her need for him to understand. "You made sure Edoline lived on."

"And then," he continued as though she hadn't spoken, looking up at the ruffling branches, "we realized we could no longer keep her safe. And we had to let our young ward go with a woman we barely knew."

"Avarielle took care of me," Cassara said.

"She did," Kaden nodded. "She made sure you survived. But Avarielle Grayloft is a warrior, and warriors, like myself, like Carsyn, try to, for better or for worse, ignore the cost of battle. Because it's what we're trained to do." She kept looking forward, toward the trees. "And it was unfair to expect you to save us all, just because you had

Graydon's magic. And then for you to sacrifice that magic to keep Siabala at bay…"

"It's fine," she said softly. "I was the only one who could do it."

"You were," Kaden said. "But it wasn't fine to ask you to do it. And it wasn't fair."

"It is what it is," Cassara said, words she'd repeated over and over again to herself. To try to ward away the memories.

"When Edoline fell, all of those memories of the Western Wars came back, for me, for Carsyn. It was unpleasant, and entirely more visceral than anticipated." He turned back to look at the trees. "And now I think of you. I imagine that if you had been expected to save the world once, and you had done it, and sacrificed the magic everyone said made you special…plus you had a tendency to think that everything depended on you because they had for so long…well, I imagine that you'd think this was on you, too, and that you could have stopped it."

He placed a hand on hers, both still looking ahead, toward the forest.

Cassara swallowed hard.

"And maybe—" Kaden's soft voice mixed with the song of dancing pine needles, "—maybe it would have helped if, back then, someone had told you that you'd done the best you could, and that was okay. Just like you told me I did for Edoline. So, I'm telling you now, Cassara. You did the best you could. And it's okay."

She didn't answer. He repeated it, gripping her hand.

And, eventually, her numbness lifted under his warmth, and tears slowly began to warm her cheeks.

They stared into the trees and growing shadows, listening to the sound of the world around them as Cassara grieved for all she'd lost, and grappled with the painful reality that she couldn't save Graydon, nor could she save everyone.

Not her people. Nor her family.

Maybe not even herself.

4 5

Shirina knelt beside the broken bodies of her adepts, making sure that each was truly dead. Avarielle doubted anyone still lived and, from the stench of things, they'd been dead a few days.

Probably since I teleported here. She looked to the mangled body of the older Orange Circle, a woman named Tisha, who had been kind to Avarielle. Her hand tightened on Graysword.

"May your path be steady," Shirina whispered, and stood, using her staff to help support her.

"None of this was your fault, Shirina."

The sorceress gave her a look that made it clear she didn't intent on discussing the matter with her. Not now, and maybe not ever.

Avarielle followed her through the outpost, as she looked at anything that might be missing.

"They took nothing," she said, voice sounding hollow. "They just killed my adepts."

"We should go," Avarielle said. "We don't know if that pit will extend out. Half your outpost is already crumbled into it."

Shirina nodded but didn't move.

"I just…I thought we'd see the attack coming."

"I know," Avarielle simply said, and made sure the sorceress followed her out of the outpost, past the broken bodies of her witches.

After some time, once surrounded by pines, Shirina's voice surprised the warrior with its softness.

"I was willing to sacrifice Rojon."

"Oh?"

"When Tally took him. It was him, or the Wall of Loss. I told Altessa not to use her magic to save him. Nor Cassara."

A moment of silence, and Avarielle shrugged. "It was a tough choice. But you'd have gone after him with everything you could. I know you."

Shirina sounded frustrated. "You're not listening. I was willing to let him die."

"You talk a good game, but you'd have never let him die if you could stop it."

"But I was willing to, Avarielle. I told them not to risk the Wall of Loss for Rojon."

"Okay," the warrior answered, wishing the sorceress would revert to sullen silence. "Do you want me to hit you? Would that make you feel atoned?"

Shirina didn't answer. Suddenly the sullen silence wasn't as welcomed as the warrior had hoped it would be. She sighed.

"Look, I know you love him, and he loves you, despite my advice otherwise. I know you'd have done everything to save him, and you did, remember? You melted your own bracers to save all of us." She paused, forced the grin to stay off her lips. "Why didn't you just pull him out? I mean, think about it. I was pretty pierced through anyway. I get you could have saved Cassara, too, for the Wall of Loss stuff. But why'd you load yourself up with all of us? Your bracers might have survived, which would have made this conflict entirely different."

More silence.

"Well? If you're going to insist on me being angry with you, find some other reason. Because as far as I'm concerned, you saved us all back there. And you sacrificed your bracers doing it." She glanced at the red, angry skin around Shirina's wrists, where the bandages had fallen off.

"It never occurred to me to leave you behind." Shirina shook her head. "I'm beginning to see why I'm not Elder material."

"If sacrificing everything is the only way to become an Elder, maybe it's better you not become one. You're doing fine with that staff, anyway."

Avarielle had a thousand questions for Shirina. Had she found Ravenhold? Had she been tested and failed? Why would the keep not see that she was trying to keep the lands intact, unlike Tally? But the sorceress, not having found what she wanted from Avarielle, had grown silent again. And the warrior decided to let her be, focusing on her surroundings again, ensuring they weren't followed as the sun began to set. Avarielle looked for any signs of recent passage, and she could only find her own tracks. Or so she hoped. At the time, she hadn't been worried about being followed. They'd thought the traitors were only targeting Massir.

That was foolish. They'd grown complacent over twenty years. They'd believed no one knew about Cassara's magic except them. That the Wall would be safe as long as she was safe.

Of course, others like Tally had known. And apparently Siabala's magic hadn't been as contained as they'd hoped.

The sorceress walked in silence behind Avarielle, content to let the warrior lead the way while she lost herself in thought. That suited Avarielle just fine. Something bothered her about the pit growing beneath the outpost. How far did it go? Did it go all the way to Massir? To the West?

Where was Siabala hiding in all of it? Or was he just mist now, a soul with no body? She'd felt something in that mist. Magic. Strength. A presence.

And, if not for Rojon and Cassara, she would have headed deeper in there. She would have hurt them, to find Siabala. She wasn't sure if it was because she'd wanted revenge or because… because of *what*? What else could it be?

She stopped, and Shirina stopped with her. Avarielle's hand rested on her sword, the magic pulsing beneath it.

Something was near.

Shirina looked around, following Avarielle's movements. The warrior cocked her head, listened intently, held her sword. She could *sense* something but couldn't see it.

"What—" Shirina's voice was cut short as she was yanked up. Avarielle lunged to grab her, tangling her hands in her cloak and pulling down, hard. Shirina tumbled down, but silver threads sliced into her flesh, robes turning red.

Avarielle didn't hesitate, striking above the fallen sorceress with Graysword. Something hissed, steam rising as silver threads were severed in two. A creature screamed, the sound like silverware scratching ceramic.

Shirina stood back up, staff in hand, back-to-back with Avarielle.

"We're surrounded," Avarielle hissed, as strange creatures, like the one from the underground village, appeared around them. Snarling, drooling mouths snapped at them. One lunged, and Avarielle cut it down. With a yelp it crumpled. Shirina grunted behind her, apparently deciding to attack one with her staff.

"Don't you have your magic?" Avarielle shouted as she knelt and plunged Graysword into the belly of another leaping creature.

"I'm trying," Shirina grunted, then started reciting

another spell. Avarielle moved sideways, trying to cover the sorceress's flank as she worked up some sort of spell.

There seemed to be no end to these creatures, and Avarielle's magic flames flared in the growing darkness. Shirina had stopped reciting.

"It's not working," she said through gritted teeth, holding her staff like a weapon.

"Great," Avarielle grunted as she cut a creature's leg, but failed to give it a killing blow. That angered it, and it managed to slam into Avarielle, knocking her down.

Eli's tits, she scrambled to get back up, but another creature leapt on her, ready to trample her.

A sharp light exploded outward, flinging the creature off Avarielle. Birds exploded in flight as three of the great, ancient nearby pine trees toppled, large root beds flying up, soil showering the new clearing and the battlefield. Avarielle grabbed Graysword and leapt to her feet. Only smoldering husks remained of the attacking creatures.

Shirina clutched her staff, its tip in the earth, eyes wide as she looked at the destruction around her.

"Was that you?"

"I think so," Shirina said, then swallowed, seemed to get her bearings. "It was."

"You couldn't have done that before I got knocked down?" Avarielle scoffed.

"I think that was it," Shirina said. "And don't take this personally, but when I saw you were in trouble, my magic exploded outward."

Avarielle's eyebrows shot up. "To save me? I didn't know you cared so deeply."

"Don't be dramatic," Shirina deadpanned. "You're my guide to Kaden's house. It was purely practical of me."

"I don't think so," Avarielle said, looking at the shaking hands of the sorceress, willing them steady with regular banter. "It's clear to me that you're emotionally attached to me."

"Hardly," Shirina said, a smile in her eyes as she looked at Avarielle. "It's clear to me what this actually means: you owe me another one."

Avarielle grinned, partly relieved that the sorceress seemed to find her footing again.

"We'll see about that. Come on. Let's go before more monsters find us."

"I've got a better idea," Shirina said. "Since I have my magic back and can't bear another moment walking with you…"

Shirina took Avarielle's arm. The sorceress's hands were cold on Avarielle's exposed arm, but the tremor seemed to be gone. Without the usual chanting, teleportation mists gathered around them both, hurtling them through the woods, and landing near Kaden's. The porch stood empty, the scent of a meal greeting them both.

Rolly the lizard looked from the trees. Shirina didn't see the creature, but Avarielle spotted it. The lizard seemed to recognize her, and continued its watch, or whatever it was doing.

The enemy had followed them by foot before, so Avarielle didn't argue with the sorceress teleporting them here. But she hoped they couldn't track her magic as easily as they had their scent.

46

Shirina stared at the staff, sitting on the porch of Kaden's small cottage, by herself. Avarielle, Cassara, and Kaden all gave her a wide berth, sensing her need for reflection. She had a problem to solve and needed the head space to do so.

The staff had worked when she'd been emotionally fraught. When her friends, or Avarielle, had been in danger. She'd reacted viscerally, not relying on her Circle training.

Sleek and dark, the staff shone like obsidian. It felt more like stone than wood, but was almost weightless. A gift from Ravenhold itself.

You worship at the altar of magic.

She still wondered what Tanja, or the keep's projection of her, had meant. Something had convinced it that this was the weapon Shirina needed. She hadn't become an

Elder, nor had she managed to restore magic for her adepts, but she'd been gifted this.

Shala, she thought, trying to reach her second. Her friend. The first adept who'd joined the Circle, trapped in Massir. Maybe dead, according to the Elder.

How could they let this happen? How could I let this happen?

"Shala," she whispered, trying to reach her, but only hearing the wind on the trees as a reply.

"Auntie Rina," Rojon said as he emerged from the forest, a bag of something in his hands. A young woman, the same one from earlier, came with him. "I'm glad you're here," he said. She nodded at him, but didn't get up.

"Are you all right?" he asked, seeing the blood and cuts on her robes.

"I am," she said, adding a weak smile to comfort him. He was nineteen and didn't need to be coddled. But she didn't want him to worry needlessly. "What did you find in the woods?"

"Mushrooms," he said. "They apparently make good soup, though they're as ugly as trilleaf root rot."

"I'm Pakana," the woman said, stepping forward and offering her hand. Shirina sighed and grasped it, though she remained seated. "It's an honor to meet you, Crimson Circle Elite Shirina."

"I'm glad to meet you, too," she said, hand back on her staff. She was tired. The wounds she'd taken from the silver threads had mostly healed with her magic, but fatigue had settled in. The last few days since leaving Massir felt like weeks, if not months, and they seemed to be catching up to her. Her wrists ached where Cassara had applied a pungent ointment and thick bandages. She wanted to rip it all off, and focused back on Rojon before she did so. He wore a long sword at his waist, like his mother. He looked more and more like her, and he seemed more like himself than he had in a while.

"Rojon," she said, "sit with me for a moment, will you."

Realizing she'd been dismissed, Pakana mumbled something about getting supper ready and headed inside.

"What is it?" he asked, pulling a chair to sit in front of her. He looked down and saw what was cradled in her hand. "You have a staff."

"A gift from Ravenhold," she said, then added with a slight grimace, "I still don't quite know how to use it."

"You'll figure it out," he said with such certainty that she allowed herself to believe him. "The one I made for you burned in the attack."

"I appreciate you making it for me, and I'm sorry I didn't get to use it. How do you feel?"

Words almost immediately slipped out of him, but then he looked into her eyes and weighed his answer more carefully. "I took the oath to protect the descendants of Grandon." Shirina simply observed him. "I thought it might help protect me from Graysword."

His words pulled at her heart and made it ache. She couldn't protect him from Siabala's magic, but he'd grown aware of it and fought hard against it.

"That was wise," Shirina said. "Avarielle felt when

Cassara was in danger in Massir. There is magic in there, somewhere."

"You think so?" The hope in his voice broke her heart even more.

"I do," she answered, not certain, but willing to believe it for his sake. "But you have to keep fighting the pull of Graysword. As Siabala grows stronger, so will it."

He nodded, looked down to her staff. "It's glowing."

She saw it then, the bright magic of Graydon dancing on its shaft, converting Elihor's magic to her own.

"So it is," she whispered, tears tugging at the corners of her eyes, where she forced them to stay.

"Rina," he said softly. "I know it's best if I separate from my mom for now." The staff grew brighter. "And I know that you'll probably be with her because you two are stronger together. But promise me you'll take care of each other. I don't want to lose either of you. I already thought I'd lost Mom once. I can't stand the thought of losing you both."

"I promise," Shirina said, looking into his eyes, their darkness illuminated by the light of her staff.

He leaned in and gathered her in a hug, and she held him back. Then he stood, nodded, and headed back in. Her staff glowed less fiercely.

Another figure came toward her, and Shirina sighed. It was impossible to find a moment to herself. She missed her garden. Her peace. Her adepts and studies.

Cassara handed her a warm cup of tea. Strong and bitter, just like Shirina liked it.

"You realize it's reacting to your emotions?" Cassara said softly.

Shirina sighed. "I was coming to that unfortunate conclusion, yes."

"You just need to allow yourself to feel, Shirina," Cassara said, with none of the sarcasm that would have dripped from Avarielle.

"That's not my strength," Shirina stated. "That's more you and Avarielle."

"I disagree." The queen cocked her head, a slight smile on her lips. "Supper will be served in a few minutes. If you don't want to come in, I'll bring you some."

And Cassara vanished back into the house. Shirina sighed again. The staff had grown dark and cold again. She took a sip of her tea, the bitter brew teasing her senses back to life.

The moon made the woods both pleasantly lit and haunted. She knew Avarielle was out there keeping watch, making sure no one would attack them. Shirina was worried about her, too, and hated it. The warrior's magic seemed to be increasing as Siabala's presumably did.

She looked down and the staff glowed vividly on her lap again.

Sighing, she stood up and headed in to share a meal with the others. Worrying about everything and everyone would hardly help her solve anything, but eating would at least help solve her very real problem of hunger.

47

If there was one thing you could count on, it was that no one could be counted on. Elder Tally had learned this a long time ago. Everything should have been finalized in Massir, in her underground hold, but they'd managed to escape.

Trying to get them to Massir had proved impossible. They were too stubborn, too difficult… in the end, it had proven much easier to move the magic to them.

Elder Tally walked through the mists of Siabala, his power glowing on her skin. She moved faster than usual, floating more than walking, supported by her Lord. She could feel him, and his strength, flowing in the wound at her neck. Cut by the same blade that had undone his body.

She stopped, used her senses to feel them above. To feel *him.*

She'd had enough of these games.

If no one else could get this done, then she would.

48

Trees loomed over her, dark shadows covering the carpet of pine needles that masked her steps. And would mask anyone else's too, something that Avarielle was all too aware of.

Hand on the pommel of Graysword, she felt its magic pulsate. Not strongly enough to alert her of a nearby monster, but enough to soothe her. Tell her it was still there.

Had the magic always done that? Sometimes, Avarielle found it hard to remember her life before her time with Rojon. She remembered fighting Siabala, but almost like in a dream. She'd been pregnant. Heartbroken. Exhausted and drawn thin after months of trying to survive, and she'd been willing to die.

Her memories were stored in different landscapes, each holding a different part of her life. The dry winds of the West, the song of the Wall of Loss up above on a clear day, the fires of Graysword against dry Elom skin.

The East, with humid air and tall trees, covered in shadows and monsters lurking beneath.

Elihor, with the stench of burning, and new growth, and cooking stews and laughter.

And now here. Kosel, her life looping back to the time when there were Eloms, and their darkness spread across Graydon like a plague. The scent of pine needles and moist earth. Of long shadows and longer memories.

Graysword's magic had reacted that way when Eloms were near, or too many in number. But she knew now that it wasn't reacting to monsters. It reacted to what she knew lurked beneath them, revealed by the pit beneath the Circle outpost.

She blinked, looked around. She'd stopped moving and had drifted off, lost in thought.

That's how people get killed.

She took a deep breath, grounded herself back in the moment, and kept walking, listening intently for any noise out of the ordinary. Anything that might cause alarm.

Her hand fell to Graysword again, her left hand, the magic soothing the scars of her arm. The throbbing power deep below must have been activating Graysword. Responding to Siabala's presence.

She'd cut him through, once. His blood had landed on her, and she'd brushed it off. Ignored it. She'd gone for the kill.

She'd killed his body, but not his soul. She could see herself standing there, scowl on her face, as Siabala fell. Heard the rumbling of laughter deep in her gut. The magic coursed more strongly, and Avarielle noticed she'd stopped moving again. She blinked, and realized she didn't know where she was.

She'd seen herself kill Siabala.

Impressive.

The rumble came from deep within her, in her mind, vibrating in her soul, her left arm cracking as energy unleashed from the bones. Energy he'd forced into her when he'd tortured her in his Rage.

Avarielle gasped, crumbled to a knee, clutching her arm. Its crisscross scars turned red with magic. New scars formed, a length of tattoo in blood red, though no blood dripped down her limb.

Red magic. Red, like Siabala.

Oh no. Realization slammed into her mind even as she felt it slip from her. Her right arm, where his blood had splashed her, turned dark red, crimson, a pattern of blood burnt onto her.

A body for a body, Oath Breaker.

She saw through his eyes now, no, through Rojon's eyes. *Siabala's eyes.* He'd wanted Rojon to kill Cassara to seal the blood oath. Elihor killing Graydon.

She saw herself stepping in front of Rojon, taking the blow in her chest, not surprised, but accepting.

Felt herself being pushed out of Rojon's body,

watching her, watching Elihor's magic, riding it, in, in, in—

Impressive. The words echoed as he slipped into the cracks and scars that had never healed, tried to never acknowledge.

Oath Breaker. She saw through her eyes, but through his, too, as he settled into her mind. She reached for Graysword, the blade welcoming her touch. She had to end it. End him. End herself.

Before he got to them.

Before he made her kill them.

She could see his plan, understand his mind. Siabala would seal the blood oath by killing Graydon and Elihor, something he'd never succeeded in his life. And her body and mind would be his.

She had taken his life, and he intended to take all of theirs.

Avarielle tried to scream, to warn them, but could only push a gurgle out. She unsheathed Graysword, tried to turn the blade toward herself as the magic lit the scars of her body and her mind... and she stopped.

Her breath grew silent as she stood back up, slowly, the hazel of her eyes lit with the same red glow of her blade.

One slow step at a time, as though fighting against herself, Avarielle Grayloft, proud daughter of the West, walked back toward the cottage.

49

Rojon stretched, and Shirina gazed at the small fire. Kaden sat beside her, having fallen asleep in the glow of the flames. Pakana placed a blanket over him, and he didn't even stir. Rojon studied a game that Pakana had tried in vain to teach him to play.

Cassara brought Rojon and Pakana another bowl of soup.

They both smiled in thanks, and Cassara returned to the oven. There was enough soup for Avarielle, and even warriors needed food. Her friend tended to push too hard. She was strong, but even she had her limits.

Besides, she could use some time outside on the porch, alone. The cottage was cozy and warm, but also crowded, and she found that the older she got, the more she craved her peace. She always had, wandering her small country by herself. Now, her world always felt too crowded, and it failed to fill the void her heart felt. It only made her mind too full.

Shirina didn't look up, lost in thought, but Pakana looked up as she headed toward the door. Rojon didn't notice, either.

Boys, Cassara mouthed, and the young woman smiled widely. For her, Pakana was the little sister she'd never had. Raised by the same men who had in a way raised her, she felt a kinship with her, and regretted not taking the time to visit her more frequently when she had been but a child.

To be a part of her life growing up.

Cassara paused at the door. Something stilled her, and it wasn't just the dreaded cool night. She took a step back and dropped the bowl of soup, her instincts screaming at her to get out of there. Shirina's head snapped up.

Before words escaped her mouth, the door flew open. Avarielle stood before her, eyes glowing, red light dancing on Graysword's blade, on the tips of her hair, on the scars lining her arm.

She looked at Cassara and smiled, but it wasn't her friend's smile. Not the grin she gave when she knew she'd succeeded in annoying Shirina, nor the genuine smile when she was pleased. She'd seen this smile before, and the way the head tilted forward in a predatory way.

She knew her enemy when she saw him, gut clenching in fear, her magic tumbling somewhere far away, out of her reach.

Siabala.

Shirina's heart dropped at the sight of Avarielle. Red magic danced all over her, and when she looked at her with the Sight, all she could see was red. Surrounding the cottage, Avarielle a glowing beacon of crimson so deep and layered that it blocked all else.

In it, she could see Siabala's form over her, engulfing her.

Siabala was in Avarielle.

In a moment, all her thoughts coalesced and Tally's plan—Siabala's plan—became perfectly clear. She'd tried beneath Massir, surrounded by the red magic of Siabala, to make Rojon kill Cassara and seal a blood oath with the shed blood of Graydon.

But his mother had stepped in and stopped him from taking an oath. Letting Graysword's magic *into* her. She'd barely needed to heal her, because Siabala's magic had done so. That's why they hadn't seen him until now. He had been weaving his web over Avarielle more tightly. That was how they'd always stayed one step ahead, seemingly knowing all their moves.

Fool.

Now Siabala had Avarielle. And he needed... he needed to kill Cassara and Rojon. That's why he'd wanted the heirs. Why Avarielle had been walking them deeper into the caves, unknowingly falling prey to Siabala's thoughts already. She would deepen her oath with him with each person she slid her blade into, each innocent that should not have died by her hand, just like her original oath to activate the magic.

And Graydon and Elihor's blood would solidify the magic so strongly that it would be impossible to save Avarielle.

"Cassara," Shirina reached for her staff, but a silver thread pulled it away, and nabbed her wrists and ankles.

"A simple staff instead of an Elder's robes," Tally said as she stepped in behind Avarielle, the warrior's hands shaking at the sound of her voice.

The warrior was still in there. She wasn't gone yet, and she was fighting with everything she had.

It won't be enough, Shirina realized. Siabala was too strong, his hold on Avarielle too deep.

"You were judged—" the Elder walked toward Shirina, "—and found unworthy."

Shirina ignored the woman, looking to Avarielle instead. Her eyes were locked with hers, and she could see her friend still in there.

"Fight him, Avarielle!" Shirina spat out. "If you're going to do anything useful in this blasted life, do this!"

The taunt energized the warrior, and her shoulders moved. Her hands shook around Graysword, her fingers flexing to drop it.

Then she screamed as red magic pummeled into her, so much that it seemed an endless source. Shirina couldn't even see the dark strands of Elihor, swallowed away, vanishing like precious air underwater.

She had no magic to draw on, even if she could get her staff.

"Don't bother," Tally sneered. Her neck moved stiffly, the skin turned to stone where Avarielle had struck it, red magic glowing beyond it, but not on it. Shirina filed the fact away, trying to grasp as much information as she could. If she lived—an unlikely event—she'd need all the knowledge she could get. "She's been his since she first took her oath. She was just too stubborn to admit it."

The Elder turned to Rojon, who struggled against the silver threads holding him and Pakana. He looked to his mother with wide eyes, mouth open, like a scream was trapped by his grief at seeing what his mother was being turned into.

"He would have taken you, but she wouldn't let him have you. Your mother was always impressive, Rojon, and is now even more so. You should be proud."

Rojon fought, unable to break free.

"Mom!" He cried out, and Avarielle's face turned to him. Shirina saw the sides of the warrior's mouth tremble, fighting for control.

She would lose. She had already lost, too much red mist surrounding her.

Realizing that she couldn't save Avarielle, that her friend was gone, made her heart break in a way it hadn't since she'd lost Ravenhold. Every detail gelled in her memory, in her mind, her magic dancing within her.

Avarielle brought up her blade, screaming in pain as it arched toward Cassara, the queen holding her ground, calm, whispering to Avarielle words that Shirina couldn't hear over the warrior's cries.

Rojon screamed. And Shirina felt the staff respond to her emotions. Her pain. Knowing she couldn't save Avarielle, the friend she loved to hate. She'd thought she'd lost her, once, but that had been a warrior's death.

This, to make her do this, obviously aware…

Magic exploded around Shirina, the silver threads burning away from her as her staff came into her hand.

And she began to draw in Siabala's magic, not caring if it would kill her.

Nothing mattered except stopping Avarielle from killing her loved ones. The battle was lost otherwise. Shirina would gladly sacrifice her life to give Rojon a chance to fight. To survive.

She hoped enough of Avarielle remained for her to realize that she owed her another one. That would make the warrior laugh, a sound the sorceress desperately wanted to hear again, one last time.

50

Time stopped for Avarielle.

Every minute became a second as she lost more and more control to Siabala, his strength coiling around her and crushing her from within.

Meeting eyes with Shirina. Seeing in them what had happened to her.

Rojon screaming her name.

Cassara telling her it was okay, pale and resolute.

It's okay. It's okay. It's okay.

As though telling her it was okay that she'd lost to Siabala. That her body was no longer hers. That she would kill her, in cold blood.

It's okay.

It wasn't okay, and everything in her fought against it, but it was like trying to hold back a mountain crumbling atop her. Her strength, her soul, her mind all minuscule and useless against such power.

Her strength didn't matter. Her will. Her heart.

All she could do was scream her agony as the blade sought out Cassara's heart, unable to stop it.

Scream, even as the queen muttered *it's okay, Avarielle, it's okay.*

Scream, as her son screamed.

Scream, as Kaden stepped in front of Cassara. Eyes closing as he took the blow.

Scream, as she smelled the burning of his flesh. By her magic.

Scream, as he slumped to the ground.

The blood on the blade turned the magic darker, stronger.

Scream, as she felt it come into her. Coil within her.

And then the screaming stopped.

51

Shirina grabbed Siabala's magic and pushed it within her staff, sensing the staff's desire to protect her, purifying the magic and changing it so that she could wield it.

She pulled the magic away from Avarielle, in a hope to buy her friend the time she needed to break free, but there was too much. Too much, and Graysword went through Kaden, red blood coating the blade.

The old man fell to the ground. Cassara stood rooted in place, looking down at him bleeding at her feet.

Like Kale, dying to save Rojon.

Graysword glowed more fiercely, and despite Shirina's attempts to pull magic away from the warrior, it now grew so thick and bright that the sorceress's eyes watered.

Avarielle stopped screaming, and Shirina understood that she'd lost. That her friend was gone. And that all she could do was save those she loved and protect them for as long as she could.

Magic pulsed through her staff, stronger than she'd ever felt, burning her palm against it.

At which altar do you worship?

Her mentor's voice whispered in her mind, and Shirina answered with her heart, her worry, her fear, her anxiety. Her sorrow, her pain, her heartbreak. Her grief. And her hope. Her belief in others.

Her hatred of Tally. Her love of the Circle.

And she found Avarielle's red eyes, focused, solid, hard.

I need magic, Shirina answered. *To save them.*

Tanja's voice vibrated from the staff into her.

You worship at the altar of magic.

She felt its strength, and so did Tally, who turned around, scowling.

Shirina grabbed the magic of Siabala and threw it at her. The Elder, powered by all the red magic, did not fall, but she did stumble. Shirina threw her hand sideways, palm open toward Rojon and Pakana. Rojon's eyes were wide, Pakana stunned at the sight of the dead Kaden.

"Run!" she screamed, pushing them far with a teleportation spell. Not as far as she'd have liked, but far enough that they could escape. If they ran in the other direction.

Rojon turned to her, screaming her name as the spell took hold.

I can't lose you and Mom.

I'm sorry, Rojon. Shirina bundled her grief at her broken promise and slammed magic into Tally again. She needed to get to Cassara. If nothing else, she needed to save the queen, and ensure that Avarielle did not claim the blood of Graydon.

Tally snarled and attacked, red coils wrapping around the cottage, crushing the walls, magic traps to stop her from teleporting again.

"Cassara!" Shirina screamed, but the queen was frozen in place, kneeling before Kaden, holding his still form. Shirina couldn't get to her, silver threads blocking her route, wires that cut through her robes and skin.

"Enough!" Shirina screamed, pouring her anger into the staff, striking the ground. The entire cottage shook, everyone falling to their knees except Avarielle, who brought up Graysword to cleave down the queen where she knelt in the blood of Kaden.

Shirina crossed the floor quickly, grabbed Cassara, yanked her back ungracefully. Graysword came down, missing her but the magic so intense it burned Shirina's arms. The sorceress had already cast a teleportation spell, ripping the red magic off the cottage to use it for her own purposes, turning the trap to her advantage.

Avarielle's eyes followed them as the cottage's roof was ripped off and Shirina whisked Cassara away, up, beyond the walls and into the sky, where Elihor's magic still waited above that of Siabala.

Her staff burned, red lines crisscrossing over it. As

they did so, the magic of Siabala around her rippled. Shrunk.

She could absorb Siabala's magic within the staff, and maybe destroy it. Or at least contain it. Trap it there. Slow the enemy down. She looked toward the West, and the Bloody Mountains. Red magic exhaled outward from the Bloody Mountains, to the north and south, over the water.

The seas began to churn.

"What's happening?" Cassara asked.

Shirina stared wide eyed, unable to answer for a few moments as a few more puzzle pieces clicked together. The monsters coming to shore, showing Siabala's reach. The city beneath them crawling back to the surface, destroying their world. The lack of other landmasses anywhere near them, or anywhere at all. The straits that kept the two lands separated by the Wall of Loss.

And now, something lurched up from beneath the water surrounding Graydon and Elihor, clawing its way toward the sky to the north and south of their lands, farther than her eyes could see.

In the distance, part of the Bloody Mountains collapsed, dust crashing up. Not beneath Stormhold, but closer to the south, scissoring Graydon into Elihor, the city beneath the West surfacing more. And another part of Massir tumbled down. Cassara gasped. And near the Southern Coalition… red cracks formed across the land, redrawing the lands of Graydon and Elihor.

And killing so many.

"Shirina?"

"It's Siabala's empire," Shirina said. "His empire is rising. It's…it's bigger than our land, Cassara. And it's, I think…I think it's all beneath it." She looked to her staff, easily drawing in the red magic. "I think I can buy us some time. But not much."

She forced her eyes away from the bubbling land mass.

"Do what you can," Cassara said softly. Shirina met her blue eyes, steady and resolute. Part of the queen had always expected to die at the hands of Siabala. And part of her still waited for that final blow.

Shirina nodded and began to pull at Siabala's magic. She hadn't been able to remove it from Avarielle, the power too concentrated, too thick from years of growing within her scars. But she could remove some from Graydon as it grew thin, spreading to the rising empire of Siabala. If she could buy everyone time by giving up the gift of Ravenhold, so be it.

Enough time to make a plan. Maybe even to fight. Or to save some people. And then, if all else failed, enough time to say goodbye.

"Wherever I bring us," Shirina said. "It will be our last stand. One without magic."

Cassara's eyes met Shirina's. There were no tears, only resolution. Acceptance.

"Then bring me home, Shirina. If this is the end, let me face it with my family. With my people."

Shirina nodded and finished her spell, bringing them

to the outpost near Massir but not in Massir itself, absorbing as much magic as possible. All around her, from Massir to the West, she drew Siabala's magic into her staff, trapping it, forcing it to remain. She could feel the web of Siabala weaken as his magic spread too thinly to erect his empire. Her stomach turned as she realized that she could only do this because Avarielle contained most of his magic, now, where his soul dwelt.

Saving the world one more time, Avarielle.

Shirina screamed her grief and anger, forcing as much of Siabala's red mists as she could into the staff, hands burning from the magic's demands to be set free. Then she slammed it into the earth, willed it to hold the magic. Cracks shimmered and then faded as it turned to stone, holding at least some of Siabala's power captive. Through the Sight she saw the red mists vanish into the staff. And then the magic left her, the staff now heavy stone.

Silent.

She'd hopefully slowed Tally down and stopped their advance to some degree. But her hope of regaining magic disintegrated as wood turned to stone, her heart crushed by the knowledge that she'd just destroyed Ravenhold's final gift to her.

Everything, it seemed, was destined to crumble with Siabala's return.

~

Rojon stumbled on the ground, the force of Shirina's spell sending them both crashing and rolling.

"Mom," Rojon whispered, trying to get his bearings. Pakana stood up faster, looked to the stars, and the trees, and gave three sharp whistles.

"We have to go back," he said, eyes wide with the need to be understood. "Mom…"

"Just killed my dad," Pakana said, her voice a whisper lacking any bite.

"She didn't…that wasn't…"

"I know," her voice trembled. "But it was. And I know that Shirina told us to run, Rojon. So, we run."

Rojon looked at her, wanting to stalk back toward the cottage. But his feet were rooted. Shirina might be dead, too. And Cassara.

Was it up to them to save everyone? How would they do that? His magic hadn't reacted, like he couldn't even touch it anymore.

Like it was gone.

"I think I've lost my magic," he said. "How are we supposed to fight Siabala without magic?"

"For now, we run," she said, and started to walk away as she whistled again.

"And then what?" He followed her, numb. Empty. Broken. And more lost than he'd ever been.

"And then," she met his eyes, hers shining. "We keep running. And when the time comes, we get our revenge on him."

"He's in my mother's body," he said weakly.

She said nothing. Siabala had killed her father.

But he'd killed his mother, too. And his father, long ago. Rojon looked up to the sky, the constellation of the Lost Lovers judging them from above, and with heavy feet and a heavier heart, followed Pakana in the shadows of Kosel.

ally hadn't fully succeeded, but Siabala could now wield his magic more effectively. She moved her neck, the stone uncomfortable, a small price to pay for life and magic.

The Westland warrior hadn't been fully taken over by her master, yet, but she would be. She just needed the blood of Graydon and Elihor, the former much easier to acquire. She had the queen's daughter waiting for them in Massir, where she had no doubt the queen would go. And what chance could they stand, now that his empire rose again from the very ground beneath their feet?

"We shall get you fully reborn, Lord Siabala," Tally said, the warrior's red eyes looking at her, before flickering back to their mundane color. "Your Empire will rule once more."

Then the Elder stepped outside the sacked cottage, not noticing the glance of hazel eyes at the old man's body on the ground, the curling of Avarielle's hand at her side, the trembling of legs before the warrior followed her into the cold, bitter night.

To be concluded in *Empire Breaker,* the final book in the *Keepers of a Broken Land* series.